Drawing Free

Ink Blot Communications

Http://www.inkblotcommunications.ca

ISBN: 978-0-9877457-7-4

Also by Elena Aitken

Nothing Stays In Vegas

Unexpected Gifts

Short Story

Betty and Veronica

*Not until we are lost do we begin
to understand ourselves.*

~Henry David Thoreau

CHAPTER ONE

There was nothing quite as wonderful as starting the day with a hot cup of coffee. Especially when that cup of coffee was enjoyed in complete silence before the rest of the house woke up. I only had a vague recollection of such moments, since it'd been years since I'd actually enjoyed one. My latest book, *The Right Foot: Setting yourself up for success*, suggested setting the alarm a half hour early, to enjoy the quiet time, and with nothing to lose, I'd done just that.

Then I hit snooze. Twice.

By the time I dragged myself out of bed, there was only about five minutes left before I'd have to wake the girls for school. But I'd take what I could get.

I ran my hand along Jordan's bedroom door as I passed. For a split second I was tempted to open it and watch her sleeping. It was my favorite way to see her, at least since she'd become a teenager. But no, I had to start my day off right, and that meant a cup of coffee, even if it was rushed. At least it would be quiet.

A crash came in the direction of the kitchen. I froze. Panic pricked at the back of my neck. What if someone was in the house? Should I hide? No. Protect the girls. I glanced behind me to Kayla's room. The door was open. It only took me three steps to reach her room. Kayla's pink comforter was crumpled on the floor, her usual nest of stuffed animals, flung around the room.

"Kayla?" I hissed under my breath.

Another crash. Then, singing.

I sighed, the vision of my coffee dimming as I walked towards the high pitched rendition of Mary Had a Little Lamb. As soon as I rounded the corner into the kitchen and splashed straight into a puddle, that vision vanished completely.

My eyes took in the wreckage. The new jug of milk I'd just bought, lay, mostly empty on the floor blocking the fridge door. The high pitched beeping of the refrigerator door alarm filled my head. Again, I cursed Jon's insistence on purchasing top of the line appliances, the stupid things were always making noise. A mixture of corn flakes, fruit loops and my favorite granola covered the counters, and most of the floor, turning into a chunky sludge where it met the milk.

My eyes came to rest on my youngest daughter, who was sitting at the table in the middle of the chaos. The singing stopped for the moment, she was munching on a mixing bowl full of cereal.

"Hi, Mommy."

"Kayla," I said very slowly, trying to keep a rein on my temper. "What on earth happened?"

"I made breakfast," she said with a mouthful. "Want some?"

I closed my eyes and tried a deep breathing technique I'd read in one of the many parenting books that lined my shelves. *Positive Parenting* stressed the importance of encouraging your children when they attempted something on their own. The author also had the foresight to instruct parents to take a moment to think about what they were going to say before they said it, lest they discourage their well meaning children.

I tried it, counting in my head. One, two, three.

"No," I said when I opened my eyes, "the last thing I want is breakfast."

So much for not discouraging my child.

Kayla's blue eyes, peeking out from under her blond

fringe, started to glisten and her lip began to quiver. "I was just trying to help."

"Well you didn't."

As soon as the words came out of my mouth I wanted them back. That happened a lot. I'd never been very good at keeping my inside voice actually inside my head. And just to concrete the fact that I felt like an awful mom, Kayla folded her arms over her cereal bowl and collapsed in a heap of tears.

Perfect. I was definitely out of the running for mother of the year.

Again.

I waited for a second. She tipped her head to the side, watching me. When I didn't respond, her wailing got louder.

I could not deal with this. Not without coffee. But it was all the way across the milky pond that strongly resembled vomit, forming on my floor. The fridge was still emitting its screech which was now combining with Kayla, creating an orchestra of pain in my head.

I took a step into the mess right as Kayla kicked her screaming into high gear. The sudden switch in volume spooked me, my feet slid out from under me and I landed on my ass with a soft plop.

Lovely.

Milk immediately seeped through my pajama pants but I didn't move.

"What the hell?" I turned to see Jordan, who at fourteen was already in full teenage angst mode and only barely tolerated anything to do with me. She was still in the tank top and shorts that she wore to bed and was standing in the doorway with her hands on her hips.

"Don't say hell," I said.

"Well, what are you doing, Mother? It looks like a bomb went off."

Jordan, in some form of teenage rebellion had started

referring to me as 'mother'. As irritating as it was, it was an improvement from her short lived phase of calling me by my first name. I'd tolerated that for an hour.

"I made breakfast," Kayla said, her tears momentarily forgotten by the appearance of her sister. Her voice wavered, but at least she wasn't screaming.

"Yeah, looks like it," Jordan said and pointed her bare foot at the lake of cereal. "What am I supposed to eat?"

"I was just trying-"

"Shut up," Jordan snapped, sparking a fresh round of tears from her sister.

"Jordan Thompson, that's enough." I pushed myself up from the floor feeling the squish of what might have been corn flakes between my fingers. "Kayla, finish eating and Jordan," I looked at my eldest who was rolling her eyes, "just go get dressed."

"Whatever," she said and spun on her heal. "I can't believe I'm related to you people." I heard her mutter as she stalked down the hall.

Oh, the next few years are going to be fun, I thought, not for the first time.

I turned back to Kayla who instead of eating, was staring at her still full bowl.

"Kayla, please finish eating."

"I'm not hungry."

"You're kidding?"

"No." She looked at me, her eyes full of sincerity, and blinked hard. She was still too close to the edge of a tantrum.

"Never mind," I said. "Go get ready for school."

Thankfully she did as she was told. I really couldn't handle more screaming. I still hadn't had any coffee. Although at that point, something stronger would have been welcomed.

Taking a deep breath, I gritted my teeth and skated my feet across the floor through the mess. I took my favorite mug out of the cupboard, grabbed the pot and

4

poured. Slightly more than a dribble.

Jon seemed to think that as long as he left a drop in the pot, he didn't have to make more.

"Fuck," I said and slammed the pot down on the counter, where a crack rippled up the side of the glass.

"I thought you said I couldn't say that word."

I turned to see Jordan standing in the doorway again. Her timing, when it suited her, was perfect.

With a smirk, she said, "I need my green shirt."

"Where is it?"

"I don't know, Mother. That's why I'm asking you."

I closed my eyes and tried very hard to remember how the book said I was supposed to deal with a difficult teen.

"Jordan, it's not okay to speak to me that way."

"Well, what am I supposed to wear then?"

"Find something."

"Whatever," she said and stalked off towards her room. No doubt to tear her closet apart in an effort to drive me crazy.

I looked down at the pathetic excuse for a cup of coffee and swallowed it in one gulp.

"Mommy, I need you to brush my hair," Kayla hollered from her room.

I grabbed the broken coffee carafe, tossed it in the garbage, and with a sigh I'm sure could be heard through the neighborhood, made my way back through the sludge to get my daughters ready for school. The good thing about starting off my day in chaos was that it couldn't get much worse.

###

It wasn't until I was pulling into the driveway, after taking the girls to school, that I realized it could, in fact, get much worse. Connie's car was parked next to the curb. With the confusion of the morning, I'd totally forgotten she was coming for a visit. It had been too long, and I normally did enjoy a visit from my step-mother, it's just, there never seemed to be -

Oh shit. The mess.

In my hurry to get the kids to school and get myself a coffee at the drive-thru, I'd left the sludgy cereal disaster for later. And by later, I meant I was hoping it would magically disappear.

I grabbed my purse and ran into the house. "Connie?" I called. "I'm so sorry." I moved through the living room, but stopped short when I got to the kitchen.

I was too late.

Piney freshness filled the room, while my sixty-seven year old step-mother scrubbed the tile floor on her hands and knees.

"You didn't have to do that," I said. But we both knew she did. Connie couldn't leave a smudge on a glass, let alone be in the middle of a major disaster zone, without jumping in.

"It's nothing," she said as she pushed herself up from the floor. I couldn't help noticing she was moving a little slower than usual. Her ankles must be bothering her again. "I hope you don't mind that I let myself in. I was going to make coffee, but..."

"Oh, right," I said, doing my best to avoid meeting her eyes. "I had a little accident this morning. How about tea?"

"That sounds lovely, dear. I'm all finished here anyway. Just let me rinse out the bucket."

I didn't bother arguing with her, there was no point. She tided up the cleaning supplies that only really got used when Connie came to visit, and stashed them away. I did my part and prepared two cups of tea, trying to forget about the coffee still in the car.

"Thanks again, Connie," I said as I sat down and placed the steaming mug in front of her.

She shrugged, because for her there was nothing

better than cleaning for those she cared about. Some people showed their love by cooking. Connie scrubbed and polished.

"I really didn't mean for you to have to do that," I said. "Honestly, I was going to take care of it when I got home but I just forgot about it and-"

"Really. It's okay. You know I don't mind." She waved her hand to dismiss my protests.

"I know, but..." I blinked, hard. For some reason I felt like I might cry. I never cried.

Ever.

Jon thought it was strange that I didn't tear up at sappy movies, or when I heard bad news. I tried to tell him that he got off easy with a wife who wasn't always blubbering. But I knew he thought it was weird. The last time I remember really crying was after each of the girls was born. But that was just hormones. I probably hadn't shed real tears since then. But for some reason, sitting across from the woman who'd helped raise me, who'd just cleaned up after my latest parenting fail, I genuinely thought I was going to lose it.

"Becca, are you okay?" Connie reached across the table and took my hand. The warmth of her skin, damp from the washing, was all it took to calm me.

I shook my head, clearing it of any left over emotion. "I'm fine," I said. It wouldn't do any good to burden Connie with my troubles right now. I decided a long time ago not to complain about my life. There were a lot worse things in the world than bratty kids and a workaholic husband. It was stupid to get upset because the girls gave me a hard time this morning. But it wasn't just this morning. It was every morning. And afternoon and -

"Becca?"

The sound of Connie's voice jerked me back into the moment. I had a tendency to zone out and miss parts of conversations. It wasn't a great trait and I was working on it. At least, I'd thought about working on it.

"Sorry," I said. "I was just thinking about something."

Connie tilted her head. She knew something was up, but would she say anything? It was hard to tell with her. After a moment, she straightened up, took a sip of her tea and said, "I was wondering if you had anything planned for your birthday?"

I had totally forgotten about my birthday. It was May. I guess it was coming up. Excellent. I'd be thirty-five, which meant I was that much closer to forty. And what, exactly, had I done with those forty years?

I shook my head. "No," I said. "To be honest, I forgot all about it, which means Jon probably did too. He's been so busy working and...well... I'm sure it'll pass quietly."

"I won't hear of it. A birthday is a birthday and we'll make sure to celebrate," Connie said. Her face lit up with the promise of an event to plan. Connie thrived when she had a project, or a party or really anything at all that she could sink her teeth into. I'd never met anyone who could multitask the way she did. I could barely manage to cook dinner and help the girls with homework, let alone orchestrate fundraising galas the way Connie did. It exhausted me to watch, so I tried not to. I also knew there was no use in fighting it. If Connie wanted to have a birthday celebration, we'd have one. Whether I liked it or not.

"We'll have you all over for dinner tomorrow. It'll be nice, I'll do a lasagna and even make a cake."

"I really don't think I need a birthday cake, Connie." I patted my stomach and felt ridiculous when I did it, but it was true. I didn't need the cake. What I needed was a diet plan and a gym membership. Cake wasn't going to help at all.

"Don't be silly, Becca. Everyone needs cake on their birthday. Besides, calories don't count when you're the one blowing out the candles."

I laughed, then groaned. "Please don't trouble with candles and singing and all of that," I said.

"Nonsense. It'll be good for your dad to see the kids. I'm sure he'll be excited."

We were both painfully aware that he probably wouldn't know who the girls were, even though it was only a few years ago that he'd taken them everywhere with him and bragged about them constantly. Nobody loved those girls more than he had. Connie and I both knew all too well that lately, more often than not, his precious granddaughters were strangers to him. But neither of us said anything.

"How is Dad?" I asked. I tried not to let the guilt I felt about not visiting for so long show on my face.

"He's doing really well." Connie's face still lit up when she talked about him. It was nice to see that after almost twenty five years of marriage, and even with his memory failing more and more every day, she still loved him as much as she had when I was a kid. I only had vague memories of my own mother, who'd died when I was five and my brother Dylan, was fifteen. We moved to Silverdale, a city five hours away, shortly after the accident and when my dad met Connie two years later, it was as she was always meant to be my mother.

"He's had a few rough days lately," she said. "But we have to expect that those are going to happen."

"It doesn't mean you have to handle it alone, Connie. It's not like it was," I said. "He's not just forgetting where he put the remote."

"Don't you think I know that?" she snapped, but at once was apologetic. "I'm sorry, Becca." She took a deep breath and patted her hair. "He's my husband. And I love him."

"I love him too, Connie. But it can't be easy, and there are -"

"No. I took vows. For better or worse. I will not put

him into a facility."

I stared at her for a moment before conceding. "Okay. But if you ever decide it's too much, please know we support you."

She smiled and the tension of the moment was gone. "I know, dear. Now, tell me what your plans are this week."

I finished my drink and looked for a long moment at the tea stains in the bottom of the mug. "Well Jordan has dance, and Kayla has her gymnastics class. Of course, both girls have dentist appointments this week, and-"

"You know that's not what I meant."

I knew. I pushed up from the table and took both cups to the sink where I ran water into them. I might as well try and keep the kitchen clean, at least for a few hours.

"Becca?" Connie's voice came from behind me. I didn't want to turn around. I knew her face would be lined with the concern I could hear in her voice. "What are *your* plans this week? Anything for you?"

I shrugged but still didn't turn around. I felt like I was ten years old again and Connie was asking me if I'd done my homework.

"I know you're busy with the girls, but last time we spoke, you thought you might like to try painting again. To start doing something for you. What did Jon say about the idea?"

I still couldn't face her. I knew she'd be disappointed. I hated disappointing Connie. "I didn't tell him."

"Becca." I didn't even have to look to know I'd done it. She was disappointed. "Why not?"

I couldn't tell her what really happened. That even though I had been excited about the idea, for awhile at least, it just didn't seem practical. I couldn't handle the girls and my responsibilities as it was. If I put one more thing on my to-do list, I'd crumble completely. I couldn't tell Connie that after we'd spoken about it, I'd tried to get down to the basement to dig out my old art supplies but something kept coming up. There wasn't time. I couldn't do it all.

"I don't think I want to bother with painting anymore," I lied.

"It's been years since you've picked up a brush," she said. "You need something for yourself. You don't have to give up your life when you have children you know."

I nodded. But we both knew I didn't agree. I hadn't planned on giving up my passion. Of course, I hadn't planned on getting pregnant and subsequently married at twenty-one either. I had planned on finishing art school and opening a gallery one day, or at least selling my work in shows. But when we found out I was pregnant with Jordan, I quit painting right away. The doctor said the oils were bad for the baby, and after she was born, there just wasn't any time. The years slipped into one another and just when I thought I could pull out my art supplies again, I missed my period. Another baby was not in the cards. Especially nine years apart. The paints stayed in the basement.

"It's just not a good time right now," I said, turning around. "There's a lot going on with the girls, and Jon's been really busy with work. Did you know that real estate has actually picked up in the last few months? I know it seemed like it never would, but-"

"Becca," her voice was soft but there was no denying the firm tone she used. "I'm worried about you."

And there it was. The I'm-Worried-About-You speech. I turned my back and rolled my eyes.

"Don't roll your eyes."

Damn, she was good.

"Come and sit."

I didn't move.

"Please, Becca."

I put down the dish rag I'd been wringing in my hands and rejoined her at the table. I had to fight the urge to close my eyes, she looked so worried. It aged her, made her look tired. She had so many other things to be worried about, she shouldn't be bothered with me.

"Connie, please. The last thing you need right now is to worry about me. Honestly, I'm fine."

"I'm not going to sit here and pretend that I know what it's like to be raising two girls, one a teenager and the other so like her mother it would be strange if she wasn't driving you insane."

"It is driving me insane." I put my head in my hands and fought the urge to slump to the table. "Some days, like today, I didn't know how I'm going to make it. It's chaos in the morning and I have full intentions to do something for me, but by the time I get the girls to school, grab the groceries or whatever else I need to get and then run home, it's already time to pick up Kayla. Some days I don't even have time for a shower." I was talking into the table, I didn't even know if Connie could hear me but it didn't matter. I kept going, "The afternoons are filled with shuttling her to dance, or piano and that's all before I have to pick up Jordan. Don't even get me started about teenagers. But I think I'd take them over one of Kayla's play dates any day. Those are the worst because then I have to sit with some strange woman and pretend that I have my life put together just as well as hers, with her homemade cupcakes and piles of scrapbooks laying around for me to look at. And I don't. And you know what?" I looked up at Connie and said, "I fucking hate those women."

I thought she might blanch at my use of language but instead she surprised me by breaking out into laughter. "Oh, Becca," she said when she'd calmed down. "Everybody hates those women."

"Everybody?"

"Everybody."

"What about their husbands?"

"I'm pretty sure even their husbands hate them a

little bit," she said and this time it was me that burst into laughter.

There was no way that Jon would hate a woman who was so put together and organized and who didn't complain about how difficult the kids were every night. No way.

"It's true," Connie said when I'd calmed down. "And you never know what goes on behind closed doors. Those women are probably closet alcoholics or miserably unhappy, crying themselves to sleep every night. They're no different from everyone else, they just put up a good front."

The thought that all mothers felt the same, struck me. "Is that what you think then? That all mothers are unhappy?" I asked and then quieter, I added, "Were you?"

Her face morphed, the laughter disappearing as she realized I was serious. "No. Not at all." She reached across the table for my hand and I let her take it. Connie's hands were always warm and soft. She squeezed mine forcing me to look at her. "You have to remember, I was a newlywed and I was madly in love with this great man and his kids. It was different for me."

"But that's just it," I said. "We weren't yours. It must have been harder for you because you didn't ask for children. You got them as part of a package deal."

"And it was a deal I wouldn't change for anything." Her smile made me believe her. I couldn't have asked for a better mother. But even though Connie had been great, I still wondered about the woman who'd given birth to me.

"Do you think my mother was miserable?"

Connie pulled back as if I'd smacked her. The smile was gone from her face. "Why would you ask?" she said.

I'd stopped asking about my mother years ago, when

it became clear my father wouldn't or couldn't talk about her. But just because I'd stopped asking, didn't mean the questions went away.

"Because she was my mother and I need to know that I'm not alone in feeling this way."

"But you're not unhappy are you? Just tired and overwhelmed, but not necessarily miserable. Right?" Connie asked the question but I could tell she didn't want to hear the answer. Something had shifted. It was always the same when I tried to talk about my mother. I guess it must be hard to be compared to a dead woman. I never wanted Connie to think I didn't love her so I'd always dropped it.

"I'm perfectly happy." I forced a smile to my face.

"Becca, you have to know that I chose motherhood when I chose your father. But I also chose myself. You don't have to give up who you are when you have children."

"Connie," I said. "There isn't time to be anything besides what I already am. And what I'm going to be, is late to pick up Kayla if I don't hurry." I looked at the clock. I still had over an hour. Connie would know that too.

"Is it that time already?" she said. "I guess you should get going then." She stood and grabbed her purse. "So we'll see you tomorrow then? For your birthday?"

"I can't wait."

CHAPTER TWO

It was quarter after twelve which meant I was late to pick up Kayla.

Again.

On the plus side, I wasn't totally lying when I told Connie I was going to be late. And I might have had a chance of being on time if hadn't stopped at the book store to lose myself in the latest self-help titles. My best friend Stephanie said I was addicted to books that gave me hope that I could change my life. She insisted that all I really needed to do was join her in a yoga and meditation class, or something like that, and I would find my center. I still wasn't sure what that meant, and I was afraid to ask, because no doubt it would launch some sort of discussion about how I was killing my body and my mind with caffeine and sugar. It was usually best to avoid those types of topics with Steph.

By the time I pulled into the parking lot of Kayla's school I was a full fifteen minutes late. I put the car in park and ran to the playground in the back. There were still a few kids playing tag or climbing on the jungle gym. Kayla was on the swings, her back to me. Her blond hair flew out behind her as she pumped her legs and went higher and higher into the air. My stomach flipped. She could fall. I knew she wouldn't. But she could. She looked so free. She tipped her head back and looked up to the sky. Pure bliss written all over her face.

I remembered the swings, they used to be my favorite. The wind whipping through my hair, the sensation that the ground was miles below me, but nothing bad could happen to me as long as I kept pumping my legs.

When was the last time I'd been on a swing? When was the last time I'd had that feeling?

Kayla must have seen me, or maybe she sensed her mother watching her. She hated it when I watched her. Her legs stopped their rhythmical pump, the motion slowed and after a moment, she jumped off. She grabbed her back pack and came to stand in front of me.

"You're late."

"I'm sorry," I said. It never failed to amaze me how my children could make me feel so small.

"I'm always the last one here," Kayla said, her lip quivering. And just like that, the freedom and bliss of the swing was gone. A tantrum likely brewing behind those blue eyes.

"Kayla, I am sorry. Grandma was over and we lost track of time." Might as well throw Connie under the bus. "Besides, you aren't the last one here." I waved my arm at all the kids still playing.

"Yeah," she said heading for the car, "but their moms are here. You forgot."

"I didn't for-" I started to explain myself again but she was already too far away. Besides, how could I defend myself when it was the truth. Kayla wasn't stupid. This wasn't the first time.

By the time I got to the car, she was already strapped into her booster seat.

"You don't have dance today. What should we do before we get your sister?" I tried to keep my voice light and fun.

"I don't know," she said. The tears had already started flowing. "You left me."

"Kayla." I turned around so the seatbelt dug painfully into my neck. "I didn't leave you."

"You did," she cried. "You left me alone, you weren't ever going to come."

"Kayla, I'm here now. See, I didn't forget you." I tried to touch her arm, to make a connection that might calm her down, but the seatbelt stopped me and I couldn't bridge the gap.

It was too late anyway. She'd been saving her fit for when she got in the car, away from the kids who might be watching. Her feet started beating against the car seat, her eyes were closed and her screams hit a remarkably high pitch.

Turning around again, I tried to collect my thoughts. Kayla's tantrums were hard to deal with at the best of times, but they were particularly bad when we were in the car. The sound of her wails in such a confined space was enough to make me want to drive off the road. And I couldn't really walk away from her and ignore her, the way *Tantrum Tamers*, my current favorite book suggested. I'd tried it once, in the parking lot of Wal-Mart. In my own defense, I didn't go far, just a few cars away, I could still see our green four door from where I hid. But I guess the lady who parked next to me didn't know I was still watching. And I don't know why I didn't notice her calling the police and trying to get the door open. It was impressive really how fast the police responded. I must have been totally zoned out thinking about my shopping list or something, because it took me a few minutes before I realized they were surrounding my car trying to jimmy the lock open.

It took me more than thirty minutes to explain to the officer that I was right there and I hadn't abandoned my child, although the way Kayla was laughing and smiling at the cops made me consider it for a moment. Jon was called and after a few weeks the whole incident became something that everyone could joke about at dinner parties, but even though I laughed along, it still bothered me. After all, it was me who abandoned her child. Even if it was only for a few minutes.

"Kayla," I tried again, raising my voice so she might

hear me over her wails. "If you stop screaming..."

I knew she'd quiet down enough to hear what I would bargain with. I tried not to bribe her, because every book I'd ever read said it was the worst thing you could do, but desperate times and all that.

"Maybe if you calm down we can go to the mall before we pick up Jordan." My bargaining had the desired effect. In seconds, Kayla's screams settled down to whimpers, her breath catching in her throat with sobs she tried hard to muffle.

"The...the mall? You mean it?"

It wasn't the mall with all the stores to browse through, or even the food court with the wide array of fast food choices to help me get fatter, that appealed to Kayla. No, it was the mini amusement park the developers had thoughtfully placed right in the middle of everything. Usually it was my worst nightmare and I would plan my shopping with precision to avoid passing the swirling rides, twinkling lights and carnival music that would guarantee either a melt down, or an unscheduled stop on the merry-go-round.

"Yes, of course I mean it."

"I can go on the ponies?"

"Yes."

"And the swings?" She sat up straighter and swiped at her tears.

"Yes."

"And get cotton candy?"

"Okay."

"Candy apple?"

"No, I think..." Kayla's eyes scrunched up. "We'll see."

"And Jordan's not coming?"

Even at the age of five, she realized the mall would be a lot more fun without a sulky teenager around.

"Nope," I said. "It'll just be us."

Okay, maybe I wasn't supposed to reward tantrums, but even I was getting caught up in the excitement. It could be a fun afternoon, and if, as an added bonus, it got her to stop crying, what was the harm?

I ended up buying the cotton candy, the ice cream, and the candy apple. There was a big bag of popcorn too, but I ate most of that because after all, popcorn was low calorie. Kayla happily munched down everything else, and maybe it wasn't the healthiest lunch, but a few treats wouldn't hurt anyone. Besides, she wasn't crying. She was actually smiling and we were having fun together. I was a good mom.

Two hours of sugar and carnival rides later, I realized if we didn't get moving we would be late to pick up Jordan. "Kayla," I called her away from the concession stand where she was watching the pink candy fluff swirl around a barrel. "We have to go, we're going to be late."

"No."

"Yes," I said. "It's time to go. We had fun though didn't we?" I tried really hard to keep my voice light, but she wasn't buying it.

"I. Want. More. Cotton. Candy." Kayla clenched her fists by her sides and stamped her feet against the tile floor.

"You've had enough, sweetie. We don't want to be late for Jordan, do we?"

"I. Want. Cotton. Candy. Now!" Kayla's face started to turn red as her volume increased.

I glanced around me. People were starting to stare. A passage from *Sugar Monsters*, a book I'd only skimmed, came to mind. "When your child has been exposed to too much sugar and begins to act in a manner that is unacceptable and unreasonable, remove him or her from the situation immediately until the behavior amends itself. Do not try to negotiate."

Well, her behavior was certainly unacceptable and unreasonable, so I took the book's advice and crouched down to look Kayla in the eye. It was time for a different approach.

"No, Kayla. No more. It's time to go," I said, in my best 'I-mean-business' voice.

She didn't react. In fact, she only stared at me, and for a half a second I felt a slight glow of pride. The book worked. I'd successfully handled the situation and it wasn't that hard at all. I stood up, adjusted my purse strap over my shoulder and without looking down, held out my hand and said, "Come on, let's go."

I waited.

She didn't take my hand.

I turned around and was totally unprepared for Kayla's face, which was an unnatural shade somewhere between fuchsia and plum purple. This was not the way it was supposed to go.

"Kayla? Honey?" I crouched in front of her again, and spoke as quickly as I could, trying to diffuse her before she blew. "Sweetie, open your eyes. We can talk about it."

Forget about not negotiating. If Kayla was holding her breath, it meant one thing; I was not going to like it when she finally took one.

"Okay, maybe we can get a little bit more cotton candy to take home."

But she didn't hear me because Kayla picked that exact moment to take her breath, followed a split second later by a glass shattering scream.

"Kayla, stop. Please stop." I reached for her and tried rubbing her arms because that sometimes worked.

She wrenched away from me and fell to the floor yelling, "Don't touch me! Don't touch me! I hate you!"

There was nothing left to do. I sank to my knees and covered my face with my hands.

Breathe. Deep breaths, I told myself. Pull yourself

together. It'll be okay. No one's watching.

"Becca?" A voice from behind me pushed past Kayla's screams.

Shit.

I didn't want to but I slid my fingers open and peered through them, directly into the perfectly painted eyes that belonged to Denise, my next door neighbor and one of the many women I loved to hate.

"You look like you could use some help," Denise said. Her gaze flicked to Kayla who was writhing on the floor hollering at top volume. "Is there anything I can do?"

I forced a smile to my face and pushed myself up. This woman did not need to see what a mess I was. "What a surprise running into you." I dusted off my knees. "Everything's just fine. Kayla's a little tired is all."

"It looks like -"

"Everything's fine, Denise," I repeated, this time with a little edge.

"Kayla, sweetie," Denise said in her sugar sweet voice. "Did you know we just got a new kitten? Maybe you could come over and see it?"

Seriously? A kitten?

With the magic promise of a baby animal, Kayla's screams lessened. She wiped her nose on her sleeve.

"What's his name?" she said.

"It's a girl. And I haven't decided on a name yet. Do you have any ideas?"

Kayla looked at my annoying neighbor and smiled. Cotton candy forgotten. Just. Like. That.

"Can I?" Kayla asked me. "Can I go see the kitten?"

"We have to get Jordan," I said. The moment the words were out of my mouth, Kayla's face began to morph again.

"Becca, surely she can come for-"

"Not today," I said.

Kayla's screaming fired up again. Stronger now.

"I just thought-"

"I know what you thought, Denise," I said.

Negotiations over, I turned my back, bent down and hoisted Kayla over my shoulder. Pinning her as best I could with one hand, I made my way to the exit. With every step I took I kept my eyes forward, avoiding the pitiful stares of the other parents who no doubt were watching my staggered procession as Kayla's fists and feet pounded into my back and chest simultaneously.

"Mother, make her stop."

"I would if I could, Jordan," I said between gritted teeth. It had taken me almost five minutes to wrestle Kayla into her car seat at the mall. But being restrained hadn't done anything to help calm her down. For such a small girl, her screams had staying power. She was still madly kicking at the back of my seat while hollering unintelligible things. Every once in awhile I could make out an, "I hate you." But mostly it was noise that was making my pulse pound in my temple, giving me a headache that not even the strongest drugs would touch.

"Do you have any idea how embarrassing it is when my friends hear that?" Jordan stabbed her finger in the air towards her sister in the back seat. "I mean, Mac was standing right there when you picked me up, Mother."

"Who's Mac?"

"You have to do something about her."

"Can't do anything," I said. "Who's Mac?"

Jordan let out a sigh that made it clear I was the un-coolest person in the universe. "Mac's a friend," she said after a moment.

I'm not stupid. A fact Jordan had yet to figure out. At a stop light I took a moment to glance over at her. Her face was flushed under the little amount of make-up I let her wear. "Just a friend?"

"Mother, please."

"You know you can talk to me." For a moment I thought I saw a change in her carefully constructed tough girl act.

"The light," she said. "It's green."

I faced forward again and pressed the gas.

"Besides," she said. "Even if there was something to talk about. You wouldn't hear me over her." Jordan spun around in her seat and yelled, "Shut up, twerp."

Out of the corner of my eye I saw Jordan reach into her back pack, pull out a pack of gum and toss it into the back seat at Kayla.

Kayla's cries turned to sniffles and I heard the sound of the wrapper tearing open.

"Thanks, Jordan," I said.

"Whatever." She turned and faced out the window.

When I looked in the rearview mirror at my youngest, tears still streaking down her face, I could've sworn I saw the glimpse of a smirk.

Maybe my girls were united in driving me crazy.

CHAPTER THREE

Jon's car was in the driveway.

Lovely.

It's not that I didn't like it when he came home early, but, well, I didn't like it. And with Kayla still sniffling in the back seat and Jordan in a mood, the last thing I needed was Jon getting in my space while I tried to cook dinner and save at least part of the day.

Before I'd even come to a complete stop, Jordan was out the car and headed up the walk. As soon as I opened Kayla's door and she hopped out.

"Daddy's home!" She ran past her sister and into the house, apparently forgetting that she was supposed to be screaming at me.

I gathered my things, as well as theirs, and followed them into the house. I walked in the door just as Jon said, "Sure you can watch TV."

"Thanks, Dad." Jordan stood on her toes to give Jon, who was holding Kayla, a kiss on the cheek.

"Wait a minute," I said, dumping the backpacks. "Don't you have homework?"

"Mother, I just-"

"Do you?"

Jordan's shoulders sagged and she narrowed her eyes in the way only a teenager can. "Yes." She bent to retrieve her bag from the floor.

"I don't see why she can't watch a little TV first," Jon said. "After all, it's been a long day. A little bit of unwind time would probably be good." He flashed his oldest a smile.

"Thanks, Dad." Jordan dropped her bag again and ran out of the room before I could argue.

"Perfect, Jon. Just perfect." I turned to squeeze past him to get to the kitchen.

"What?"

"Would it kill you to back me up once in awhile?"

"I don't see what the big deal is," he said behind me. Then to Kayla he said, "Why don't you go watch TV with your sister for a bit. I need to talk to Mom."

Kayla knew she wasn't allowed to watch television after a freak out. I stopped and listened, but didn't turn around.

"Okay, Daddy," she said and I heard her footsteps running down the hall.

Whatever. I rubbed my temple. I needed something for the throbbing that would not stop.

I continued walking.

"Rough day?" Jon asked as I opened the cupboard and reached for the Advil bottle.

I filled a glass of water, swallowed two pills and slumped into a chair at the table before answering him. "Yup, Kayla was in fine form. How was yours?"

"Not too bad, signed a new client today. It should be a good commission and a pretty easy sell." Jon had been in real estate since I'd met him and he was good at it too. Even with the whole world in a recession, he somehow managed to continue buying and selling houses. I'm sure his success had something to do with his charm, and his natural knack for flirting probably didn't hurt either. It used to bother me when I saw him with clients, but I'd learned to ignore it. I'd learned to ignore a lot of things.

"I'm glad you had a good day," I said and put my head down on the table.

"Hey, it can't be that bad," Jon said, and a moment later his hands were on my shoulders, working out the tension. I groaned. His fingers were like magic, melting my muscles. "Feel good?" he asked and the tone of his voice shifted. I ignored it.

"It does, thank you."

"Wanna talk about it?"

"No." I shook my head. "I really don't."

"Okay, well the girls are happy now." He stopped rubbing and slid into a chair across from me.

"I really don't know why I bother," I said. "Kayla knows she's not allowed screens after a tantrum and Jordan has homework, I told you that."

"I'm sorry," he said and picked up the newspaper.

"You're sorry?"

"Sure." He shrugged. "I was just trying to help. You looked like you could use it. But if you don't want my help, I won't."

"Really?" I said. "Did you just say that?"

I waited for him to put down the paper. When he didn't, I snatched it from him. "You think I can't handle my kids, don't you? Do I tell you how to do your job, Mr. Real Estate?"

"Wait a minute." He held his hands in front of him. "That's not what I said at all. I think you do a great job with the kids. But everyone needs a little help once in awhile, and it's okay. Even I have an assistant."

Oh, I knew Donna all right. A tiny little blond bitch. To be fair, she'd never been anything but sweet as honey to me, but anyone who's a size two with boobs that big, has to be a bitch. Jon should have known better than to mention her to me. It didn't take a genius to figure out his assistant was interested in assisting him with a whole lot more than just paperwork. Once, when I'd told Jon what I thought, he'd laughed. Maybe a little too much.

"Becca," he said, clearly realizing his mistake. "Like I said, everyone needs a little help once in awhile especially when Kayla fires up. What set it off this time?"

I shot him a look, but let it go. "The mall," I said and waved my hand. "It doesn't matter anymore. But my head..."

Jon pushed up from the table. "That I can help with," he said and went to the counter. He grabbed a bottle of wine we'd started a few nights ago, took two glasses out of the cupboard and poured us each one.

"It's not even five," I said when he handed me the wine.

"Cheers." Jon smiled and held his glass out.

What the hell.

I raised my glass. "Cheers."

Jon ordered a pizza for dinner. I'm sure he recognized that I was not about to cook anything. Besides, he knew me well enough to know that if I'd had a particularly rough day with the girls, it was take-out or peanut butter sandwiches.

God forbid he cook anything. I even bought him a cookbook once, as a hint. *Grill Zone: A man's guide to embracing the flame.* I thought he'd like it, after all didn't most men like to be master of the grill? He never said, but I'm pretty sure he thought I was insulting his somewhat lame efforts of contributing to hamburger night. He was right of course. At any rate, he never did make anything out of it.

By the time dinner arrived, Kayla had completely calmed down and had forgotten about her meltdown. Jordan was happy because we were having pizza and she'd even promised Kayla to braid her hair after bath time. It was almost happy. I liked moments like those. Too bad they didn't happen more often.

"I'm stuffed," Jon said at the exact moment that I reached for another piece of double pepperoni. "You must be hungry tonight," he added.

I dropped the pizza and glared at him. "What does that mean?"

"It means you must be hungry," Jon said.

"Just because I'm having another piece?" I pushed my plate away and got up from the table. I knew I shouldn't have another piece; I'd already had two, but I didn't need Jon commenting on it.

"Becca."

"I'm not hungry any more," I said. "It's getting late anyway, Kayla needs to have a bath and get ready for bed." I gathered up the dishes.

"I wasn't trying to-" Jon said, but I cut him off with a look.

"Daddy, will you give me my bath?" Kayla asked.

He looked at me one more time and for a moment I thought he was going to try to say something else. He knew how sensitive I was about the extra pounds that wouldn't seem to budge after Kayla was born. I didn't care how many times he said they made me look curvy. I didn't believe him.

"Come on, Kay," he said looking away from me. "Let's get you cleaned up."

"Will you tuck me in too?"

"You know I will, kiddo." He ruffled her hair and they left. I took the plates to the counter and loaded them into the dishwasher. When I turned around to get the last piece of pizza after all, it and Jordan were gone.

I didn't have a chance to talk to Jon again until after Kayla was in bed and Jordan was locked up in her room listening to music. I was stuffing ham and cheese sandwiches into baggies for the kids' lunches when I heard him come in. I had my back to him and I wasn't ready for him to slide up behind me. He wrapped his arms around my waist, pulled me close against him and nuzzled into my neck.

I jumped a bit, but didn't pull away. He must have felt bad about his comment earlier. When his lips kissed the sensitive skin behind my ear, I couldn't help the low sound that came from deep in my throat. He knew it was my sweet spot. I stretched my neck to the side a little, opening it up to him.

It had been a long time since we'd made love. Too long I knew. And it wasn't for lack of trying on Jon's part. I felt bad about that, but even though I hated to, I kept making excuses. Even after fifteen years of marriage, Jon still looked great. He stayed in shape and took care of himself. It wasn't him. I knew he wasn't the problem.

"Come on, Becca." His kisses moved lower. He pushed himself closer to me and started kissing the base of my neck again, this time working his way up to my earlobe where he bit down with just enough pressure, the way he knew I liked.

My body was winning the battle with my mind and I groaned a little more as it responded to his touch. I arched my neck further and this time he responded by spinning me around, pressing me back against the counter, and meeting my lips with his own. I couldn't remember the last time we'd kissed more than a quick peck, and I let myself sink into it.

His mouth never left mine and his hands started exploring my body. It was like he couldn't remember what I felt like. And to be honest, he probably couldn't. His touch felt good. More than good.

I gripped his back in encouragement.

"Oh God, Becca, I want you so bad."

And he did. I could feel feel his want.

My hands moved up his back and when they cupped the base of his neck, he let out his own moan and I pulled him close for a deeper kiss. His hands found their way under my t-shirt and tugged it over my head, breaking our lips apart momentarily. As if they had never left, his hands found me again, and this time shocked me with their chill on my bare skin. He didn't waste anytime unhooking my bra, leaving my breasts totally exposed.

I swallowed hard and tried to stay relaxed and go with the moment. I squeezed my eyes closed and tried not to think of the list of reasons we shouldn't be doing this in the kitchen. Jordan could come in. Were the blinds open? Jon trailed kisses from my neck to my bare chest and his hands held me firm around the waist.

I felt him pull away and my eyes snapped open. He was staring at me. I was half naked in the kitchen and he'd stopped kissing me to stare at me.

"What?" I said.

"You're beautiful."

"Beautiful?" I swallowed hard. "Right."

"You are."

I couldn't tell if he was serious or not. He had no reason to lie, except to get lucky. His gaze made me uncomfortable. I was too exposed. When he didn't say anything else, my arms flew up to my chest, trying in vain to cover my breasts and stomach at the same time.

"Don't," I muttered.

"Don't what?"

"Don't tell me things you don't mean." I bent to retrieve my t-shirt off the floor.

"Becca."

I turned my back to him and tugged the shirt over my head.

"Becca," he said again and his hand reached out and spun me around to face him. "Look at me."

I did. I looked up and met his eyes. I blinked hard. He might have thought I was going to cry. But he knew better. I looked away again.

"I do mean it," he said softly. "You're beautiful."

"Stop it."

"You are."

"Stop it," I said, louder this time. "Stop telling me things that aren't true. You know they're not true." I wrenched my arm away from him. "I'm not the same person I used to be. I'm fat and ugly, and that's the truth."

As soon as the words came out of my mouth I stopped. I didn't really feel that way about myself. Did I?

"That's enough," he said and anger flared in his usually serene eyes. "I'm sick of you putting yourself down all the time. I think you're as beautiful as the day I met you, more so. But that's not enough for you. It's never enough."

I opened my mouth to say something, but closed it again. I didn't know why I said those things. I watched as he refilled his wine glass, splashing liquid over the rim. I still couldn't find any words. He took a few healthy swallows before turning back to me.

"Do you know how long it's been since we've made love?" he asked.

I shook my head but wouldn't meet his eyes. I knew.

"Six months, Becca. Six months." He took another swallow of wine. "You're always tired or not feeling well, or...or...unhappy with yourself, or some other excuse. I love you dammit, but I'm getting fed up. I've tried my best to be understanding, really I have."

I looked at my feet and traced the pattern of the floor tile with my toe.

"Is it me?" His voice dropped, the anger draining away as quickly as it came. "Don't you find me attractive anymore? Is there someone else, Becca? Tell me."

My head snapped up. "No," I said. "God no, Jon. Of course there's nobody else. You can't really think that."

He shook his head and his shoulders fell. "Of course not, I just..." Jon put his glass down and wrapped me in my arms holding me close. "I love you, Becca." His voice was muffled in my hair and for a second I thought he might cry.

I let him hold me for a moment before I pulled back.

"I know you love me," I said.

"Then what's going on?"

"I told you." I looked down again. His eyes were too full of emotion. I couldn't tell him the real reason. That I was too tired. Too disgusted with myself, who I'd become. There was nothing sexy about my life and it was hard to get in the mood when the daily monotony wore me down. "I don't like it when you say things you don't mean," I said. I knew it was a cop out answer. And he knew it too.

For a long moment he didn't say anything. I lifted my gaze to find him glaring at me. It was definitely a glare. I'd never seen him look at me like that before.

"Jon?" My voice shook and I hated it.

When he finally spoke, his voice was tightly controlled, the anger barely contained. "I don't say things I think you want to hear. I never say anything I don't mean. If you don't believe me... well, I don't know anymore how to make you see what I see. I don't know how much I can take, Becca. I don't know what else to do."

I opened my mouth to tell him I loved him and I did find him attractive. I opened my mouth because I was going to tell him that I was sorry and I was being stupid and insecure and it wasn't him, it was me and my life. But when I opened my mouth, my throat tightened. Nothing came out.

He stood, waiting, and when I didn't say anything he said, "Forget it."

When he turned, I let my hand reach out as if to grab him and turn him around again.

"I'm going to bed," he said.

I let my hand drop as he walked away.

CHAPTER FOUR

9:00 AM. It must have been a record. I'd managed to get the kids to school without any tantrums or major embarrassing moments. Jon had left before I'd even gotten out of bed, but it was probably better that way.

I refused to dwell on what happened. There was no point. I don't think I'd ever seen Jon so angry, but if I ignored it, maybe things would go back to normal.

Whatever normal was.

I flicked the switch on the new coffee pot and sat down with the paper. I couldn't remember the last time I'd read it. I usually threw it into the recycling bin as I walked to the car. There was never any time to catch up on world news, even if I'd wanted to.

Flipping through the sections, I realized I didn't want to. Between the natural disasters and countries fighting amongst themselves, there was really nothing worth reading about. I grabbed the travel section. There was a story featuring the Swiss Alps on the cover. The mountain peaks surrounding the green, lush fields were gorgeous. The story that went with the pictures talked about a hiking holiday.

Hiking? If I was in the Swiss Alps I think I might just like to sit and look at the view. Forget hiking.

I turned the pages without really looking at them. The breakfast dishes were still piled in the sink and the vacuum stood in the middle of the living room floor, where I'd left it yesterday. I needed to make a trip to the grocery store. I flipped to the entertainment section.

A few more pages and then I'd decide what to do.

As it turned out, I didn't have to make a decision. The doorbell rang through the house.

I stood, tried to straighten my hair and went to the door, ready to tell whatever salesman was trying to push his wares on me, that I wasn't interested.

But when I opened the door to tell him just where he could go, it was Steph.

"Hey, honey. I'm home," she said in a singsong voice.

"Steph?"

"It's Wednesday, right? You did tell me to come over Wednesday morning. You said, and I quote 'I don't have anywhere to be on Wednesday, we can catch up' and really, Becca. We need to catch up. It's been way too long."

"I said that?"

Steph moved past me into the house and past the vacuum. "Of course you did that whole, 'I'm not as busy as usual on Wednesday' thing. But I knew you meant it was time to have a coffee. Look at that," she said looking around the living room, "you always say how hard it is to keep everything clean, but it looks good to me. Let's get a drink. And snacks. I'm hungry."

I looked at my best friend of almost twenty years and sighed. That's just the way Steph was. I should be used to it. So much for a morning to myself. I followed her into the kitchen just as she said, "Oh, and Becca, I'm off coffee. It's herbal tea for me. Do you have any?"

If Steph remembered that I'd told her to come by on Wednesday, I must have mentioned it somewhere along the line. It wouldn't be the first time I'd forgotten an appointment.

I dug up some peppermint tea in the pantry. I'd likely bought it after one of her lectures on eliminating caffeine from my life.

With coffee and tea in front of us, I sat at the table. I'd rather catch up with Steph than do dishes or run errands anyway. She was my oldest friend and besides Jon, Steph knew me better than anyone. Maybe even better than Jon, if last night was any indication.

"So," Steph was saying. "How are you? How're my girls?"

"They're good, driving me up the wall as usual. Maybe they need a little time with Auntie Steph."

"I'd love that," Steph said as she rummaged around in her bag. "But things might be a bit crazy for me in the next little while." She produced a small bottle from her purse.

"What's that?"

"Stevia," Steph said as she squirted a few drops into her tea. "But you didn't answer my question. How are *you* doing?"

Steph looked at me the way she always did when she was trying to figure out what was going on in my head. I looked away. I didn't want to tell her about what happened with Jon. She'd probably just tell me to go buy some slutty lingerie or something to make me feel better about myself. But what I really needed was to find a minute to figure out how to feel anything about exhaustion. A little spark of desire would go a long way, but I didn't need to hear her opinions about that either. I should probably have told her how Connie had a theory that all mothers were miserably unhappy, and she was right, I was. I should have told her all of that.

"What's Stevia?"

"Becca," Steph sighed. "It's a natural sweetener." She popped the bottle back into her bag. "It's good to talk about your feelings, you know?"

"I'm fine." I scooped two large spoonfuls of sugar into my mug and stirred.

"You shouldn't use so much sugar, it's like white poison. Besides, don't you usually drink your coffee black?"

"I feel like sugar today."

Steph shot me a look that I pretended not to notice and then said, "So aren't you going to ask me why I'm going to be busy for awhile?"

"Right." Good, she was done grilling me. "What's going on with you?" I took a sip of coffee and tried not to grimace at the sweetness.

"Well, I'm glad you asked," she said, and flipped her long immaculate braid behind her. "I'm going away."

"Okay." I should have probably tried to sound more interested, but Steph always had a new plan, a new idea, a new something. It was hard to keep up, let alone feign excitement for each new thing. I reached for a celery stick on the plate I'd put out. It was impossible to find snacks that fit whatever low fat, no gluten, soy only, diet Steph was on at any given time. Vegetables may not be elaborate, but they worked. The ranch dressing I coated the celery in was strictly for me. "Where are you going?" I said, after I'd sucked all the dressing off.

"I thought you'd never ask," she said. "I'm going to back pack around Europe. Well, maybe not all of Europe, but Italy for sure. I guess it depends on my mood and where I feel like going when I get there."

"Europe, huh?" I examined my naked piece of celery. I hated celery. "Sounds fun."

"Becca, you're not even listening."

"I am," I said dipping the offending vegetable in the ranch again. "Italy. It sounds fun. When are you leaving?" This was the part of the story I was waiting for. Knowing Steph it would involve some elaborate plan with a job she heard about that was a sure thing and an easy way to get overseas. She'd probably thought she'd be able to travel for free and live a life of leisure. Steph had always been lucky. I don't know how she did it, but she had a never ending stream of men who liked to take her places or set her up in great jobs that she'd work at for a few months until she got bored.

"In a few weeks. I have some money saved up, quite a bit really, and I need a change. Don't you ever just feel like you're trapped and you need to get away?"

"You have no idea," I muttered. "What do you mean you have money saved up?"

"I've been putting away for awhile and my grandma left me some money a few years back. Besides, since I'm not at the radio station anymore, I thought-"

"Why did you quit that job again?"

"They wouldn't let me speak on air," she said. "I told you. Anyway, that's not the point. The point is, I'm ready for a change."

There was something in her voice. She sounded serious and she actually wasn't relying on someone else to get her there. Maybe she really was going to go.

My mind drifted. What would it be like to travel by myself to Europe? See the canals in Venice. Maybe go to Paris and sit under the Eiffel Tower, drinking cafe au lait and eating croissants. What would it be like to wake up in the morning and only worry about myself? Maybe even paint something again?

"So," Steph was talking. "What do you think?"

"I think it sounds amazing." I took another sip of my coffee, trying to cover the envy that most certainly showed on my face. Of course I was envious. Steph was free to do what she wanted. She was the cool 'auntie' who showed up to take my girls shopping, or to the movies, but never had to deal with the daily crap that went along with being a mom. And now, it seemed, she was running off to Europe.

"You should come," she said.

I almost spat out my sugary coffee and I should have, because forcing it down my throat only made me choke. It took me a moment to get the coughing under control. Once I'd regained control, Steph brought it up again.

"Well, why not, Becca?"

"Why not? Because I have two kids, a husband and a

life. I can't just pick up and go to Europe." As much as I'd like to.

"Sure you can. Maybe not for six months like me. But surely for-"

"Six months? I wish."

"Maybe not so long," she said. "But why not a few weeks? I bet Connie could come and help look after the girls. You need a break now and then too, you know?"

I did know. That was the problem. For the last few years, all I'd dealt with was tantrums, homework, planning dinners, Jon working late, and the general monotony of being a mother. There was no question I needed a break. But the reality was, I wasn't going to get one.

"It sounds great, Steph. And believe me when I say that I'd join you if I could. But escaping to Europe is the last thing that will happen right now."

I grabbed a carrot stick. Anything to keep me from telling her I would go. That I would leave everything and go traveling with her, as if I were twenty-one again.

"Becca," Steph said, her tone turned serious. "Don't you ever find it all too much? I mean, I just don't know how you do it all. Don't get me wrong, I admire you for everything you do around here. You're a great mom." I tried not to laugh. "And you keep this house running, and you've always been there for Jon, but..."

"What?"

"I don't know how to say it," she said.

I sighed. Not speaking her mind had never been Steph's problem. "Just spit it out."

"I don't think I could do it," she said. "I don't think I could sacrifice myself the way you have. Maybe that's why I don't think I'll ever be a mom."

I felt like I'd been punched. I sucked in deeply.

"Sacrifice myself?" I managed to get out.

She had the decency to look abashed but she didn't take it back. "What I mean is, you've given up everything, Becca. You're like a totally different person."

"I am not. I'm still the same person, I just look after more people."

"When was the last time you painted anything?" Steph's green eyes flared with the challenge in the question and I stared at her for a minute instead of answering.

After a moment I said, "I thought we were talking about your trip to Europe."

She picked up her mug of tea but watched me carefully as she took a sip. "We were," she said.

The idea of going with Steph to Europe was ridiculous. I knew it was. It didn't make sense in any way.

So why couldn't I get our chat out of my head? All afternoon, it was the only thing I could think of. It wasn't even the idea of getting away, although that was appealing. It was that she'd said I'd changed. That I wasn't me anymore. Of course I was me. What did she mean? I wasn't anyone different just because I had children. Was I?

I didn't want to dwell on it. I knew the answer.

"Becca?" Jon's voice called out.

If he was home from the store with Kayla, it meant it was almost time to go for my birthday dinner. He always left shopping for my present until the last minute and this year he'd taken Kayla to help him choose something. No doubt it would a vase or a big piece of costume jewelry. Not that it mattered.

"I'm in here," I called to him and pushed up from the bedroom floor.

"Becca?" Jon opened the door. "What are you doing in here?"

"Just sitting."

"On the floor? Are you okay?"

"Of course I am. I was just..." I wasn't really sure what I was doing on the floor. I'd gone to get socks and I'd just ended up sitting, staring at the carpet. That happened sometimes. How was I supposed to explain that to Jon?

"Is everyone ready to go?" I asked instead.

"Of course." Jon didn't look convinced that I was okay, but he wouldn't start anything. We were expected at Connie and Dad's for dinner in twenty minutes. "We're just waiting for you. The kids are in the car."

I accepted his outstretched hand and let him pull me up. We hadn't touched at all since our fight but he didn't let me go right away as he usually did. Instead, he wrapped his arms around me and pulled me closer. "You're sure you're okay?"

I nodded. It was hard, but I forced myself not to pull away. He was trying. It was more than I was doing. It's not that I didn't want to fix things, I just...it was hard. Things had been strained between us to say the least, and not just in the last few days. It had been longer than that.

"Maybe later..." Jon nibbled my neck and shivers ran through me.

"Maybe later I can get a good night's sleep?" I smiled, trying to make the joke.

He pulled away. "Right, Becca. It's your birthday. If that's what you want..."

The look in his eyes, the rejection. I hated it. "Jon," I said. "It's not what I-"

"No. I get it." He dropped his arms and turned to leave. "We should go."

"Jon." I grabbed his arm. "Don't."

When he spun around I wasn't ready for the anger in his eyes. "Don't what, Becca? Don't try and be close to you? Don't try and show you affection? I've tried everything I know how to do and you keep pulling away. What is it about me?"

"It's not you," I said. "It's just..." It's just what? What was I supposed to say? I should be able to tell him that I was so tired that all I wanted to do was sleep when I got into bed. And besides that, I didn't want him to see me naked. How was I supposed to tell him that the thought of sex exhausted me? That I couldn't imagine summoning enough energy, let alone any desire. And why would he want to have sex with a shapeless, boring, house mom?

I looked at him, he was waiting for me to explain. I couldn't.

I let my arm fall to my side. Jon's shoulders sagged, and he said, "We should go."

I watched him walk out of the bedroom, leaving only my reflection, exhausted, fat and frumpy in my rumpled blouse, staring back at me in the mirror.

The drive to Dad and Connie's took fifteen minutes, which was not long enough for me to think of a way to tell Jon that I wasn't trying to avoid him. I missed him. I missed being close to him and hanging out on the couch, just talking and laughing. When was the last time we'd done that? Maybe if he just looked at me in that way he used to? It seemed more like it was the idea of sex in general that he wanted, not necessarily with me. How could I explain to him that sometimes I just wanted to snuggle and feel close? Why did it always have to be about sex?

I could've laughed at myself, and I would have too if I were alone. The idea was ridiculous. Of course it had to be about sex. Jon and I had always had a great sex life. At least until Kayla was born. Things had been going downhill for the last six years. It just got worse the longer nothing went on. Every time I turned him down, the distance between us grew larger. Even when I did relent, things never turned out the way they were supposed to. I always felt like something was missing. A connection that used to be there.

"Mother," Jordan said from the back seat. "Did you hear me?"

I looked over at Jon for help. He shrugged and offered me a small smile to let me know he was on my side whatever it was.

"No, sorry, I was daydreaming," I said. "What were you saying?"

Jordan sighed as if I'd just said the most ridiculous thing. "I asked you if I could go to a movie tonight. Liz said she'd meet me there if you could drop me off. The show doesn't start until 7:30 and this thing at Grandma and Grandpa's can't possibly take-"

"This 'thing'," Jon interrupted, "is your mother's birthday dinner. It'll take as long as it takes."

Jon glanced at me and the rush of warmth I felt for him took me by surprise. I put my hand on his leg and gave it a squeeze.

"Whatever," Jordan said. "Can I go or not?"

"The attitude isn't helping," Jon said.

"No, Jon," I said before she could launch into a full scale pout. "She can go." I turned to look at Jordan who was trying to suppress a smile. Kayla sat quietly watching the situation play out. Sometimes I thought she was taking notes for when she got older. "You can go."

In *Teen Time: Successfully parenting your terrific teen,* the author talked about picking your battles so your child felt like they were in control of even a few things in a world that was largely out of their control. Besides, it might be nice to play good cop for once.

"Really? I can go?"

Jon looked at me out of the corner of his eye as he took the familiar turn to Connie and Dad's. I knew what he was thinking. He thought I'd caved. But he wouldn't say anything.

"You can go," I said again. "We'll drop you off on the way home. But Jordan?"

"What?"

"Best behavior tonight," I said. "And I'm picking you up as soon as the movie's over."

"Whatever, sure. Can I use your phone to tell Liz? Because I still don't have my own," she added pointedly.

I handed over my cell, ignoring her comment. To hear Jordan tell it, she was the only kid in the ninth grade who didn't have their own phone. But that was a fight I was saving for another day.

CHAPTER FIVE

"He's not having a great day," Connie said to me after we arrived. The girls had retreated to the living room, where Connie kept books and games for them when they came to visit. Jordan liked to pretend she was too old for them, but, just like Kayla, she ran to the room to see what was new every time. Jon had brought his toolbox, and armed with a list from Connie, he was tackling some of the home repairs that my dad either didn't have time to get to, or more likely, couldn't handle anymore.

"What do you mean?" I asked, following her into the kitchen. "Where is he?"

"Where else?" I followed her gaze and saw Dad sitting in his chair on the deck. He sat in the same spot, looking over the gardens that Connie still tended with care. It was his spot. When I was young he'd retreat there at the end of the day with his newspaper. More often than not, he'd abandon the paper and world news and simply stare at the flowers, watching the birds or just disappearing into his own thoughts. Lately, as his memory failed more, the deck and the gardens seemed to be the only place he liked to be. On a good day, I could sit with him and get him to talk, or at least listen, while I told him about the girls and filled him in on any news that he might be interested in. On a bad day, he didn't know who I was. He'd stare at me blankly, or even get angry because I was bothering him. He knew enough that he knew he should remember me, but the fact that he couldn't, just angered him.

There had been more bad days than good lately. I wasn't sure if I could handle it today.

"It's okay," Connie said, reading my mind. "It's not too bad. He knows you're coming. He knows it's your birthday. He just seems agitated about something. But he's expecting you. Why don't you go out and say hi?"

I turned away from the window and looked at Connie. "Are you sure you don't need any help in here?"

"Becca," she said and put her hand on mine. "He's your dad. Go sit with him."

Pockets of irises, lilies and dozens of other plants I couldn't identify filled the garden and lined the pathways through the yard. Connie was featured on the community garden tour every year, and for good reason. It was only the end of May, and already the space was in full bloom, showcasing her love and attention in every corner.

Dad didn't look up as I got close. I pulled a chair over so I was sitting next to him, not in front of him. His gaze was fixed straight ahead, focused on a flowering shrub of some kind.

"Hi, Dad."

"Vicki?" He glanced in my direction.

"No, Dad."

It was hardest when he thought I was my mother. I turned so he could see me clearly. "It's me, Becca."

Vicki, I'm so glad you're here. You look beautiful. You always look so beautiful." He gripped my hand and looked into my eyes with so much adoration I didn't have the heart to correct him. I tried to loosen his grip on me, but I didn't pull away.

We sat in silence for a few moments before he spoke again, "You're not Vicki are you?" His voice cracked and I couldn't look at him.

His hand slid out of my mine and I said, "No, Dad. It's me, Becca."

I stared straight ahead and it was a few moments before I realized his shoulders were shaking slightly. When I looked over I could see the silent tears streaming down his cheeks.

There was nothing I could say, so I let him cry until the tears dried on their own.

It didn't take long. He sniffed and blew his nose into a handkerchief he pulled out of his pocket and said, "I'm sorry, Becca. You just look...you remind me so much... I'm sorry, I get confused."

"I know you do. It's okay."

That was the moment when I should have done what I usually do and start talking about the girls, about our boring life, about anything at all to change the subject so he didn't have to remember to feel bad. But I couldn't. I was tired. I tried to think of something to say, but I had nothing. So I let the silence grow. He turned back to the garden and all I could do was take his hand again. We sat that way for a few minutes and after awhile I thought maybe he might have fallen asleep so I slipped my hand from his to make my exit.

He tightened his grip, pulling me back down into the chair. "Where are you going?" he said.

"I'm-"

"Vicki, don't go."

"Dad, it's me, Becca."

"Please, you don't have to run away. Stay. I can make you happy."

There didn't seem to be much point in correcting him again. The sadness in his eyes was second only to the deep pleading as he held my gaze.

"Vicki, stay." His voice was thick with emotion and I had the odd sensation that I was an intruder in a private moment.

I peeled my hand away from his. The look of hurt deepened.

"I have to go," I said. "I-"

"Please don't say that." Tears pooled in his eyes.

My skin itched with discomfort.

"You always say that, but you don't have to go. Stay. Stay with me. Please."

"I'm sorry," I said.

And like ripping off a band aid, I left him sitting, alone with his memories.

When I went back in the house, Connie was still busy in the kitchen. I could hear Jon whistling as he changed lightbulbs in the bedroom and the girls were still nowhere to be seen. I didn't think I could face anyone. The living room was the safest place to go.

It was a comfortable room, with overstuffed couches, pillows and the plants Connie loved inside as well as out. On the two bookcases at the back of the room, Connie kept dozens of framed pictures. She said it was to help them remember the good times, but I think secretly she was trying to help Dad remember any time at all. It was hard for me to be mistaken for my dead mother, but for Connie, it must be excruciating.

I usually avoided looking at the photos, but with nothing else to occupy me, I was drawn to them. Moving to the shelves, I picked up a large picture in a jewel encrusted frame. In it my father wore a bright smile, and an equally bright purple tie that matched Connie's flowing dress. Dylan stood next to him in a shirt of the same shade and I held Connie's hand dressed in a white eyelet dress with a wide purple sash. Connie had insisted their wedding day would be fun and full of color; no boring white dress for her. I couldn't help but smile at the memory. I was only ten when they got married, but Connie made sure I felt included in her special day. For me, being a flower girl was as special as it got.

In contrast to the bright picture, was my own wedding portrait in a heavy silver frame. We'd opted for the more traditional route. Jon wore a tuxedo, and I had a long white dress that camouflaged my expanding belly. I loved that particular picture, because I had no idea it had been taken. In the shot, we were gazing into each other's eyes as the photographer captured what was an intimate moment. I remembered it well. It had been an overwhelming day, with people demanding things from me wherever I turned. Jon rescued me by grabbing my hand and sneaking me into a quiet corner of the botanical gardens that were the back drop for our photos.

"It's such a crazy day," I'd said blinking back tears of exhaustion.

"It's only going to get crazier."

"It is, isn't it?"

Jon laughed and kissed me.

When I pulled away, I smiled at him, more relaxed, "I still can't believe we're doing this."

Jon took my face in his hands and stared into my eyes, the laughter was gone from his voice as he said, "I can't imagine doing anything else."

We didn't know we were being watched, the photographer had snapped the picture using his zoom lens. It was one of my most cherished memories from that day.

I ran my finger down the side of the frame, remembering. It seemed like a life time ago. But then again, it was. We'd been married almost fourteen years. Most of my adult life. I put the frame back on the shelf, this time placing it at the front.

Jon's whistling came closer and I turned toward the hallway as he walked past. He stopped and gave me a quick smile. Even though things had been tense with us, he was still on my side. He knew seeing my father wasn't easy.

When he left, I returned my attention to the bookshelf. There were quite a few pictures of Dad and Connie together over the years, most of them taken on their many travels together. A few more family shots from when we were kids, taken before Dylan had graduated and moved away. He rarely came to visit, but we lived vicariously through the postcards that he sent on his journeys as a travel writer.

There were various shots of Dad posed with Jordan and Kayla. It was easy to see what a doting grandfather he was, at least before he'd started forgetting so much. One special photo of Jordan sitting next to him in his garden, was taken the summer before. For reasons I couldn't explain, Jordan enjoyed sitting with him, and even though he often had no idea who she was, he seemed to tolerate her presence and would tell her stories from when he was a child. It was magical that he could still recall events from long ago, but not what he'd had for breakfast. And that my angst filled teenager, loved it.

A picture pushed towards the back, caught my eye and I picked it up to get a closer look. It was posed portrait that was meant to be a three generation shot. It was taken when Kayla was still a baby.

I'd never liked it.

"Are you feeling okay, Becca?" Dad had asked as we were getting into position. He'd taken the baby from my arms. "You seem tired. Are you getting enough sleep?"

"She's fine, Rick. Just the usual new mom tiredness," Connie had chastised him. "Leave her be."

I'd grabbed Kayla from him again. "Stop it, Dad."

"Stop what? I'm just concerned is all."

Tears had sprung to my eyes the way they always did after Kayla was born. "Stop judging me. Stop looking at me that way. You're always watching me." I couldn't look at him so I'd turned my attention to the baby's dress which was bulging awkwardly over her diaper, and blinked hard against the burn in my eyes.

"Becca," Jon had said. His voice was calm. "Honey, nobody is judging you." He'd helped straighten Kayla's dress and positioned Jordan next to me.

"I think she smells," Jordan had said and wrinkled her nose.

"Can we just take the picture please?"

Connie did take the picture then. Kayla squirmed at the last minute causing her dress to hitch up again, Jordan was looking down at her shoes, my eyes were red rimmed with black smudges under them, and instead of looking at the camera, Dad was watching me with a strange, unreadable expression on his face.

I put the picture down and pushed it where it belonged, at the back.

There was a snapshot with me and my father taken at my high school graduation. In this one, Dad's eyes held the adoration and pride I'd always remembered and this picture was the perfect reminder of how things used to be. I put it right up front.

"Becca?" Connie interrupted my memories. "It's time for dinner." She crossed the room to me and rubbed my arms. "Are you okay? I know it's not easy sometimes with your dad."

"No." I shook my head. "No, it's not. But it's nice to look at these pictures and remember." I tried to smile. "Connie, I don't know how you do it."

"You have to remember, it's not like that for me. I see him everyday. I guess it's one of those situations where the monotony of daily life can pay off." She laughed and I felt better. I had no reason to dwell on the past and what couldn't be changed, especially if Connie could find the light side. "You know what?" Connie said. "I have a box of old pictures and some of your dad's papers and things from years ago. I think you should have them?"

"Thank you," I said, and meant it. It might help to

remember Dad the way he was, instead of what he was becoming. "That would be nice."

"Good," Connie said. "I'll have Jon take it out to the car. Now come on." She put her arm around me. "Let's go celebrate your birthday."

CHAPTER SIX

Dinner wasn't as bad as I thought it would be, which was probably a bad way to look at your birthday dinner, but with Dad the way he was, Jordan itching to leave, things rough between Jon and I and well, Kayla being Kayla, it wasn't a stretch to think things might not go well. Everyone must have been on their best behavior for my birthday, because Kayla hadn't blown a fit all day and Jordan even presented me with a card. I know Jon bought it for her to sign, but still, she managed to hand it to me without any attitude. That was gift enough for me.

Connie and Dad gave me a gift certificate for my favorite book store, which couldn't be more perfect because I knew I was going to need a new book soon. Maybe something to improve things with Jon. I'd never checked out the sexual relationships section before. Somebody, somewhere, must have written a book that could help me figure things out. I let my mind drift to the store with its rows and rows of bound pages, ready to offer me advice.

I wasn't paying attention, but I shouldn't have been surprised when Connie came out of the kitchen carrying a beautiful cake. It was Connie. She wouldn't let a birthday go by without a homemade cake. It looked delicious, but by the time she'd lit the candles, the birthday magic had worn off. Dad had returned to the deck and his garden, and the girls were more interested in the icing than singing. They sang a half hearted rendition of Happy Birthday and I was ready to go. So was Jordan.

"Mother, if we don't leave soon, I'll be late," she said as Connie started to cut slices.

"Jordan," Jon said, "I think we have time to enjoy your mother's birthday cake."

"Dad, we don't. I'm going to miss the previews."

"I want cake," Kayla whined and grabbed the plate Connie handed her.

"Eat," Connie and I said at the same time.

"Mother, it's not fair." Jordan pushed away from the table and ran out of the dining room.

"That's great," I said to Jon. "We should just go."

We did go. Mostly because I was tired. Tired of listening to Jordan's whining, tired of pretending I was happy about turning thirty-five, and well, just tired.

Kayla left without a fight, mostly because Connie gave her another piece of cake to take home with her and I had to promise she could take it to school for a snack. I was pretty sure I'd get a note home from the teacher about healthy snacks and the importance of including all the food groups every day, but I didn't care.

We dropped Jordan off at the movie theater on the way home. I knew her friend, Liz well. They'd been friends since kindergarten. I didn't see her waiting outside, but Jordan assured me Liz would be waiting inside, saving seats for them since she was so late. I gave her final instructions to meet me out front after the movie and she was gone, sprinting from the car and into the theater.

"Do you think she's too young?" I asked Jon.

"For a movie? We've let her go before," he said and turned the car out of the parking lot and towards home.

"I know, it's just..." I couldn't explain it. Maybe I was being silly but she seemed to be growing up too fast. I was probably just feeling old since it was my birthday. "I don't know, it's nothing I guess."

Jon gave me a side-long look. He was always trying to tell me that Jordan needed more freedom and if I smothered her she'd only rebel. I didn't think I smothered her. I was just trying my best to be a good mother, something Jordan reminded me every day that I was failing at miserably.

I glanced behind me. Kayla had fallen asleep, cuddled up to her stuffed dog, Pup-Pup, who managed to come everywhere with us. She looked so sweet when she was sleeping. Like an angel. An angel that was reenergizing her powers ready to attack when she was rested.

It was an awful way to think, but even when she was in peaceful slumber, I was on guard for her next tantrum. *Spirited Children,* the book our doctor recommended to me, suggested taking a picture of your child when they were at peace so you could look at it during moments when things were getting out of control. I tried it a few times, but I think the only thing it did was desensitize me, so it didn't matter when I looked at Kayla, all I could see was the cherubic face that could easily twist into a demonic mask with the least little prompting. I'm sure just thinking that way put me on some kind of bad mother list, but I couldn't help it.

"I'll carry her up to her bed," Jon whispered when we pulled into the driveway.

I nodded and gathered our things from the back seat.

I was putting the leftover cake into the fridge when Jon came into the kitchen with a wrapped box.

"You didn't think I forgot about your present did you?"

I did think that. "Of course not," I said.

"Come here," he said and put the box on the table.

I went to him and let him pull me into his arms. I inhaled his musky familiar scent and closed my eyes. It was nice. Especially after our argument. Maybe he did understand that I just wanted to feel close to him. I needed to remember that feeling. Sex would come. I nuzzled into his shoulder and let him hold me. Too soon, he released me, and handed me the box.

It was beautiful. Obviously a professional job because Jon couldn't even square the corners of the wrapping, let alone manage the curly ribbons that adorned the package.

"It looks fancy," I said and ran my fingers along the shiny surface

"Open it, I think you'll like it." He tried to suppress his smile. His excitement was contagious. I smiled and my fingers shook a bit when I slid them under the paper, popping open the seam.

Carefully, I peeled the wrapping away and exposed a pink box. It should have looked familiar, but I was too caught up in Jon's excitement. I lifted the lid, pushed back the pink tissue and-

Lifted out a nightie. It was red. It was silk. It was small. It was nothing I would wear.

Ever.

I held it out by the straps staring at it as if it would slink away. It didn't.

"Well," Jon said. "What do you think?"

I looked from the nightie to Jon. "Really?"

"Do you like it?"

He looked so eager, so earnest, that for a moment I thought I shouldn't say anything. I had the sudden and completely bizarre notion of not upsetting him. Upsetting him. As if that was the problem.

"It's a..."

"Negligee," he finished for me. "I got the matching robe too." He reached into the box and pulled out a scrap of fabric that must have been the robe. He smiled as he held it out to me.

"Why?" I managed to say.

That's when he looked at me, really looked at me. "You don't like it?"

"I don't...I guess... I don't understand it."

The smile fell off his face and guilt flooded through me. I should have liked his gift. But...it was a negligee. Was I really supposed to like a present so obviously for him?

"I thought it might make you feel better about yourself," he said. "You know, sexy. The salesgirl said every woman should feel sexy about themselves, especially on their birthdays."

"You discussed me with the sales girl?" I balled up the negligee and dropped it back into the box.

"Well, of course," he said. "I mean, I had to get you a gift."

"And when you thought of the perfect thing to get me for my thirty-fifth birthday, a silk nightie came to mind?" I couldn't keep the edge out of my voice.

Jon held out the robe again. Instead of taking it from him, I let it fall to the floor. "I was just trying to get you something nice," he said. "I thought you'd like it." He kicked the puddle of silk and moved past me to the wine cabinet.

"Why would you think that?" I spun around to face him. "Do I usually walk around in silk lingerie two sizes too small?"

"Well, maybe you should," Jon said as he popped the cork on a bottle of wine. He didn't offer me any but poured himself a glass and drank deep. "Maybe if you wore something besides your sweat pants and old t-shirts to bed you might be in the mood for sex once in awhile."

"I knew it," I said. "That's what this is all about. It wasn't a gift for me at all was it?" Anger boiled through me. It was my birthday, for god's sake, and he was thinking only of himself and his need to get laid. I snatched the nightie from the box and threw it at him.

"If you like it so much, you wear it."

Jon's wine splashed over the rim of his glass as he moved to catch it with one hand. "Becca, you're being ridiculous."

"Am I? Because I thought it was my birthday and this is quite clearly a gift for you. At least you might think it was until you saw me try and squeeze into it. Maybe I should put it on just so you can see what a bad idea it was. Here." I tried to snatch the nightie back from him but he held it tight.

"Cut it out." His voice was low with warning. Jon turned his back to me and tipped his head, draining his glass. He had no reason to be angry with me. I hadn't bought him lingerie. My own anger burned brighter.

"I'm serious," I said, not ready to let it go. "You know how I feel about my body, about...what the hell were you thinking?"

Jon slammed down his glass. "What the hell was I thinking? Maybe that I can't remember the last time I had sex with my wife and that it used to be something we both enjoyed. Lately all you do is bitch and moan about how tired you are, or how you look, and I, for one, think you look fantastic."

"Stop it." I wrapped my arms around my middle.

"I won't." His face was hard. "I thought maybe if I bought you something beautiful to wear, you might feel good about yourself and maybe even a little sexy. And before you can say it again, I was not thinking of myself. It's not just about sex, Becca. It's about a whole lot more than that."

I stared at him. There was nothing to say. My rage had burned out as quickly as the fuse had lit, leaving me with a headache that pulsed in my temples. I knew he was right. This wasn't about lingerie anymore. I hated the gulf growing between us. We'd been inseparable from the time I'd met him in my second year of art college. He was in his senior year of commerce and ready to take on the world. Or at least the real estate world. He was handsome, charming and the exact opposite of the art majors I'd dated. Jon had dreams and goals, but more than that, he cared about mine too. Laying in his arms after making love every night, he'd stroke my hair while we talked. He'd ask me questions. So many questions. He wanted to learn everything. And he did. In only a few months it felt like I'd been with him forever and I couldn't imagine my life without him in it.

The memory of those days, so long ago, flashed sudden and unexpected. Looking at him, standing in the kitchen with anger burning in his eyes, his posture hard and cold towards me, it was impossible to remember that time. The girls had been a blessing in our lives but they'd also been the start of a life I was never sure I wanted. Jon was right, this was about more than just sex. A lot more.

We'd been happy. Foolish, young and in love. When he graduated, Jon had taken a position at a local real estate firm so I could finish my art degree. He never told me pursuing painting was silly, in fact he encouraged it. And for awhile, everything was perfect. But two months into my final year, I missed my period. I was pregnant. Jon wanted to get married right away, so I dropped out of school, moved into a house on the edge of town and planned our wedding in record time. At the time, I was so busy with wedding and baby preparations, I didn't have time to think about everything I was giving up. No one realized until Jordan was born six months later, why we rushed things. I hadn't picked up a paint brush since, and the days of laying in each other's arms talking, were a distant memory.

"You don't have anything to say?" he asked me, jolting me out of my thoughts.

There was so much that should have been said. So

much that we should have told each other. I looked at him and willed myself to say what I had been feeling. That I wanted that again. Those moments, the closeness. I wanted them back. And I wanted myself back too.

I blinked hard and opened my mouth to tell him. "I'll go pick up Jordan," I said and looked away.

Before he could answer, I grabbed my purse from the table and left.

When I got to the theater, I still had thirty minutes before the movie was finished, so I parked and went next door to the book store. I might as well spend the gift certificate from Connie and Dad. As I pushed through the main doors, I inhaled deeply. I loved the scent of books. It calmed me. There was so much promise in all those printed pages.

I'd barely made it past the magazine rack when my cell phone rang. So much for a moment of peace.

"Becca?" Steph's voice crackled over the line. "Happy birthday. I tried you at home, but you weren't there."

"Which is why you're calling me on my cell."

"Jon said you went out. He sounded mad. Or drunk. Or both," Steph said. "What's going on?"

I steered myself straight to the self-help section of the store. It'd been years since I'd read a novel.

"Nothing's going on," I said. "I didn't like the present he got me and he got upset." It wasn't a total lie.

"Well what did he get you? A power tool or something?"

"Worse, lingerie."

"That's awesome," Steph squealed. "And you didn't like it?"

"Of course I didn't like it." I stopped and made a detour into the sexual health section. I picked up a title. *Lighting the Spark: Rediscovering the passion for your partner.* I put it back. I needed more than a spark. As Jon had pointed out, whatever was going on wasn't about sex.

"Maybe you should tell him you want to come to Europe with me. Now that, would be a good birthday present. Imagine, the art galleries. The history. You'd love it."

Of course I'd love it. I walked towards the travel section. Another area of the store I was unfamiliar with.

"So," Steph was still talking. "What do you think?"

I tucked the phone under my chin and reached for the travel guide to Paris. "I think," I said, as I opened the book landing on a page of the Louvre. So much inspiration within the walls, artists gathered outside, soaking up the greatness inside by sheer proximity. "It sounds great," I said with a sigh. "But it won't happen. I have kids, remember?"

I closed the book and returned it to the shelf. It was a nice dream. But it didn't matter. I didn't paint anymore.

"Well, it's something to think about," Steph said.

Because that's what I needed, something else to think about.

"There's no point," I said.

I hadn't realized I'd spoken out loud until Steph said, "Of course there's a point. Maybe that's what you need to get started painting again."

"You don't understand," I said. "It's not that easy."

"Sure it is. Pick up a brush and get to it." Steph laughed. She was always doing that. Making light of my life and how I handled it.

I stopped and watched a mother pull down a book for her young son. She handed it to him and hand in hand, they walked away. "You have no idea what it's like," I snapped. "You don't have kids or a husband so you can't possibly understand the demands I have on me everyday."

"Becca-"

"No, you think it's so easy to just drop everything and run off to Europe. Well, it's not, Steph. That might be your life, but it's not mine."

"That's not fair." I could hear the hurt in her voice and instantly regretted my outburst, but I couldn't bring myself to apologize. What I'd said was true, she didn't have a clue what it was like to be me.

"Steph, I gotta go," I said instead. "I have to pick up Jordan in a few minutes."

I clicked off the phone before she could say anything else. Or me. I'd already said too much.

A quick glance of my watch showed I wasn't late yet. The movie would be finishing any minute, which meant it would take Jordan another five, to get outside. I still needed a book.

I left the travel section and made my way back to the self-help aisle I was more familiar with. I ignored the parenting books for today. While that was usually the pressing issue, clearly, other matters had taken priority.

A red spine caught my eye. *Reenergizing the Connection: Reconnecting with your spouse.* Perfect. Maybe there was something more I could do? Of course there was something more I could do. It wasn't just Jon's fault we were so far apart. I was mature enough to shoulder some of the blame. Sometimes.

Flipping through the pages, a chapter heading jumped out at me. *When Sex is a Chore - How to bring back the fire.* I took it, and another book that caught my eye, *Relationship Repair: How to heal life's important relationships,* to the front of the store. Maybe that one would have something on apologizing to a best friend.

The line at the till took longer than normal, but mostly because I stopped to flip through the magazines before I got there. I couldn't help it, something about the glossy covers, showcasing delicious looking dinners and perfectly put together living rooms, drew me in. I never actually bought them. I'd stopped doing that years ago. The magazines filled with pictures and articles on how to be a perfect wife and mother depressed me rather than inspired me. And the last thing I needed was anything else to feel bad about.

I was ten minutes late by the time I left the store and headed down the sidewalk to pick up Jordan. I knew she'd be mad, and packing attitude, so I braced myself for the teenage monster I was sure to meet. I was ready for a hormonal meltdown. I was ready to deal with crossed arms and eye rolling. What I was not ready for, was what I saw instead.

"I don't know what the big deal is," Jordan yelled, as she stormed into the house.

"The big deal?" I said when I caught up with her. "Really?"

Jon came out from the kitchen and met us in the living room. "What's going on? What's the big deal?"

"There isn't one," Jordan said. She threw her hoodie on the couch and moved to go to her room.

"Where do you think you're going? We're not done here."

"Becca, calm down," Jon said and put his hands on my forearms. "Now, tell me, what's going on?"

"My mother is freaking out because I have a boyfriend and she totally embarrassed me in front of him," Jordan moaned. "I should be the one freaking out, not her." She jabbed a finger in my direction.

"A boyfriend?" Jon asked and raised his eyebrows in my direction. "This is new."

"I wouldn't call him a boy," I said. "And you are not old enough to be doing what I just saw."

The image of Jordan lip-locked with a cross between a man and a boy, flashed through my head again. She was way too young for that type of intimacy. The man-child had the decency to stop kissing her when they spotted me, but I hadn't missed his hand on her rear end. It wasn't appropriate.

"Oh really." Jon looked at Jordan. "How old is this guy? And how come we haven't heard about him before now?" Oh good, Jon was going to be the protective father. There was no way he would want his little girl locking lips with some half grown, testosterone loaded man-child. I crossed my arms over my chest and waited for the answer.

"He's sixteen, mother," Jordan spat the answer at me, even though it was her father who'd asked.

"That's not so bad," Jon said.

"Really? Are you serious?"

"Becca, it's not unheard of for girls to date older boys. Sixteen is only two years different."

"There is no way that kid is sixteen," I said. "You didn't see him, Jon. I don't like it, I think she's too young."

"You're unbelievable," Jordan said. "That's so not fair."

Jon sat on the edge of the couch and took Jordan's hand. "No one is saying you can't date him."

"That's exactly what she said."

"I think everyone needs to calm down," Jon said. "Why don't you get some sleep and your mother and I will talk about it?"

Jordan glanced between us. She glared at me, but when her eyes fixed on her father, they softened. "Fine," she said. "Good night, Daddy." She gave her dad a hug and without another look at me, jumped up and disappeared down the hall into her room.

Excellent. Happy birthday to me.

"Maybe we can have a little time alone together now?" Jon asked, as he got up and crossed the floor to me. He wrapped his arms around me and whispered in my ear. "I'm sorry for your present."

He'd waved the white flag. Offered me a chance to save the birthday that couldn't get much worse. I should have accepted. I should have put all thoughts of our argument and the blow up with Jordan out of my head. Instead, I pushed him away. I needed to breathe.

"What was that for?"

"You can't be serious," I said. "Our little girl is making out with a much older guy, you blow it off, make me look like the bad parent and now you want to cuddle? Please tell me you're not serious. Sex is the last thing I want."

"Oh I'm well aware of that," Jon muttered. "I wasn't looking for sex. I got that message loud and clear earlier. But we do need to talk, Becca."

Talk? Alarm bells went off in my head. I turned to make my escape to the kitchen.

"Sit down, Becca."

"I'm tired, Jon. Can we do this later?"

"It's always later with you," he said. "Whether you want to now or not, we need to deal with this." His voice was hard.

I spun and faced him. His eyes held the same angry expression I'd seen earlier. "Fine. Say what you need to say." I knew what was coming. I knew he'd tell me that he needed sex. That he had needs. I'd put him off long enough. I braced myself for what was coming.

"We can't go on like this, Becca. Something has to change."

"What?"

"I said-"

"I heard you," I said. "I just don't understand."

"I love you, Becca, but sometimes I just don't know who you are anymore."

I almost laughed. Of course he didn't know who I was. I didn't even know.

I swallowed hard but couldn't say anything.

"I don't know if I can keep doing this."

"What are you saying? Do you want a divorce?" I grabbed onto the back of the couch as the room tilted.

Jon dropped his arms, his shoulders sagged and he looked at me with an expression I couldn't read. He was supposed to say, 'No'. He was supposed to say, 'We'll make it better together, we'll work on it.'

He didn't.

He didn't say anything. It was the look on his face that told me everything he didn't have to say.

"No," I said.

The room spun around me.

"Becca, it's not that I want a divorce," he said. "I don't know. Maybe we could talk to someone."

I couldn't look at him. "You don't know?"

"Maybe we should try a separation," he said. My stomach flipped, I thought for a brief horrifying moment that I might throw up.

There was no air. I couldn't breathe. I fumbled a few steps grabbing on the table. A stack of books toppled to the floor.

Air. I needed air.

"Becca."

I couldn't look at him. But I could feel him standing next to me.

"Are you okay?" he asked.

It was such a stupid question that I had to look at him then. Tipping my head just enough so I could peer at him from under my hair. He looked like shit which made me feel slightly better. "You didn't seriously ask me that did you?"

"Becca, I'm sorry. It's just...are you?"

His hands fluttered in front of him as he tried not to touch me. It was an interesting change to see him flustered. Usually so self assured, it was kind of nice, in a twisted way, to see that our total marriage break down was affecting him too. Even a little.

"I can't do this right now," I said.

"Becca, please."

Any energy I had, left my body in a rush and I slumped to the couch and put my head in my hands. "Leave me alone, Jon."

"I think we should talk about this."

"I think you should leave me alone."

I didn't look up, but after a moment I heard him make a noise somewhere between a sigh and a cry, then I felt the slight breeze as he walked past me. It wasn't until I heard the click of our bedroom door that I opened my eyes again.

My thoughts flashed to the books I'd just bought. Somehow I didn't think reading a few chapters would be an adequate solution for my latest problem. A hysterical and totally inappropriate giggle burbled out of me. I cut it off as quickly as it started, but it was too late, I hadn't heard the door open.

"Mommy?"

I needed a drink.

I pushed myself up off the couch and turned to see Kayla leaning against the wall, Pup-Pup clutched in her arms. "What are you doing up, sweetie?" I tried my best to sound casual.

"You didn't tuck me in."

"Daddy said he put you to bed," I said. I took her hand to lead her back to her room.

"But you didn't tuck me in," she said again. This time her voice cracked.

I crouched in front of her. "I'm sorry about that. Let's fix that right now. Okay?"

She nodded and I kissed her nose. I could save one situation at least.

After I had Kayla tucked under her quilt just right

and I arranged her stuffed animals so they surrounded her just the way she liked, with Pup-Pup by her head, I sat next to her. "Are you ready for kisses?" I asked.

She nodded, her eyes barely more than slits.

I bent and dropped a kiss first on her right cheek, then her left, her forehead and finally her lips. Just the way I had since she was a baby. "Good night, sweetheart," I whispered.

Her eyes were closed. She had fallen asleep before I'd even finished with the kisses. I tiptoed through the toys strewn on the floor and was almost out the door when I heard her.

"Mommy?"

"Yes, sweetie."

"Happy birthday, Mommy."

When I left Kayla's room, our door was still closed and there was no light coming from under the door. Jon had obviously taken me seriously when I told him to leave me alone. There was no way I could sleep next to him, not when I knew how he really felt. Besides, I wasn't ready for sleep. It was still my birthday, despite the complete ruin it had turned out to be. I'd always been superstitious and if I didn't toast to the new year ahead of me, if might turn out to be even more of a mess than the last one.

In the kitchen I found the bottle of red wine Jon had opened earlier.

I hoisted my full glass. "Happy birthday, Becca. May the coming year be less of shit show."

I clinked the air and took a healthy swallow. Then I looked around. The house was a disaster. Dishes from lunch were still stacked in the sink, the girls' school bags were on the floor and laundry was piled on the couch in the living room. I refused to clean on my birthday.

With my wine glass in one hand, I grabbed the bottle with the other, and side stepping the mess, went down the hall to Jon's office. The mess would still be there when I was ready to deal with it. Besides, without access to a good book, I needed Google. Maybe I could find some insight into why my life was falling apart.

I usually tried not to go into Jon's office much. It was so organized and clean all the time with everything in place, it bothered me. How could there be such a contrast from the rest of the house right behind one door? Probably because his office was the only room Jon ever lifted a finger in. The only thing out of place was the box Connie had sent home. Jon must have brought it in from the car for me to deal with. I put the wine down on his mahogany desk without using a coaster and took the lid off it. It was as good a time as any to look at it, besides, I needed something to distract me. At least for a minute.

I flipped through some photos. Many were duplicates of the ones on Connie's shelf. I shoved our wedding photo to the bottom and focused on the older pictures. But those weren't holding my attention either. I grabbed a pile of files that were under the photographs. Connie had saved all sorts of stuff. A newspaper clipping announcing their wedding. And even an article that Dad was featured in when he and some buddies raised a bunch of money for a local family in need.

Expecting more of the same, I opened the next file. But it was different. The paper on top looked to be the deed to a house. Maybe Connie had misfiled it. But when I looked closer, I saw it wasn't their house. The document was for a house in a town called Rainbow Valley. Turning to the next page, there was what looked to be an old rental contract with directions and small faded photograph stapled to the corner. There was a contract agreement with the Rainbow Valley General Store, as well. I scanned the page. Then again. I didn't understand.

I didn't know anything about a vacation property. And in the mountains? Dad hated the mountains. Even though they were only a few hours away, we never went. Even as kids, when we wanted to camp, Dad always said there was no point going into the woods, they were just full of trouble. He told us it was silly to sleep in a tent when we had a perfectly good house and warm beds.

I stared at the picture of the house. It was more like a cabin, really, with a large covered deck surrounded by a field of wildflowers. Even though the photo was old, I could see the flowers were beautiful and in full color they would be dazzling. The contract agreement stated that the Rainbow Valley General Store would act as the agent to handle any and all rentals for the house.

It didn't make sense. A rental house? It must be a mistake. Connie probably had put it into the box thinking it was something else. But Connie didn't make mistakes like that.

I picked up my wine glass and drained it in a few gulps.

I closed the folder, but didn't put it back in the box. I'd take it and ask Dad or more likely, Connie, about it when I had a chance. I shoved it across the desk and flicked on the computer. There were more important issues to take care of first.

CHAPTER SEVEN

I couldn't be sure if it was the article I read the night before about ways to show your husband you care, or maybe it was the forum for disillusioned mothers I'd stumbled across sometime after midnight. Or, maybe it was the fact that sleeping on the couch had given me a sore neck. Whatever it was, I was up before six, with a fresh resolve.

After stretching out some of the kinks in my back, I slipped into the kitchen, started a fresh pot of coffee and poured a glass of orange juice.

"It's going to be a good day today." My voice sounded hollow and tinny in the empty room.

Affirmations were important. It was essential to start out each day with a purpose, an intent. It had been awhile since I'd used the techniques outlined in *Daily Destinations: How to live every day with purpose*. But today seemed like the perfect time to start again.

I swallowed the last of my orange juice just as the coffee finished percolating and tried to remember what the book had said about how to use affirmations. There was something about designing your day simply by harnessing the power of positive thinking.

If I visualized how my day would go, I could control my destiny.

It was worth a try anyway, things couldn't get too much worse. So I leaned back against the counter, closed my eyes, and tried to picture the perfect day. In my mind I saw Jon walking into the kitchen, falling to his knees and begging me for forgiveness. He'd say, "I can't believe we ever went to bed angry with each other. And on your birthday. I'm so sorry, Becca." Or something like that. It didn't have to be exact.

I, of course, would pull him up, where he would crush me in an embrace.

"Oh Becca, my darling, my love. Can you ever forgive me?"

Then, once I'd forgiven him, Kayla and Jordan would come in. Kayla's hair would be perfectly combed and pulled back, despite the early hour. And Jordan would be apologetic for her behavior from the night before, as well as her teenage attitude would completely dissolve.

"I'll be happy to eat whatever you've made for breakfast, Mommy," Kayla would say.

"And after breakfast, I'll clean up my dishes and tidy my room too," Jordan would add.

It was perfect. I popped my eyes open and couldn't stop the smile that formed.

Well, it might be a little over the top, but there wasn't any harm in wishing for perfection. Even if my morning went a little bit like that, it would be great. And there's no way I could have a bad day if it started so well. It was so simple. Why hadn't I tried it before?

I poured myself a cup of steaming coffee and inhaled the aroma. It was going to be a great day.

"What are you doing, Mommy?"

Startled, I splashed some coffee on my bare toe. I put my mug down with a bit more force than necessary, sloshing even more coffee on the counter and hopped on one foot, turning to see Kayla standing in front of me.

Her hair was matted in the back and sticking up in the impossibly strange angles that only her hair seemed capable of first thing in the morning.

Apparently, I hadn't worked hard enough on that part of the visualization. Oh well, it was only a small detail. Kayla's hair wasn't going to derail me from what was going to be a great day.

"I was just waiting here for you to wake up, sweetie." I bent down to kiss her on the cheek. "Did you have a good sleep?"

Kayla nodded. "Yeah, but I'm hungry. What's for breakfast?"

I smiled.

"I thought we'd have scrambled eggs and bacon today. Your favorite."

Kayla was guaranteed to agree to her favorite breakfast. So what if I stacked the odds in my favor a little bit? After all, this was all about having a good day.

"No."

"No?"

"No. I hate scrambled eggs. I want pancakes."

"Kayla, you love scrambled eggs. Just last week, you told me they were your favorite."

"Not anymore. Pancakes are my favorite. I want pancakes."

I sighed, squeezed my eyes tight for a moment and quickly modified the visualization. I could adjust. I was an adaptable woman. Such a small detail would not throw me.

I opened my eyes and pasted a huge smile on my face. My cheeks hurt from stretching. "Sure. Pancakes it is. It'll take a few minutes, why don't you go watch cartoons until it's time to eat?"

Kayla didn't need to be asked twice. She turned and ran for the living room.

I looked at the clock. There was no time for homemade so I pulled a box of mix from the cupboard. Aunt Jemima would have to do today. I got to work mixing up the batter, and while I worked, I returned to the image of Jon begging for forgiveness. That part of my plan was bound to go right. Especially if I made him breakfast too. He would see what an excellent wife and mother I was and would fall to his knees admitting how wrong he'd been, telling me he didn't mean anything that he said. How could he not?

Giving the box a shake, I added more mix to the bowl. It was better to have too much, than not enough. Plopping the box down in a cloud of flour, I stopped in the middle of stirring.

The box.

Shit.

He'd know they weren't homemade. What kind of perfect wife doesn't make pancakes from scratch?

My hands started to shake and my eyes darted to the door. Jon was going to wake up soon. There was no way I had all the ingredients to make anything from scratch. Even if I did, I didn't have the first idea how to do it. Kitchen skills were not my strength.

In a flash of brilliance, I dropped the spoon in the bowl and raced to the drawer where I kept the baking supplies. It was actually a drawer with a bunch of odds and ends, since not much baking ever happened in my kitchen. Keeping an ear out for Jon, I grabbed anything that remotely resembled a tool that could be used to bake something.

Measuring cups, spoons and a whisk.

But they were clean. Baking tools should never be clean. I threw them in the sink, went to the fridge and grabbed the carton of eggs. I cracked a half a dozen or so on top of the tools, took the box of pancake mix and poured some onto of the egg mixture creating a gooey paste. Inspired, and on a roll, I shook some more mix over the counter and smeared some on my face before burying the box at the bottom of the garbage bin.

There. Now Jon would be impressed.

Everything was still going according to plan. After my quick thinking, I finished mixing the batter, heated the griddle and scooped out four perfect circles onto the hot surface. I poured myself another cup of coffee and put a fresh pot on so Jon would be able to smell it when he walked in.

He would be so impressed. The morning was going just as I'd imagined.

And then the phone rang.

It was only 6:30, who could be calling so early?

I grabbed the cordless receiver and pushed talk. "Hello?"

"Rebecca? Is that you?"

"Yes, Dad. Is everything okay?"

"Where the hell have you been?"

"Pardon me?" It was too early to deal with my dad.

"Are you hard of hearing?" he barked. "I asked you where the hell you've been?"

"I-" Shit. The pancakes were burning. I lunged for the spatula and flipped them. Not too bad, just a little black.

"Rebecca, are you listening to me?"

"I am," I said, and turned my attention back to the phone. "What's the problem? Where's Connie."

"The problem is, that you seem to have forgotten you have a father. I'm all alone here and you don't give a shit."

"Calm down, you're not alone. And don't swear at me." He never used to swear, he considered it to be bad taste; but lately, curse words were a regular part of his vocabulary. "I do come visit you. I was there yesterday, remember?"

"Don't lie to me." His voice rose a little more. "I may not have the best memory, but I'm not senile yet. It's been over two weeks since you've been here."

I tried to stifle a sigh. "Dad, put Connie on the phone."

"Who's Connie?"

Oh, it was one of those days. "Okay, look I'm sorry. It's been busy and-"

"I don't want to hear your excuses, Rebecca. I'm a lonely old man and dammit, I would like some company."

I tucked the receiver between my ear and shoulder while I flipped the pancakes off the griddle and spooned out more batter.

"Maybe you should stop swearing at me and I'll come visit." I tried teasing him into a better mood because clearly logic wasn't the way to go.

It worked.

"Okay, okay. I'll watch my mouth. Vicki's always getting after me for that too."

"Vicki?" Oh no, it really was a bad day. "You mean Connie, Dad."

"Who are you talking to?" Jon asked as he entered the kitchen. "What's burning?"

"Nothing's burning."

Crap, the pancakes were burning.

Again.

I rushed to flip the new batch which were now as black on the bottom as the last ones.

"What's burning?" Dad asked over the phone.

"Who are you talking to?" Jon asked again.

"Oh, for God's sake. Nothing's burning." I yelled into the phone before turning to Jon, "And I'm talking to my father."

"Is this a bad time?"

"Something is burning."

Both the men spoke at the same time.

I squeezed my eyes shut, trying to block them both out for a moment. I took a few deep breaths in an effort to stay calm.

After I exhaled, I turned first to Jon. "Can you please wake up Jordan and get Kayla for breakfast while I finish up with Dad?" Even to my own ears, I sounded much calmer then I felt.

When he left, I returned my focus to Dad who was in the middle of a rant. He was probably pacing his living room getting all worked up.

"-I'm always such an inconvenience these days. You don't visit and then I call and it's a bad time. I'm just an old man with a daughter who doesn't give a shit about me. You might as well lock me up and-"

"Dad, you done?"

"Well, it's true isn't it?"

I was fresh out of energy to argue. "Look, will you be happy if I promise to visit later?"

"I guess it'll have to do."

"Fine. I'll come this morning while Kayla's at school."

"Good."

The line went dead.

It wasn't exactly the way I was hoping to spend my morning, with my confused dad, but it didn't seem like I had much of a choice. Besides, it would give me a chance to talk to Connie about the property in the mountains. Maybe she knew something. From the sounds of things, it wasn't likely Dad would remember anything.

I put the phone on the counter and a wave of exhaustion took over. I crossed my arms on the granite countertop and rested my head, right in a puddle of batter.

"I told you something was burning." Jon's voice came from behind.

I lurched upright and swiped at my forehead. When I turned around Jon was standing there, both girls flanking him. He sniffed the air and Kayla pinched her nose shut. Jordan looked as if she'd just rolled out of bed and was less than impressed about it.

It was too late, but I rushed to flip the last batch of charred pancakes. I tossed them directly into the sink on top of the gooey, egg mess I'd created earlier.

"I've never seen such a mess for pancakes before," Jon said.

The beginning pulses of a headache started in my temple. In a last ditch effort I closed my eyes and fiercely tried to recreate my visualization.

"What are you doing, Mother?" Jordan asked.

"She was doing this earlier," Kayla chipped in.

Slowly, I opened my eyes and stared at my family. "If you must know, I'm trying out a visualization technique. Is that okay?" I stared hard at Jon waiting for him to say something. When he didn't, I added, "Do you have something you want to say?"

Jon's face hardened. "No."

"No?"

He was supposed to get down on his knees now. Surely this part of the morning would go right.

"No. There's nothing I want to say right now."

He was supposed to apologize.

Jon continued, "Becca, of course we have a lot to talk about it."

"Okay, we'll talk."

Jon glanced at the girls. "I don't think now is the time," he said, "I have to run anyway." He bent down to kiss Kayla on the forehead and gave Jordan a peck on the cheek. She would have murdered me if I'd tried that.

"Where are you going?" I asked, and hated the whine in my voice.

He wasn't supposed to leave. This was going to be a happy family breakfast.

"I have an early meeting with that potential buyer I was telling you about. The one who's interested in the Old MacDonald farm." He grabbed a banana from the fruit basket before he snatched up his brief case and left.

I stared after him, waiting for him to come back. When he didn't, I took a moment to regroup before turning towards the girls. The day wasn't totally ruined yet. I forced a cheerfulness into my voice that I certainly didn't feel. "Okay, who's ready for breakfast?"

"Mother, seriously, you have goop on your forehead," Jordan said and left the room.

"What about you, Kayla. I made your favorite.

Pancakes."

"I hate pancakes. Scrambled eggs are my favorite."

CHAPTER EIGHT

I could have thought of a hundred other things I needed to do, including cleaning the kitchen after the breakfast fiasco, but after dropping the girls at school, I went to visit Dad. The last thing I needed was another ill-timed phone call.

Connie's car was in the drive when I pulled in, so I knocked and walked in the front door the way I had since I'd moved out. It's a funny thing when your childhood home stops being your house.

"Connie?" I called as I made my way into the kitchen, the most likely place to find her.

She was standing at the window looking out to the garden. Her back was to me but she had the look of a woman who would fall over if the wind blew too hard. I didn't want to startle her. "Connie," I said again, this time quieter.

She turned around so fast I was afraid she might actually fall.

"Oh, Becca," she said. "I didn't hear you come in." She put her hand up to her head, patting her hair that was desperately out of place. After a second she gave up and wrapped her robe around her a little tighter. "I'm afraid it's been a bit of a rough morning. I haven't had a chance to get ready for the day yet."

"Is everything okay?" I asked. I looked past her through the window and saw Dad. He was sitting in the chair, his leg bouncing so hard and fast I thought he might break the deck. "Dad looks...well..." Before I could finish, he bolted out of his chair and started pacing through the garden. His mouth was moving, it looked like he was yelling, but I couldn't hear through the closed window. I turned back to face Connie.

"He's been like this all morning," she said. Her voice was tired, defeated. "I tried to make him stop, or at least quiet down. I mean, the neighbors...I don't know what to do."

Connie always knew what to do.

I reached an arm out for her, but withdrew it before touching her. How was I supposed to know what to do? I was the child. I wasn't expected to deal with this type of thing. Was I supposed to go talk to him? Calm him down? Or stay here and comfort the woman who had always been the one doing the comforting?

"I'll go talk to him," I heard myself say.

I expected her to tell me not to worry, that it was okay, she'd handle it.

"Thank you, Becca," she said. Tears and exhaustion glistened in her eyes. I couldn't change my mind.

I put on a brave face, or at least I thought it was brave, tugged my purse higher over my shoulder and went out to the deck to face Dad.

Once I pushed open the screen doors I could hear quite clearly what he was saying. But it didn't make any sense.

"Carnations should be pink! Not red. Those miserable thieves took my pink carnations and gave me red ones. Red carnations aren't natural."

"Dad?"

"Vicki." He stormed straight at me, before stopping only inches from my face. I was afraid he might fall into me. But he stood straight, impossibly tall and imposing for a man who was failing so monumentally. I tipped my head to look up to him.

"Dad, it's me, Becca."

He reached out, his hand rested on my cheek in a way he'd never done before. A romantic touch. A gesture not meant for father and daughter. "Vicki, you look beautiful today. Have you been painting?"

I stared at him but didn't move his hand. At least he wasn't hollering anymore. I kept my voice low and said, "No, I haven't painted in years. You know that."

Dad dropped his hand and took a step back. Shock lined his face, and something else, concern maybe? But then again, it wasn't me he was talking to.

"Not painting? Maybe it's time for a trip to the cabin. Would that help, darling?"

"The cabin?"

"We can go up for a long weekend," he said, my voice hadn't registered with him. "The fresh mountain air will be just what you need to recharge."

I glanced at my purse, that I'd tossed on a lounge chair when I came outside. I'd stuck the folder in there last night before falling asleep.

"Hold on," I said and crossed the deck to grab the file.

"You mean this house?" I pulled out the paper with the photo and showed it to him.

Dad chuckled a bit and it sounded so good to hear him laugh that I forgot for a moment what I was doing. "Of course that's the house," he said. "Your house. Should we go? I just need to make some calls and..." the smile faded from his face.

"Dad?"

"You're not Vicki." His shoulders slumped and the broken, deflated version of my father returned.

"No, Dad. I'm not." I put the paper away. Obviously the house had something to do with my mother, but I knew enough to know it wasn't the right time to ask him about it. He wouldn't be able to tell me anything.

I took him by the hand. He let me lead him across the deck to his chair where he sat. Sagging into himself, his head tucked to his chest, he began to cry. His body shock gently with his sobs. Helpless, I sat on the chair across from him, held his hand and closed my eyes so I wouldn't have to watch.

After Dad calmed down and the tears stopped, I left him in his chair and returned to the kitchen to find Connie dressed. She didn't look as put together as normal, but it was a marked improvement.

"Thank you," she said, when I walked in kitchen.

"I didn't do anything."

"You were there," she said. "You came today and you were there for him. Thank you."

Connie looked like she might start to cry so I turned and got a bottle of water out of the fridge. One parent crying a day was my limit.

"I've been thinking," Connie said behind me. "Maybe it is time. For a facility I mean."

I whirled around. "Really? Just the other day you said-"

"I know what I said, Becca." She was tired, just as defeated as Dad. I could hear it in her voice. More than that, I could see it lined across her face. "I didn't know what to do today," she continued, "so I didn't do anything. If you hadn't come, well...I don't know what I would have done."

And then it happened. Tears from parent number two.

It's awkward when a parent cries, especially for me. So I did what I thought I should and I put my water down and hugged her.

Should I say something? Should I keep hugging? I never knew quite what to do. It wasn't natural to comfort a parent.

Fortunately, Connie pulled herself together and untangled herself from my arms first. "I'm sorry, Becca," she said. "I know this can't be easy for you either. I shouldn't burden you with such things." She wiped her eyes and turned back toward the window.

"You know I'll support whatever you decide," I said.

It was weak. I should have said something more. After all, it was my father we were talking about putting in a home. Where was Dylan when I needed him? He might be able to help, or at least help us make the decision.

She nodded, and when she turned back to face me, she looked like Connie again. Any sign of being upset or out of control, were gone. "So, do you have time for a cup of tea?"

I glanced at my watch.

"Crap. I'm going to be late. Again."

"Is it that time already? The morning went so quickly."

"Half day kindergarten is definitely not all it's cracked up to be."

11:45

"Damn it."

I turned the key in the ignition and accelerated backwards out of the drive way narrowly missing an elderly lady walking down the sidewalk.

"Get out of the way," I yelled out the window. "Sorry," I added, and pressed down on the gas.

Even if I had managed to navigate the side streets that led to the main thoroughfare with no further incidents, it would still have taken another twenty minutes once I got on the freeway, which would make me a full half hour late for pick up. My tardiness was beginning to turn into a habit.

When my cell phone rang, I didn't even look at the caller ID screen, fully expecting it to be the school. I answered it and automatically said, "I'm so sorry."

"Becca?"

"Jon?"

"You're sorry? So we can talk?"

"No." Shit, not Jon, not now. "I mean, yes. I mean, I

don't know right now."

"What?"

"Never mind. This isn't a good time." I swerved around a slow moving car.

"Becca, it's never a good time."

"Seriously, Jon. Do we have to do this right now?"

"If not now, when?"

I accelerated, trying to beat the car beside me which was trying to merge. "Jon, I know what you're going to say, and honestly, I can't hear it right now. My dad's not well, Connie's at the end of her rope and-"

"Look, I was just calling because I wanted to make sure you're okay and-"

"Okay? You wanted to make sure I was okay?" I almost laughed with the absurdity of his comment.

I could hear his sigh of exasperation across the extension before he said, "Come on. Don't be like that. I just wanted to make sure you'd be home tonight so we could talk."

"Really, where else would I be?" I wedged the phone under my shoulder so I could take the wheel in both hands.

He sighed again. "So, tonight? Can we talk?"

"Whatever." I was only half listening as I slammed on the brakes. The seatbelt bit into my shoulder as the cars in front of me came to a screeching halt. "Shit."

"What? Are you okay?"

The line of red tail lights in front of me told me I'd be even later than thirty minutes.

"Yes, I'm fine. I mean, no. I mean..." I took a deep breath and squeezed my eyes shut. Coming to a split second decision, I said, "you know what, Jon? You need to pick up Kayla today."

"What? Pick up Kayla?"

"That's what I said. I'm stuck in traffic and I'm not going to make it on time. You need to get her, you're closer."

"Becca, I can't. I have meetings. I have a showing in fifteen minutes."

"I don't give a fuck about your showing. Go get your daughter."

I gazed out at the line of cars. Horns were honking. I could hear sirens wailing in the distance.

"Becca-"

"Look, this isn't really a good time to talk. Just pick her up. You have a car seat, use it."

"But, I-"

"Good."

The minutes ticked by, and the longer I sat in traffic, the worse the pounding in my head got. The pain that had begun at breakfast was in full bloom. I rubbed my eyes and forced myself to take a deep breath.

More sirens wailed in the distance.

Perfect, it was a big accident.

I scanned the rows of traffic. If I didn't get out of there soon, my head just might explode. There was an off-ramp to my right. Some of the other drivers were using it as an escape route, but it lead to the highway.

Was it better to take a detour and back track? It might take just as long if I was going to wait for traffic to move. My eyes fell to the folder on the passenger seat. It must have fallen out of my purse. Damn, I hadn't had the chance to ask Connie what she knew about the house after all.

I grabbed the paper and pulled out the sheet titled, 'Renter's Information'. I had looked at the faded picture clipped to the top, a few times now, but there was something about it that drew me. The cabin stood in a small meadow overgrown by a mass of wildflowers in brilliant shades of red, orange, yellow and blue. A large covered porch extended off the front of the house, creating a pier into the sea of flowers. A dense mixture of pines and mountain ash trees created a wall around the clearing and the cottage. Something in the photo had a hypnotic effect; despite the old colors, I couldn't remember the last time I'd see such a stunning place.

The sound of the ambulance sirens racing past the car jolted me from my trance and I scanned the page again, looking at the words I'd read the night before. It was basic information; driving directions, where to buy groceries, that type of thing.

Rainbow Valley. I didn't even know such a place existed, but according to the sheet it was only a four hour drive into the mountains. I lowered the paper and looked at the off-ramp again. The phone rang. This time I looked at the caller ID, Brookfield Elementary flashed on the screen.

Great, Kayla probably got sick of waiting and went into the office to make sure I was coming. I put my cell down without answering it. Jon was on his way there. Let him deal with her tantrum. Of course he would probably tell her it was my fault.

I scanned the snaking line of tail lights.

Something inside snapped.

"Forget it," I said aloud.

I shifted into gear and turned the wheel sharply to the right. The phone's incessant ringing filled the car. With a smooth acceleration, I navigated onto the off-ramp that took me away from the chaos and out of town towards the highway.

CHAPTER NINE

I'd been driving for a little over an hour. The houses and strip malls had thinned out and were replaced by the occasional gas station and road side turnout. Grassy fields, dotted with cows, stretched over the rolling hills that flanked both sides of the single lane highway. With every mile that passed, I could feel a little more tension release from my shoulders. Even my hands loosened their grip on the steering wheel and that persistent ache behind my eyes started to slide away.

With the radio off, I should have been enveloped in thick silence. Instead, there was the light whistle of the wind slipping through the window seal that Jon hadn't gotten around to fixing. Instead of annoying me the way it usually did, I let the simple sound wash over me and fill the cavities of my mind, leaving no room for thoughts of what I'd just done and what I'd left behind.

The simultaneous ding and red warning light flashing on the dashboard interrupted my peace.

Dammit. Gas.

The needle hovered just over empty, a detail I'd overlooked. I scanned the landscape until I found what I was looking for.

"Fill it up, please," I told the teenage attendant.

The boy shoved the nozzle into the tank and leaned back against the door. Taking the opportunity, I grabbed my purse and slipped out to visit the restroom.

Roadside bathrooms made me cringe. It was never clear when they were last cleaned, despite the chart on the back of the door proudly proclaiming they'd been sanitized on the hour, every hour, followed by employee initials. I'd read in *Hidden Dangers* that public bathrooms were breeding grounds for the worst kinds of germs.

Trying not to touch anything, I hovered over the toilet, used my foot to flush, and skipped the sink all together, opting instead for the hand sanitizer in my purse.

I backed out of the bathroom to avoid touching the handle.

"It's fifty bucks," the teenager said when he spotted me.

"Even?"

"Fifty, even."

I fished the bills from my wallet as I walked to the car. I glanced at the pump that read $46.67 and handed him the bills. "Remarkable," I said.

"I thought so." He grinned at me and stuffed the money in his pocket. "Hey, my little sister has a toy like that." He pointed to the backseat and wandered off to help the next customer.

My stomach flipped and for a second I thought I might actually be sick. I didn't have to turn around to see what he'd pointed at, I knew.

Pup-Pup.

Shit.

When I built up my courage, I looked into back seat only to confirm what I already knew. That morning, on the way to school, Kayla had decided she wanted to take Pup-Pup to class but at the last minute, by some miracle, I'd managed to convince her to leave him in the car.

Shit. Kayla couldn't sleep without him.

I pulled my phone out of my purse and stared at the blank screen. Dead.

I got in the car, slammed the door and stared out the

windshield. The mountains weren't too far away now. I could be there in under an hour if I kept going. I reached around to the seat behind me and grabbed the toy. Visions of my little girl crying herself to sleep filled my brain. Would Jordan lend Kayla her special stuffed animal? Would Jon know she liked the pink elephant almost as much?

I'm sure they'll manage, I thought. It's not like I've never gone out before.

But I've never run away before. The thought popped into my mind before I could stop it.

The more I tried to block the image of Kayla crying at the loss of Pup-Pup, the more it persisted. I squeezed my eyes shut trying to force it out. My stomach twisted and my fingers went numb from clenching the stuffed toy. When I opened my eyes, I was staring into the rearview mirror. I'd have to turn around.

A rapping at the window startled me, breaking my trance. The teenage attendant was gesturing for me to unroll the window.

"You need something else?" he asked when I managed to start the car and get the window down.

"My phone is dead." I felt like a moron but I held it out.

He gave me a strange look and for a minute I thought he might tell me to move my car, but instead, he said, "Let me see." He took the phone and walked away. And I let him. It was the only thing I could think to do, so I sat and continued to stare out the window, stroking Pup-Pup's fur.

A few minutes later, he returned with my cell and a black cord. "Here," he said, and thrust it at me.

"What is it?"

"It's a car charger, Lady." He looked at me much the way Jordan did when I said something she thought was intensely stupid. "You plug it into the lighter."

I shook my head in an effort to wake up my body. "I

know that." I took the phone from him. "What I meant was, where did you get it?"

"Don't worry about it." He shrugged. "Some dude left it here."

"How much?"

"On the house." The boy jammed his hands into his jeans. "Like I said, some guy left it here."

I eyed him. "Thanks."

"Hey, you okay?"

"Yeah." I shoved the charger into the lighter. "I'm good."

"Here," he said, and pulled his hand from his pocket holding it out to me. "Your change."

Through my daze I managed a smile. "Keep it. For the charger."

"Thanks." He pushed his hands back into his pockets and shrugged. "If you need anything..."

"I'll be okay now." I slid the car into gear, and drove to the corner of the parking lot.

Once I got the phone plugged in and powered up, it started ringing right away.

Jon.

I flipped it open. "Have you been trying to call?"

"Jesus Christ, Becca. Yes, I've been trying to call. Where are you?"

"The battery in my phone died. I didn't notice." I rubbed my temple, feeling the headache start behind my eyes again.

"I've been worried sick. Where are you?"

"I'm fine."

"It's been over an hour, Becca. You can't still be stuck in traffic. I've been waiting for you to get home. I have meetings. Where the hell are you?"

"I told you, I'm fine."

"Okay, good." Jon softened. "I mean, it's good that you're fine, obviously. Where are you? How long till you get here?"

"I'm going away for a few days." I squeezed Pup-Pup's ear.

"What? Where are you going? Becca, what's going on?"

"I need a break. It's too much."

"What's too much? Look, I know we left things badly last night and I was a jerk this morning. We need to talk. But we can't talk if you're running away."

"I'm not running away," I whispered.

That was exactly what I was doing.

"Just come home and we can sort it out," Jon continued, "running away won't solve anything, we need to work through this together." His voice was quiet and soothing, the way he spoke to the girls to pacify them.

"You're not listening." I took a deep breath. "I need to think for a few days. Just leave it, okay?"

"Leave it?" Jon's voice broke, his calm veneer cracking. "You're just going to run away from your life? From me? And you want me to 'leave it'?

"Jon."

"What about the girls?" he whispered, Kayla must have been in the room.

"I'm not leaving forever. I'm sure you can handle things for a little while."

"When will you be back?" His voice started to take on an edge. "Where are you?"

I ignored him. "I'm sure spending some time with the girls will be good for all of you. Oh, and, I just realized I have Pup-Pup. I'll send him."

"You have Pup-Pup?"

"Yes, he was in the car."

"Pup-Pup?" Kayla's little voice in the background.

"You'll send him?"

"Pup-Pup," Kayla started wailing.

"Just give her that elephant that's on her shelf. She

likes that one too. And if Jordan lets her sleep with one of her old stuffed animals, that will help too. Just tell her Pup-Pup is having a sleepover." I looked out the window and noticed a Greyhound sign. "Jon, I'll send him right now. He'll be there by tomorrow morning."

I had to squeeze my eyes against the sound of Kayla's cries and the pounding in my head. "Don't forget to brush Kayla's teeth, she thinks she can do it herself, but you'll have to check them. And Jordan will have homework. Even if she tells you she doesn't. Oh, and you'll have to make lunch for her tomorrow. Just don't send peanut butter. Kayla can eat with you after you pick her up. And don't-"

"Becca, I can't do this. Just come home. Don't send the stupid dog, bring him home."

I took a deep breath. "Of course you can do this."

I would have said more, but I'd said everything I could think of and just then the teenager stepped out of the building and leaned up against the brick wall. "Jon, I have to go. Don't forget to pick Jordan up at three. And tell the girls I love them."

I clicked the phone shut before he could protest further and tossed it on the front seat. I grabbed Pup-Pup and headed across the parking lot.

The teenager smiled cautiously when he saw me approaching. I'd probably freaked him out enough for one day.

"Can I help you with something?"

"Yes," I said. "I need to send the dog." I held up the stuffed animal. "The bus goes into the city, right?"

"You bet." He looked at his watch. "Should be here in an hour or so. You want me to..." He gestured to the dog.

I held Pup-Pup to my chest. "No, I couldn't possibly."

"You said you needed to send it. Your kid's right? My little sister can't sleep without hers."

I nodded. "My daughter," I said. "I can do it. I'll just

go-"

"I'll take good care of him," he said reaching his hand out. "Besides, Christy, the girl who works inside," he said, and a slight blush tinted his cheeks, "she's pretty cute."

I gave the dog another squeeze. "You promise you'll take care of him?"

"Lady, I get it. My sister goes crazy over hers."

I glanced again at the Greyhound office. A pretty girl with a blonde ponytail was working at the counter inside. I turned towards the mountains. They were so close. Finally, my decision made, I turned back to the teenager. "Okay." I rummaged in my purse until I found an old receipt that I scratched my address on and gave it to the boy along with two twenty dollar bills.

"I promise I'll take care of him."

I gave Pup-Pup a kiss and entrusted him to the eager teenager who immediately headed inside with him. I watched him saunter into the office and talk to the girl. He put Pup-Pup on the counter and waved out the window to me. It was done. Kayla would get her stuffie in the morning and I could go to the cabin without guilt. Well, with less guilt.

I raised my hand, waved to the boy, and returned to the car.

I followed the twisty highway west and it wasn't long before I was surrounded by towering walls of stone. The mountains rose on both sides of the road, imposing in their solid presence. I tried to recall the last time I'd been to the forest, but I couldn't remember. Surely not since Kayla was born? When Jordan was a baby, we'd make the effort to go for picnics and short hikes, but it seemed like too much work with more than one. Everything seemed like too much work with more than one child.

Just being close to the mountains felt therapeutic. The further I drove, the more my head cleared, until the headache that had built while I was talking to Jon, faded completely. I unrolled the window and a blast of piney sharpness hit me with force. I inhaled deeply and let the scent surround me. A quick look into the rearview mirror revealed Kayla's empty car seat and a fresh flash of pain struck me in the chest. It wasn't a new feeling. I'd been experiencing what I referred to as guilt pain since before Jordan was born. Whenever I drank a coffee or ate soft cheese, or whatever else I wasn't supposed to do when pregnant, the pangs would start. At first I thought it was heartburn or something worse. It took me three trips to the doctor to rule out anything serious before he kindly pointed out that the pain might be in my head.

Only a week ago, on one of the rare occasions that I'd been early to pick up Kayla, I overheard a group of women talking. They weren't the kind of ladies I usually tried to make conversation with because they were the annoying type that always looked put together, with full make-up and wrinkle free clothes. As a general rule, I tried to avoid them. I was leaning up against the wall, trying not to attract any attention, while they were talking about mother guilt of all things. As if any of them knew what that was. One woman described it as feeling nauseous whenever she thought she should be doing something for her daughter, like steaming fresh organic beans instead of serving frozen. Another lady said it was more like a constant niggling in the back of her brain whenever she left her children with a babysitter so she could get her shopping done. To me, mother guilt felt more like someone had stuffed my heart in a vice, occasionally giving it a twist to squeeze it tighter. For me, the pain didn't happen once in awhile, it was a state of being.

The pain I thought was heartburn when I was pregnant only got worse when Jordan was born. The aching started when I couldn't quite get the hang of breast feeding, leaving me with chapped, bleeding nipples and engorged, leaky breasts. Instead of the close mother-child bond I'd anticipated, I was left with a screaming, starving infant on my lap and the dull ache of guilt. Books, like *Breast is Best* and *Mother's Milk*, only brushed over nursing difficulties, suggesting a lactation consultant to solve any problems. But there was no way I was going to drag my newborn to a clinic. I was already embarrassed enough with my total failure at the basics of motherhood. It was easier to switch to formula. And really, it's not like anyone but me cared.

That's what I thought anyway, until I went to baby group. The guilt grew deeper, and the pain sharper when the other mothers asked me about the bottles and then launched into a lecture about the benefits of breast milk. I hoped it would get better when Jordan started on solids, but the first time I whipped out a jar of mushed peaches to the incredulous stares of the other mothers, I was not at all prepared for the fall out. Not only was I not preparing my own organic peaches, but I had broken the cardinal rule of *Feeding Baby's Health: The bible of baby food*, by introducing fruit before vegetables. It wasn't long after that episode that I stopped going all together. When Kayla was born, I didn't bother looking into the groups. After all, despite my failings, Jordan had survived.

I wasn't sure if it was normal for mother guilt to manifest as physical pain, but after fourteen years of motherhood, it certainly wasn't subsiding.

Lost in thought, I almost missed the sign marking Rainbow Valley. It was wooden and weather-worn and looked like it was once brightly painted with a carved rainbow on one side. Now the colors were chipped and faded, with bits of paint still clinging to the wood. The sign heralding my arrival wasn't much, but there was no way I could miss the magnificent entrance to the valley. It was far better than any signage. Throughout the four hour drive, I'd alternately climbed and descended as I'd navigated the numerous valleys and passes of the mountain range. Now, the road curved sharply and hugged the mountainside spiraling down into the town. As the car rounded the bend, the trees dropped away on one side to reveal the valley below. Rainbow Valley.

The view was so spectacular, I had to pull off onto the shoulder to fully appreciate it. The road spiraled down into the valley, where the trees swallowed it again. A lush blanket of pines and aspens covered the mountainside and a river sliced its way through the green carpet. To the left of the river was a cluster of buildings and houses. The town. For a few minutes I sat motionless, absorbing the sight below. It was hard to believe that someplace so beautiful existed so close to home. The fingers on my right hand twitched. What would it be like to paint the scene? The thought was so sudden and unexpected, it shocked me. I hadn't painted anything in years. I had barely even sketched pictures for the girls. Hadn't wanted to. But I couldn't deny that the feeling was strong. Just the way I remembered it years ago. An eagle soared overhead, letting out a shriek that broke my reverie. I cleared the image of a brush meeting canvas from my mind, put the car into gear and began the steep descent down the mountainside.

CHAPTER TEN

The directions on the sheet instructed renters to go to the general store to pick up the keys from a woman named Sheena. Once I got into town, it didn't take me long to find the store. The road led straight into Rainbow Valley, passing only a handful of old houses, most with large vegetable gardens, laundry on the line, and the occasional goat or chicken running around the yards. Besides a gas station, a small cafe and an antiques shop, the only other building on Main Street was the general store. There wasn't much to it, but I liked what I saw. The same sense of peace that filled me driving, settled around me.

By the time I parked my car and stepped out, the sun was low in the sky. The scent of pine and fresh earth filled my senses and any tension I had left in my neck had vanished.

The store front was neatly kept, with a large veranda stretching out on either side of the door. A log bench sat beneath the window and the rails were draped in what looked like tied-dyed cloths in every possible shade of the rainbow. An array of wind chimes hung from the eves, creating what should have been an overwhelming mixture of noise. Instead the sounds complemented each other with their difference, creating a beautiful melody. Another set of bells tinkled when I opened the door and I was in for another surprise.

What looked like a small, unassuming store from the outside, was anything but. I couldn't help but stare in amazement at the sheer amount of stuff crammed inside the space. There was a grocery section to the left, with a variety of cans, boxes and bags all pushed together on the shelves in no particular order. A large deep-freeze with the words MEAT-FISH-BIRDS, scrawled on the front in black marker sat against the far wall. A fridge with the word FRESH, next to it. The other side of the store resembled a flea market, with items like hammers and nails shoved up against bird baths and baskets of yarn. Hanging from the open rafters were tennis rackets, fishing nets, hammocks, kites and every possible size of wicker baskets.

"Jason?" A voice called from somewhere behind a curtain. "Jason, is that you?"

I picked my way towards the back of the store, and the voice.

"It's about time, would you get back here and help me out? For the love of all things holy -" The woman's voice was swallowed by a loud crash.

I froze next to a barrel of dried flowers. "Hello?" I called out. "Are you okay?"

"Good lovin', you're not Jason." The woman's head peaked out from behind a beaded curtain. At first glance I thought she might be in her thirties or early forties, but as she emerged from the back room and into view, I could see that the green scarf tied around her thick black hair didn't quite cover all of the silver streaks. A crystal jewel sparkled from her nose, catching the light and detracting from the deep lines etched in her tanned skin. It was hard to tell, but she was probably in her sixties.

"Hello," she said. "I wasn't expecting any visitors today." The skin around her eyes crinkled when she smiled, which only accented the cool depth of some of the bluest eyes I'd ever seen. I tried not to stare, but there was something about her face that drew me in. I felt like I should know her. "Sorry to startle you," she said. "I thought you might be Jason. He was supposed to be here helping me with this load of boxes, but wouldn't you know it, he's late again." The woman wiped her palms on her peasant skirt and extended her hand. "I'm Sheena."

"Oh, you're Sheena?" I took her hand and she squeezed.

She didn't let go of me the way I thought she might. Instead she wrapped both her hands around mine and looked into my eyes.

"Have we met before, Sunshine?" she asked.

I shook my head.

She laughed, a hearty sound, straight from her belly that broke me from whatever trance I'd found myself in.

"Sorry," I said. "No, we haven't met before."

She released me but didn't move away. "Well, we might have. In another life. Spirits are funny things, drawing together past connections into the present."

I took a step back, putting space between us. Before I could ask her what she meant, she asked, "So, why is your spirt seeking mine today?"

"My spirit is," I started. "I mean, I'm looking for you because, well it's kind of strange, but I came up to stay at a house and I think you might have the keys?"

"There's nothing strange about that at all," Sheena said. She moved back around the counter, leaving a waft of patchouli in her wake. "What house are you staying at?"

"There's more than one?"

"I look after a handful of rental cabins. You didn't think this was all there was, did you?" Sheena waved her arm, encompassing the contents of the store.

"Well no, I mean, it's..."

"Don't worry, I'm just teasing, Sunshine. I'll help you figure it out. Who sent you? Whose place is it?"

"Well, no one sent me really. But it's Rick Saunder's place."

Sheena's face flickered and the sparkle in her eyes

dimmed. But it might have been my imagination, because after a split second her smile was back and she said, "I know just the place you're talking about. I have the keys right here." Sheena crouched down and disappeared under the counter, when she emerged a few seconds later, she held a single key attached to a stained glass rainbow keychain.

"I didn't think the Saunder's cabin was rented right now."

"It's not," I said. "I mean, well, I don't know if it is. I didn't check."

"Are you a new renter then?"

"Well, I guess I am," I said. "Rick Saunders is my father. So I guess I'm just borrowing the place for a little bit."

"Holy Mother of Earth." Sheena's face stripped of color, she dropped the key where it clattered on the counter and her hand flew to her mouth.

"Are you okay?"

She grabbed a cord that was around her neck and tugged a little pouch out from beneath her blouse. I watched, mesmerized while she kissed it and muttered something to herself that I couldn't quite make out. "Is everything okay?" I asked again.

Sheena gave her head a shake and tucked the pouch away. "Yes." Her voice faltered and cracked. "Everything's fine," she said, stronger this time. "I know your...well, knew your father. But it was a long time ago."

"Really?" I had a strong urge to grab the key and run out of the shop. I didn't want to have an awkward discussion about Dad and how he was. Besides, I couldn't imagine my straight laced father ever being friends with such a strange woman. I glanced around, looking for someone, anyone to interrupt the conversation, but the store was still empty.

"And your mother?" Sheena asked. "How is..." She

trailed off and stared just past me. I turned to see what she was looking at and half expected to see a ghost, or something equally bizarre, standing behind me.

"She's dead," I said. "Well, my mother is. My step-mom, Connie, she's fine. Did you know her as well?"

"Yes." Sheena's eyes snapped back to focus on me. "Your mother, I mean. I knew her very well. I was devastated to hear of her early calling back to the Mother Earth. She was a gifted artist."

"An artist? I didn't know her. She died when I was very young. Connie's my mother." The last part came out much harder than I'd intended, but Sheena didn't seem to notice, she was staring at me intently.

"I can't believe I didn't see it earlier."

"See what?"

Sheena didn't answer. Instead she stepped around the counter and wrapped me in a tight embrace.

"You look just like Rick," she muttered into my hair.

"Pardon?" I managed to squeak despite the crushing grip around my chest.

"And your brother?"

"Dylan? He's fine."

She released me and I sucked in a breath. For such a small woman, her strength was shocking. I watched as she again pulled out the sack from the cord around her neck and brought it to her lips before looking to the ceiling. She tucked it away but didn't say anything. Sheena stared at me again, her face an unreadable expression.

It was awkward. I felt like I should say something but I've never been good at filling silences, especially with strange women who knew uncomfortable details about my family.

"So," I started and took a step towards the counter and the key. "Is there anything I need to know?"

She blinked hard then shook her head and herself, out of whatever trance she'd been in.

"I'm sorry, Sunshine. I don't know what came over me." With a swish of her skirts, she moved and handed me the key. "I assume you have the directions to get there? It's a few minutes out of town." I patted my purse and forced a smile. "And I should tell you," she continued, "there isn't a phone up there and the cell coverage can be spotty at best. I suppose it depends on how the stars are aligned."

"That's okay, I don't really want to talk to anybody anyway." I took the key and squeezed it in my palm.

"Just like your mother." She spoke so softly I wasn't sure I heard her correctly, but I didn't have the energy to ask her to repeat herself.

"Thanks." I turned and started across the floor, eager for the sanctuary of my car.

"Sunshine?"

"My name is Becca." It came out harsher than I'd intended it. I turned around and added, "It's short for Rebecca."

"Of course it is."

"My father named me."

Sheena nodded, a small smile playing at her lips.

"My middle name is Meadow," I blurted out. I don't know why I said it. I didn't like anyone to know my hippie middle name.

Sheena smiled and said, "It's perfect, isn't it?"

I didn't know what to say in response so I looked at my feet and kicked at a dust ball on the floor. "Okay, well, I should go." It was strange, but the desire to leave and find the cabin was suddenly just as strong as the pull to stay in the cluttered shop.

"Go with blessings and sunbeams," Sheena said. She closed her eyes and tipped her head as if to pray. That was my cue, so clutching the key, I crossed the floor and let the screen door clatter behind me as I took a desperate breath of fresh air.

###

I followed the hand drawn map that was part of the file. The rough pavement gave way to gravel and it wasn't long before the trees crowded in on both sides. The mass of green was mesmerizing and I almost missed the plank bridge that spanned the river. At the last moment, I jammed on the brakes and assessed the flimsy looking bridge. It seemed solid enough, and the water wasn't raging. It was probably safe. Besides, there didn't seem to be another way across. I put the car in gear again and edged my way onto the wood and over the river.

Safely on the other side, I laughed aloud at my worry. Jordan would have called me a chicken, especially if she'd seen me holding my breath. I tried my best to close my mind to thoughts of the girls.

The road wound upwards on a one lane path, that was well worn and easier to navigate than I would have thought. Occasionally, a side road, marked with a name or number jutted from the main trail, leading to properties hiding in the trees.

After five minutes of bumping over the gravel, I noticed a small wooden sign marking another side road. Although it was faded with age, I could still make out the colors of a rainbow, similar to the one I'd seen on the highway. According to the directions, it was my turn.

The aspens and pines thinned a little on both sides of the lane, enough to allow streams of the late afternoon sunlight through, showcasing a smattering of wildflowers in a variety of brilliant colors. I took my time edging the car down the road. It wasn't too late to turn around. I could still go back. But even as the thoughts popped into my head, I knew I wouldn't. And when I rounded a corner in the road and the trees abruptly gave way to an open field, carpeted in flowers, my decision was made.

Wildflowers in every shade of the rainbow blanketed the meadow, shocking me with the intensity of pure color. The driveway circled around to a little wooden house. It was so plain in comparison to the field, it almost blended into the trees behind it.

I left the car parked at the side of the house and stepped onto the porch. It was huge, probably almost the same size of the house itself. Most of the deck was covered by a wooden roof, as if whoever had built it simply forgot to put the walls up. I took my time crossing to the front door, passing by two large wooden chairs sitting in the middle of the space, with a small wrought iron table between them. It was the rocking chair, worn with age and exposure to the elements, that drew me. It was positioned close to the edge, so the occupant could sit and stare into the field of flowers. I ran my hand along the smooth weathered wood, gave it a slight push, and letting it rock gently, turned toward the cabin.

Although old, it was easy to see the house had been well cared for. The boards had received a fresh layer of stain recently, and the front door gleamed with bright yellow paint. To the right of the door, a wooden rainbow hung from a nail. I was starting to sense a theme. I ran my fingers over the sign and smiled.

Like a child on Christmas morning, I was entranced by the wrapping, but I still needed to know what was inside. I fit the key Sheena gave me into the lock and stepped inside. I don't know what I expected, but given that my father owned it, I guess I thought it might have at least a little bit of his influence.

What I saw was the exact opposite of anything my father would have chosen. My childhood home was always tidy, and well-planned, with everything in its place. Dad insisted on an ordered environment, and Connie obliged him by choosing matching throw cushions, tables and lamps that mirrored one another on either side of the couch. It was nothing like the hippie-influenced living room I saw. A low couch that looked as if the legs had been cut off was pushed up against one wall. It was impossible to tell what color the upholstery was because it'd been draped in layers of large cloths. They were the size of bed sheets, but each one was dyed in a different vibrant color, some with patches sewn on.

The setting sun light shone through the windows. The colored glass fragments and woven dream catchers that hung in almost all the windows refracted the light, throwing it around the space in elaborate bursts of color. It was like being inside a kaleidoscope. The large front pane was the only window without adornment. I crossed the room and looked out at the spectacular display of nature's floral arrangement. The entire cabin had been designed around the field of wildflowers.

I knew I'd have plenty of time to enjoy the view. But first, I needed to finish exploring.

The small kitchen in the corner was decorated with multi-colored cupboards lining the walls above the stove and sink. On each bright door there was a painting of a different type of flower. I recognized a few, but I had no idea what they were called. There were two more doors off the main room. One opened to a bathroom, the other to a tiny bedroom with nothing more than a simple oak bed, and a wardrobe pushed in the corner. A large antique trunk acted as a nightstand, and like the bed, was covered in cloths similar to those I'd seen on the couch.

There wasn't much to the house. It was perfect. I couldn't have imagined a better place to escape to. I returned to the porch and sat in the rocking chair. The sun was starting to slip behind the mountains. The whole afternoon had passed so quickly. I couldn't help but wonder what Jon had told the girls. How would he explain where I was? I knew I should call. It would have been the right thing to do. But hadn't Sheena said that cell coverage wasn't very reliable?

The hypnotizing colors of the flowers, now muted by the dusk, were no less mesmerizing. With every rock of the chair I could feel the peacefulness of the place take over. I was tired. It had been a long day. Jon could wait. I closed my eyes and let my body relax.

CHAPTER ELEVEN

I must have drifted off. The slam of a truck door startled me into awareness, but it took me a second to remember where I was. The porch was almost completely dark. I sat up, body tensed, straining to see something in the blackness. I listened. Nothing.

The only thing I could hear were the crickets in the field.

I let out a breath. I must have been dreaming. It was entirely possible. My dreams had woken me more than once before.

The crunch of footsteps on gravel jerked me out of the chair. That wasn't a dream. I scanned the porch, looking for something to use as a weapon.

How stupid could I be? Driving out to the middle of nowhere, not telling anyone where I was going and then falling asleep totally exposed in the middle of the forest. Idiot.

My eyes fell on a long hiking stick propped in the corner. It would only take two steps to reach it. The footsteps grew closer.

"Hello?" A man's voice called from the darkness. At the same moment that his foot fell on the wooden deck, I lunged for the stick.

Grasping the solid wood in both hands, I swung towards the shadowy figure and let a scream rip from my throat.

"Whoa."

"Get away from me," I screeched. "I swear, I'll kill you. I swear it."

"Okay, okay," the voice said. "I give. I won't come any closer, but I have something for you."

"What?" I asked, and raised the stick a little higher.

"I brought you a few things." He took another step towards me. His face was cloaked in the shadows.

"Don't move," I said, and hoped I sounded braver than I felt. "I'll swing."

The man laughed, and despite the fact that I was freaked out and ready to maim him, I couldn't help notice that it didn't sound very threatening.

"Don't waste your energy on me," he said. "I promise, I come in peace." He took another step forward and I could make out the features of his face in the light from the moon. He had one of those sexy, rustic beards that meant he hadn't seen a razor in a few days. The kind I would never let Jon grow, but then again, Jon didn't live in the mountains. The stranger's hair was shaggy, past his ears, curling up at his collar. He was tall, probably six -two, and despite the broad shoulders, and the muscles that were straining against his thin t-shirt, he really didn't seem very dangerous. He held a cardboard box in front of him and a smile he wasn't even trying to hide, played on his lips.

He didn't look like he meant me any harm. But I wasn't a fool. I watched the news and I knew better than to trust a strange man, in the dark, in a secluded location. Even if he was as handsome as the one that stood in front of me.

I took a step back. "Back off. I swear I'll hit you if you take another step."

"Okay, Becca," he said. "I may not look it, but I'm smart enough to know when to leave a lady alone." He raised his hands in surrender and turned to leave.

I lowered the stick. It was getting heavy anyway. "Wait," I said. "How did you know my name?"

He turned slowly, probably so I wouldn't whack him. "Sheena told me. She sent me up with a few things she thought you might need."

"Sheena sent you?" I let the stick fall to my side. I was probably being ridiculous, but Sheena had given me a strange feeling since I'd met her. A feeling I couldn't shake. "Who are you?" I asked him.

"The name's Jason," he said. He shifted the box to one arm and offered me his hand. "Nice to meet you."

I stared at his hand, but didn't take it.

"I didn't mean to scare you," he said. "I really didn't. I'm a lot of things, but a creep isn't one of them. Had I known you were sitting in the dark, I would've waited till morning. But Sheena asked me to bring you these things."

"No," I said. "I'm sorry. I shouldn't have threatened you. Hold on." I backed up towards the door. "There must be a light switch here somewhere."

"Just on the wall there, by the door," he said.

I found the switch and in an instant the porch was illuminated with a soft glow. "How did you know?"

He shrugged and I took a good look at him for the first time. The man oozed sexuality and even more troubling, he carried it with confidence. His eyes met mine and I didn't look away, the way I usually would.

"Where do you want this?" he asked.

I cleared my throat and looked away. "What is it?"

He tilted his head, but didn't comment on my rudeness. "Just a few things, Sheena said you didn't look very prepared."

What exactly did I need to be prepared for? I thought.

I tried to peer into the box, but he was too tall and I didn't want to seem obvious.

"I think it's food, mostly," Jason said.

Food? I hadn't thought about food since breakfast. My stomach grumbled at the idea of something to eat.

I wrapped my arm around my middle, but not before Jason smiled knowingly and gestured towards the door.

"May I? Sheena would be very upset to learn that I dumped the box on the porch. And I swear, I really do come in peace."

He seemed harmless enough, and the promise of food was strong incentive, but I kept my grip on the stick as I pushed open the door and led the way into the dark cabin. I scrambled along the wall, looking for a light switch. Instead of finding one, I managed to bang my shins on the couch and two tables.

"Damn," I muttered. "Where is the-"

The room filled with the soft glow of the lamp Jason stood next to.

"-light," I finished lamely.

He'd deposited the box on the counter and I watched while he moved around the room, turning on two more lamps.

"I've been here a few times." He shrugged apologetically. "I help Sheena out sometimes, so I know my way around pretty well." He stopped in front of me. He was so close I could smell him. The scent of pine needles clung to him, like a natural cologne.

"Of course," I said, and swallowed hard. The room suddenly seemed too small for both of us. I shifted towards the door and adjusted my hands around the stick again.

Jason saw the movement, and said, "I'll go. No need to use the stick again." He smiled.

I backed away from the door, trying to give him as much space as possible.

"It was nice to meet you, Becca. I'm sure I'll see you around."

I didn't say anything. Instead, I stood, mute, and watched him walk across the porch before he slipped into the darkness on the other side. It wasn't until after I heard the roar of his truck fade away down the mountain that I carefully propped the stick against the wall, locked the door behind me and released the breath

I was holding.

CHAPTER TWELVE

The sun shone through the gauzy scarves that covered the windows, and cast the room in a warm glow. I sighed and stretched my arms over my head. What time was it? Kayla never let me sleep past six. And if she did, it inevitably ended in some sort of catastrophe.

My mind flew back to the memory of my youngest sitting at the table among of sea of mushy cereal. Was that really only a few days ago?

Would Kayla have to get her own breakfast without me there? Would Jon remember to brush her hair before school? Jordan wouldn't let her little sister leave the house without her hair done. But if Jordan was in a mood...

"No." I pulled a pillow over my head and willed my brain to change channels. Jon could handle the girls. I was on a break. The guilt pain in my chest sparked to life. I needed a break, dammit. Everyone got a day off once in awhile, why should it be different for mothers?

Giving up on further sleep, I flung the pillow to the side and heaved myself out of bed. With my toe I pushed at the pile of clothes I'd thrown on the floor the night before. I hadn't thought of fresh clothes.

I hadn't thought of anything.

There was no other choice, I pulled on the dirty jeans and t-shirt. They weren't too bad, and really, it wasn't like I hadn't worn clothes two days in a row before. I went into the bathroom and cleaned my teeth the best I could without an actual toothbrush or toothpaste.

At least there was food. Thanks to Sheena, and Jason too, I had something to eat. In the kitchen I grabbed the bottle of milk and a chicken sandwich. There'd also been a dish of tuna casserole, but I'd devoured it before going to bed. I unwrapped the sandwich and took a bite. The bread was so fresh it practically melted in my mouth, and the cheese. Was that goat cheese? It was delicious, and I polished it off in only a few bites, washing it down with the creamy milk.

The empty box sat next to the now empty fridge. There was no doubt about it, I was going to need supplies if I intended to stay.

Did I intend to stay?

I stared out the front window and took in the field of flowers awash in the sun. I listened to the silence around me. No children fighting, no phone ringing, no angry husband.

I took a deep breath, letting my lungs fill completely.

Yes, I thought as I let out a long, slow exhale, I intended to stay.

I wasn't excited to see Sheena again. It was more than a little unnerving the way she'd looked at me as if she could read my thoughts. And when she started talking to herself? That was even weirder. But at the same time, even as she made me want to run and hide, she drew me in. I couldn't understand the strange push-pull I felt, but then again, I didn't understand a lot of my feelings. Besides, there wasn't a choice. From what I could tell, there was only one store in Rainbow Valley.

The parking lot was almost empty when I pulled into the gravel lot in front of Sheena's. The lack of people suited me just fine. Sheena and Jason had been more than enough for me to take in. I glanced at my cell phone, still powered off on the front seat, where I'd left it the night before. I knew I should check in. That I should do the responsible thing, and call Jon to let him know I was fine and to tell the girls I loved them. I reached across the car, grabbed my phone and stuffed it in my purse.

I'd call later.

The inside of the store was just as quiet and deserted as the outside, so I grabbed a wicker basket from the corner and started my search through the clutter.

I was only half way down the first aisle when a voice interrupted my silence.

"Good afternoon."

I gripped my basket and turned around, looking for the source of the voice I recognized.

"I heard the bells when you came in," Jason's voice preceded him from behind the counter.

"Hi," I said. "I'm glad I ran into you." To my horror, and total surprise, I could feel my face flush. I never blushed. I bent to retrieve a bottle of shampoo from the bottom shelf.

"Oh?"

"I didn't thank you for the food last night." I straightened up and hoped my face wasn't still too red.

"It was nothing," he said. "Sheena put it together, I was just the messenger."

"Either way, it was great." I turned to look at him then, and my brain caught up with me. "Wait. Did you say good afternoon?"

"Sure did." He smiled and leaned back against a shelf crossing his arms. "It's quarter after one. It wouldn't make much sense to say good morning, would it?"

"Afternoon? You're kidding." I hadn't looked at a watch, but I'd come down to town right after I woke up. I never slept so late. Ever. "Are you sure?"

"Absolutely. Take a look." Jason pointed to the wall behind him.

I didn't bother looking. He wasn't lying. Why would he? Instead, I turned towards the fridge labeled

'FRESH.' I opened the door expecting to discover eggs, milk, cheese and other perishables to fill my basket with.

It was empty.

I looked back to Jason who only shrugged and said, "It's not Saturday."

"What does that have to do with anything?"

"Everything." Jason pushed himself off the shelf and walked closer to the fridge. And me. "Eddie provides us with all the dairy, some of the eggs and most of the produce. He has an organic farm down the valley."

"Again," I said, trying to control the waver in my voice. "What does that have to do with Saturday?"

"The thing is, Ol' Eddie doesn't like to leave the farm. He's a little paranoid. Probably did a few too many drugs in his day," Jason said. "So he only leaves the property on Saturdays, something about good cosmic energy."

I looked back at the bare fridge. "Seriously? I can't get anything for two more days?"

"Check the freezer, usually there's something in there."

There was. I found some chicken breasts and a pork cutlet and tossed them into the basket.

"Most of the meat is from right here in the valley. Sheena likes to buy local," Jason said.

"Let me guess, organic?"

"Absolutely," he said. His eyes sparkled with flashes of gold when he smiled. Not that I normally noticed that type of thing. It must have been the way the light reflected in the store. "The bread is fresh too," he said, "baked this morning by Moonbeam."

"Moonbeam?"

"What can I say? Rainbow Valley is full of old hippies. There's good karma in the valley though." He grabbed a box of cans from a pallet on the floor and began lining them up on a shelf while I watched.

"Watch out for the brownies," he said, over his shoulder.

I shook my head and turned down a different aisle. I needed space. Jason's presence made me nervous, but more frustrating, I didn't know why. He was sexy, there was no doubt. But it was more than that. Good looking guys, didn't usually make me act like a total idiot. But then again, I didn't usually get much attention from men, especially ones that looked like Jason.

I turned my attention to the shelves, taking my time picking out a variety of foods and toiletries that I'd need. I tried my best to ignore Jason, who'd finished with the cans and had moved on to sweeping the floors. I didn't look. I didn't need to. I could feel him watching me.

"Don't you have something to do?" I asked, after a few moments of unsuccessfully ignoring him.

"I'm doing it."

The bells over the door jingled, and Sheena, loaded down with an armload of what looked like more batik and tie dyed cloth, burst into the store. "Jason, come grab these. I need you to take them up to the cabin for Be-"

Jason barely had time to drop the broom and catch the bundle Sheena thrust it at him. "She's right here," he said. "You can give them to her yourself."

Sheena spun around, noticing me for the first time. "For Lord's sake, Sunshine. I didn't see you there. I'm so sorry, I thought I had more time."

"Time for what?" I asked.

"To get things organized," she said. "I thought you'd sleep a lot longer."

"I don't think that's possible," I said, trying to laugh. The sound came out as a mixture between a strangle and a squeak.

"You needed a good long rest," Sheena said, ignoring my strange noise. "It looked as if you hadn't slept in quite a while. I expected you down here late afternoon. I wanted to be here to help you get what you needed."

I stared at the other woman and goosebumps popped up on my arms. Her eyes gave away nothing and her smile was warm, but I still couldn't shake the unnerving feeling. I turned my attention to the few contents in my basket. "I'm fine," I said after a moment, and turned back towards the shelf. I didn't need these strange people knowing anything about me or why I was here. "I just forgot a few things."

"It looks like you forgot more than a few things," Sheena said. Her voice was kind and soft. It really wasn't fair of me to be rude to her. I looked up and shrugged.

"I hope Jason's been helping you out."

"He's been...he...he told me to stay away from the brownies." I could feel the burn flame to life on my cheeks again.

I didn't even have to look to know he was laughing at me.

"Well, I'm glad he was helpful." Sheena glanced between us, a smirk of her own on her face.

"Sheena, what do you want me to do with these?" Jason raised the bundle in his arms.

"Right," she said, remembering. "I brought you some things to wear, Becca. They should fit you fine and get you through the next few days."

"Really? I don't...you didn't have to-"

"Nonsense. It's the least I can do." Sheena grasped my arm and gazed into my eyes. I blinked hard and looked away, squirming out of her grip.

"It's been fun," Jason said. "But I have to run."

"Of course," Sheena said, and just like that, the strange tension was gone. "You have things to get to. Just put those on the counter, I'll take care of them myself. Thanks, love."

"Bye, ladies. I'll see you around, Becca."

After the door swung shut behind him, Sheena said,

"Jason will be out at your place later if that's okay? We thought the house would be empty for a bit longer, and he has a few projects that need to get done. I am sorry about the disruption, but he's promised to stay out of your way and leave you alone."

"It's fine, really," I said, trying not to sound disappointed. The last thing I wanted was a strange man, even a gorgeous one, okay, especially a gorgeous one, hanging around. "I'm not really doing much up there anyway. It'll be fine." I forced a smile that I'm sure Sheena could tell was fake, and returned to my shopping with a new urgency. The faster I finished, the faster I could get out of there, and back to the solitude of the cabin.

It didn't take me long to get totally overwhelmed by the store. It wasn't so much that there were too many things crammed into the small space, even though there was. It was that I had absolutely no idea what to buy when I was only cooking only for myself. I didn't have to worry about catering to three other, somewhat picky people. I didn't have to concern myself over tomato sauce versus a creamy sauce. Or crusts on the bread. Or putting onions on only half the pizza. No, it was just me. I could eat whatever I wanted. And faced with nothing but options, I couldn't think of anything I wanted.

I ended up grabbing a few packaged pastas, cans of soup and a loaf of fresh bread. After the sandwich I'd had that morning, I figured I could happily live on bread. My shopping finally finished, I hauled my basket to the counter where Sheena was wrapping bundles of fresh lavender with satin ribbons. The sweet fragrance hung in the air like a gentle cloud.

I took a deep breath, letting it fill my lungs. "That

smells divine."

"Grown right here," Sheena said. "In my back garden. Lavender is very relaxing to the senses. I'll toss in a bundle for you."

"Thank you, but that's not..." I didn't bother finishing my thought because the kind smile on Sheena's face stopped me. I looked away so she wouldn't see the embarrassment that must have shown in my eyes. "What's this?" I asked picking up a small pillow embroidered with tiny purple flowers.

"I make those sachets for babies. Lavender is the perfect scent for the little ones because it naturally soothes."

I lifted it to my nose, inhaled deeply, and asked, "Do you think it works on children as well?"

"Of course," she said. "The power of lavender works on everyone."

I looked up and met her eyes. They were full of concern. She reminded me of someone I knew. Connie maybe. She looked at me that way a lot. Like I might breakdown at any moment.

"Is there anyway I can send this to someone?"

"Of course," Sheena said. "For a friend or family?"

"No." I dropped the sachet. "I mean, yes."

Seriously, I was losing my mind. It wasn't like Sheena could have known I had abandoned my children. I took a deep breath, picked up the sachet, and said, "It's for a friend. And this as well." I picked up a small bottle of lavender oil and put the two items to the side of the counter. Maybe Jordan would like it.

"Why don't you leave me the address and I'll take care of it for you? The mail is usually picked up after lunch. It can go out today.

I nodded and scratched down my home address, putting Kayla and Jordan's name at the top.

"You look like you could use some air, Sunshine," Sheena said, when I was finished. "Take yourself outside, and I'll finish up in here. The fresh air will do you some good." She reached for my basket of shopping, and like a little girl, I did what I was told. I handed it over with a sigh of relief, and went outside.

As soon as I stepped outside, I could feel my head clear. The air was heavy with the sharp scent of pine, and the sun warmed my skin. I sat on the log bench in front of the store window, leaned my head back against the glass and looked up into the cloudless sky.

I rolled my neck, stretched and stared down the empty road. There was no where I had to be, no schedule to keep, no one to look after. It was just me, alone. My head spun with the thought. I was completely free.

Except I wasn't.

The dizzy feeling of freedom was short-lived as the familiar guilt pain crashed through me. I'd left Kayla at school. Jon didn't know where I was. What kind of mother did that? What kind of person did that?

I dug through my purse for my phone and powered it up. The red message light started blinking right away.

Ignoring the messages, I dialed the numbers for Jon's cell phone, then hesitated, my finger hovering over the send button. After a moment, I hit end, clearing the numbers from the screen.

The message light flashed relentlessly. It was hypnotic with its blinking rhythm. How many times had he called?

Only one way to find out.

I punched in the code to my voicemail.

"You have six messages," the computerized voice said, "first message."

"Becca, it's Jon. Why aren't you answering your phone? Do you know how worried I am? And what about the girls? For God's sake. You can't just run away from your problems. Come home. I don't even know where you are."

"Second message."

"Becca?" Steph's voice came on the line. "Good Lord. What's going on? Jon called and said you left him. That you abandoned Kayla at school, and just took off. Is that true? Call me. He said you didn't take anything with you except your purse. I'm worried. Call me, okay?"

"Third Message."

"Becca, for Christ's sake, answer the phone. Kayla's been screaming for you all fucking night and Jordan's going on about some guy. What the hell am I supposed to tell the girls? Answer the God damned phone."

"Fourth message."

"I'm sorry. I shouldn't have yelled. I'm sorry, I'm just so...Becca, come home. I love you."

I entered the code to erase the rest of the messages and dropped my phone into my purse. I closed my eyes, and tried to block Jon's voice from my head.

"Becca?"

I snapped my eyes open to find Sheena watching me with two large paper bags at her feet. I hadn't heard her come up.

"Are you okay, Sunshine?"

"I'm fine." I rubbed my eyes, trying my best to look normal. "Why do you call me Sunshine?" I asked, changing the subject.

Sheena smiled. "Does it bother you?"

"No." I shook my head. "I just don't understand. There's so much I don't understand."

She placed her hand on my leg and patted gently. "I don't know if I can help you with all the answers you seek," she said, "but I can at least I can help with this one. I call you Sunshine because there's a light in you. It's trying to break free, just like the sun."

I looked up from my lap and stared at her. "There's a light in me?"

Sheena nodded.

"Ha. I don't know about that. I'm certainly not feeling very light or sunshiny right now."

"It' s not always easy," she said. "I understand if you don't want to talk about it." Sheena's voice was warm and kind. "Sometimes it helps to talk," she said, and sat on the bench next to me. "Talking about your problems, releases them to the spirits so they have no control over you in the physical realm."

I wasn't exactly sure what she was talking about, but I had a strong urge to lay my head on her shoulder and let her comfort me.

Instead, I pointed to the bags and asked, "How much do I owe you?"

"Not a thing, Sunshine. Your money is no good here."

"How did you know her? Vicki, I mean. Who was she?" The questions came out so suddenly, they even shocked me. "I mean, I didn't even know about this place until the other day. Dad never said anything and Connie never mentioned it."

"No." Sheena shook her head slowly. "I imagine they wouldn't."

"But, why?"

She didn't answer, just shook her head again and the action irritated me. "I don't understand. Why so many secrets?"

"I can't answer that, Sunshine."

"Can't? Or won't?" I jumped up, no longer able to sit still. "I can't stand all the lies. All the..." I stopped myself. It wasn't fair to Sheena to direct my anger at her. "I have to go." I snatched up the bags and started to the car.

I put my groceries in the back seat and turned to apologize to Sheena, but she was gone.

CHAPTER THIRTEEN

It didn't take long to unpack my bags at the cabin. After all that shopping, I still didn't look like I had much. But at least it was something. The second bag held the clothes Sheena had lent me. I took it into the bedroom and dumped it on the bed. A sprig of lavender lay among the items and the sweet smell permeated the room. I lifted it to my nose and inhaled deeply.

Maybe lavender did have soothing properties.

I placed the sprig on my pillow and shook out the first article of clothing in the pile. The skirt was long and bright and the fabric flowed when I swung it back and forth. It was like nothing I'd ever wear. Stephanie would probably love it. She'd tell me it was enlightening and would let my spirit be free. In fact, I'm pretty sure I'd seen a very similar look on Steph before.

At least it was clean, and it did look comfortable.

I tugged off my jeans and pulled the skirt on. I couldn't help it, but the moment I put it on, I had to spin. The blue and green fabric swirled around me. The silver threads caught the light and sparkled in the sunlight streaming through the window.

I laughed at myself and grabbed a blouse from the pile. There were three of them, all made of a thin, gauzy white cotton. Lavender flowers had been embroidered on the hem of the one I held, daises on another, and a red flower of some kind on the third.

Trading the blouse for my t-shirt, I felt lighter right away. Even if I looked like a hippie, the clothes were comfortable and I didn't have to deal with an annoying waistband that felt a little too tight. I yanked the elastic out of my ponytail and using my new brush, picked out the tangles, letting my hair hang loose around my shoulders.

I felt a little like I was playing dress-up, but there had been nothing normal about the last few days anyway, so why not?

My little bedroom was a mess, and while a stack of clothes on an unmade bed at home, would have been the norm, it bothered me to have the serene environment of the cabin messy. I grabbed a few hangers and hung everything up in the wardrobe, bundling up my dirty jeans, I tucked them inside as well.

The bed was completely disheveled. I couldn't remember my dreams, but by the looks of things, I'd had a rough sleep. I reached to straighten the blankets, and a flash caught my eye.

A silver key lay in the middle of the bed. It must have fallen out of the bag. I held it between two fingers and examined it. It was too small to be a house key, and not the right type to fit into a padlock. Strange.

Sheena must have dropped it in the bag by mistake. I left the room and put the key on the kitchen counter so I would remember to take it to her when I went back to town.

The view of the meadow beckoned to me through the window, and with nothing left to do, I pushed open the screen door and went to sit in the rocking chair.

I had no idea what time it was. Kayla would be done school. Had Jon picked her up? Did he remember to take her to dance class? I should call.

I looked back to the house where my phone was. What would I say? He'd tell me to come home. How could I tell him I didn't want to? I couldn't tell him that all I wanted, was to be alone.

"No," I said aloud. "I'll call later."

I was probably lying. But even I knew I'd have to call Jon at some point.

For the moment, I forced my mind to shift gears and decided to try a relaxation technique I'd read about in *Meditating Mommies*. The book suggested focusing on one image, the first one that came to mind, until it became so clear that it took over all other thoughts, releasing stress.

I closed my eyes. It was worth a try.

A picture of a pick-up truck appeared in my mind. An older model, blue truck. Exactly like the one that had been parked in front of Sheena's store earlier.

A strange choice to meditate on, but I went with it.

I focused on the outline of the truck, the unrolled windows. The tool box in the back. The roar of the engine.

The slamming of a door jarred me from my meditation and I opened my eyes. Craning my neck, I could see the same blue truck parked down the lane, close to the tree line.

"Bizarre," I said, and shook my head. "This meditation stuff works a little too well."

I watched, and a moment later, Jason appeared from the driver's side.

Of course. It had to have been Jason's truck I'd seen at the store.

He pulled out a chain saw and wheelbarrow from the back, heaving the heavy equipment with ease. Even from a distance, I could see the muscles of his back straining against the fabric of his shirt. His masculinity was obvious and raw. Very different from Jon's perfectly groomed good looks. Very different.

He must have sensed my eyes on him because he turned around and smiled. Damn it if my stomach didn't flutter a bit.

"Hello there," he called. "Hope I didn't scare you this time."

"Nope. Of course, it helps when I know you're coming."

He loaded his wheelbarrow and, pushing it, made his way closer to the deck, and me. "It looks good on you," Jason said, gesturing to my outfit.

"I don't know about that." I laughed, surprising myself. "It's not really the type of thing I'm used to. But it's comfortable. And clean."

"What are you used to?" He asked. He leaned against the deck railing, crossed his arms and looked up at me. "I mean, what's your story? Why're you here?"

My laughter caught in my throat. "I don't think that's any of your business," I choked. I turned away, focusing my attention on a bumblebee nestling into a yellow blossom.

"Wow, that was rude of me," he said. "I'm sorry." He sounded genuine, so I turned back to face him.

"It was rude of you."

"I really am sorry, Becca. I have a way of sticking my foot in my mouth sometimes. It's not my best feature. That and my terrible singing. I'm working on it. The rudeness, I mean." Jason smiled again and I let myself smile in return. "Besides, Sheena told me to leave you alone."

"She did?" When he didn't answer, I added, "It's okay, I should probably apologize too for the way I acted last night. I guess it's not very polite to threaten kindness with violence."

"Forget about it." He waved his hand, dismissing my apology. "So, what do you think of Rainbow Valley so far?"

I sat back in the rocker and gazed over the field into the trees. "I love it," I breathed, mostly to myself.

"Well, it's not too bad for a town of old hippies," he said.

"So there are lots of hippies here? I've hardly seen anyone at all."

"Are you kidding me? Pretty much everyone here is some sort of free spirit communing with nature. Why do you think the town is called Rainbow Valley? It's not because there are actually rainbows. It's because years ago the hippies saw rainbows when they were tripping on whatever drugs they'd taken."

"That's not true." I pretended to cover my ears. "Don't ruin it for me."

"Actually, I don't know if it's true or not," Jason conceded. "But that's what I like to think. It's more interesting than just seeing a rainbow in the valley, don't you think?"

He looked so cute, trying to keep a straight face. Cute in a deadly handsome way, I couldn't help it and I burst into laughter.

No sooner had the sound bubbled from my mouth, that I stopped it. Or tried to. The result was a gagging snort.

"Hey," Jason said. "Don't stop on my account. It's funny."

The burble welling inside me burst forth and I let myself laugh. Really laugh. Even if I'd wanted to, I couldn't contain it, so I let go and doubled over in my chair holding my stomach.

It had been months since I'd had a good laugh, and longer still since my stomach muscles hurt from the effort.

After a few moments, I recovered enough to sit up and I saw Jason watching me with a grin on his face.

I covered my mouth with my hand and swallowed hard.

"I'm sorry," I managed. "I don't know why I did that."

"No," he said. "I told you, it's okay to let it out, the whole place is kind of bizarre. I'd laugh too." He grabbed a tool belt from the wheelbarrow and fastened it around his waist, where it hung low on his hips. "Besides," he added, "you look like you needed it."

I had needed it but I didn't like having it pointed out. He held my gaze for a minute, but I had to turn away.

"I have to take care of the deadfall next to Prince's Pond," Jason said, changing tracks. "I should probably get going and leave you alone."

When I looked up again he was tucking a pair of work gloves into his back pocket.

"Thank you," I said, and got up from the chair.

"For the deadfall?"

"No." I smoothed my skirt but couldn't bring myself to thank him for making me laugh. "Just, thanks."

He shrugged. "For the record, you have a beautiful smile and an amazing laugh. I get the feeling you don't use them nearly enough." He turned away and picked up the wheelbarrow handles.

I took a step back, rolling his words around in my brain.

"Hey, Becca?" Jason called, before he turned to go. "Have you seen Prince's Pond yet?"

I shook my head, too shocked from his earlier comment to speak.

"Want to come along? It's beautiful."

I hesitated. He unsettled me, but at the same time, being around him kind of made me feel like I was free falling off a cliff into the unknown. And I liked it.

"It's even more beautiful than this." He waved his arm encompassing the meadow that had entranced me.

"I don't think that's possible."

His eyes challenged me and he said, "Then why don't you come see for yourself?"

I never would have seen the path in the tree line if I hadn't been following Jason. It was well hidden by a cover of shrubs, and while it looked worn, it probably hadn't seen much traffic in a while. Once we pushed past the low hanging branches and overgrown bushes, the trail was easier to follow and wide enough for Jason to maneuver his wheelbarrow, only occasionally getting hung up on a root or large rock.

We walked in silence, mostly because I didn't know what to say.

After a few minutes, Jason called over his shoulder. "It's not much further."

"That's good."

He stopped and turned around. "Don't tell me you're one of those women who don't like to walk."

"I walk lots, thank you very much." I straightened my shoulders and tried to hide my breathing, that had become noticeably heavier in my effort to keep up to his quick pace.

"Don't worry, we're close," he said, and continued walking. "It's not a place we tell the renters about. Some discover it on their own, of course, but most don't."

Jason held back a branch for me and I ducked my head to push past. "Why wouldn't you..." My words drifted away as I stepped out of the woods into a clearing.

The thick trees of the forest had thinned to reveal grassy banks that sloped down to a crystal clear pool of water. It wasn't a huge lake, but it wasn't the pond I'd pictured either. Delicate ferns laced the edges of the tree line with clusters of red flowers dotting the banks.

"So." Jason came behind me and asked, "What do you think?"

"I..I...it's stunning."

"You like it then?"

I let my eyes drift over the scene in front of me. It was like a screen shot from a Disney movie. I expected birds to fly down from the tree tops at any moment and start singing to me.

"I wasn't expecting this," I admitted. "When you said pond, I had an image of lily pads and algae. This is something else all together."

"I like it," he said, and leaving his wheelbarrow, he moved past me towards the waters edge. "It's actually not really a pond, but more of a lake. I'm not sure of the definition exactly. The water's fresh and clean, and that's all that matters to me."

"You don't actually swim in it do you?" I ventured closer, knelt in the grass and stuck my hand in the water prepared to be shocked. "Oh," I said and looked up at Jason. "It's not all that cold."

"It's actually fed by underground springs and one of them must be a natural hot spring, because it keeps the water at a decent temperature. It's no hot tub, that's for sure," he said. "But it's perfect for cooling off on a warm day without freezing to death."

"It would be." I watched my hand moved under the surface of the water.

"So what do you think? Want to go for a dip?"

"Oh, no." I snatched my hand back. "I don't have a suit."

"Who needs a suit?" Jason unhooked his tool belt and dropped it the ground before reaching for the hem of his shirt. In one quick motion he peeled it over his head and was half naked in front of me.

I felt the heat in my cheeks but I couldn't stop staring at his chiseled stomach. He had a body like an underwear model. A really hot underwear model.

I made myself turn away, so I wouldn't keep staring like a teenage girl. "I couldn't do that," I said.

"Why not? It's a warm day. It would be good to cool off a little," he said. "Besides, it's not like we know each other."

"That's just it." I turned around to face him at the exact moment he started unbuttoning his jeans. The heat in my face flared and I spun again, focusing on the ground. "I don't even know you."

"That's the point, Becca. We have no preconceived

ideas about each other. No strings."

No strings? Did he just say that? It's not like we were in a relationship, or going to have one. I was about to tell him just that when I heard a splash. I turned around in time to see him break the surface, water dripping from his shaggy locks. He shook his head and drops went flying. "Come on."

It did look refreshing. I glanced over at the pile of clothes he'd left. It would feel good to swim. A heat flushed through my body.

"I don't think so," I called to him. "I'm not that type of woman."

"Not the type to swim?" Jason moved his hands back and forth, keeping himself afloat effortlessly. "You don't know how?"

I crossed my arms over my chest. "Of course I know how to swim."

There was a naked man only a few feet from me. An extremely well built, naked man. A naked man who was not my husband.

"I'm not the type to go skinny dipping with a complete stranger," I said. "Besides, I feel like going for a walk."

"Suit yourself...Ma'am." He added the last word before diving under the water.

I watched as he surfaced a few feet away, and with easy strokes, swam across the pond. For a moment I was torn between screaming at him that I didn't need to prove myself and tearing my own clothes off to join him.

It was hard not to be completely and totally aware of a naked man slicing through the water only a few feet away, but I did my best as I picked my way along the banks of the pond. I made an effort to keep my back to

Jason so I wouldn't catch an accidental glimpse. Not that I didn't want to, but...

A cluster of the same bright red flowers I'd noticed earlier caught my eye, and I focused on them, settling into the soft grass, thankful for a distraction of any kind. I'd already counted four different types of flowers around the water. There were definitely fewer varieties growing in the shade of the woods than in the field, but there was something about the wildflowers thriving, with such minimal sunlight, that fascinated me.

I hadn't always been a flower person, but on our very first date, Jon had brought me a bouquet, and after that I was a convert. It was such a simple thoughtful act, and relatively cliche, but it didn't matter. It was sweet. After that first date, he would make a point to give me flowers on a regular basis. It made Steph jealous, because the men she dated either didn't believe in romantic gestures or were too absorbed in themselves to consider that she might like some.

Even after we were married, Jon would still bring me bouquets, although they didn't seem to come with the same frequency. Occasionally he would surprise me with roses, or my favorites, daises, on our weekly date night.

We'd started our special Friday night dates when it became clear that married life was different than the fun and carefree college days. Especially with a baby on the way. With Jon busy working on his career, and me focusing on getting ready to be a mom, it was easy for the two of us to get lost in our daily lives and forget about each other.

We made it our mission to reconnect every Friday night after work by going for dinner at a new place. We did our best to try every restaurant in town, even the little diners and hole in the wall pubs. If they served food, they were fair game. I used to love our nights out and the satisfaction there was in turning down invitations from other couples, because I knew I already had the hottest date in town.

When had they stopped? Those dates seemed so long ago. It had been years since we'd laughed over menus, deciding on appetizers to share and which entree sounded best.

I wrapped my arms around my knees, remembering. After Jordan was born, I'd been buried in overwhelming feelings of being trapped by a new little being and the guilt that came from thinking thoughts like that. I knew I'd pushed him away. And after Kayla was born, it'd only gotten worse. More than once, over the years he tried to take me out for a date. I bent to inhale the fragrance of the wildflowers. I knew exactly when the last time Jon asked me to go out was. How could I forget?

"Hey," Jon had said. He'd come up behind me while I was folding a basket of Kayla's tiny clothes. "I have an idea." He'd slid his arms around me, and nuzzled my neck. "Let's start up date nights again. I miss you."

I'd pulled my head away, his breath on my neck irritated me. "I don't know. I don't think it's a good idea."

"Why not?" He had squeezed me in a gentle hug. "Steph would watch the girls."

I'd twisted out of his grip, and said, "I have nothing to wear. Nothing fits."

"So, go buy something."

The thought of shopping, trying on clothes that were too tight in the harsh lights of the change room had made me wince. "I don't have time for that."

"Come on, Becca. It's been too long since we've been out. And the company Christmas party doesn't count."

No, it didn't count. His party had been torturous, with all Jon's associates' wives, with their professionally styled hair, their tiny bodies in revealing, glittery dresses. They'd all toasted their husbands with countless glasses of champagne while I'd felt like a stuffed olive in my green satin dress, too tight on the arms, clinging to all the wrong places. I'd hidden in the ladies' room until Jon sent his assistant in to find me and haul me back out. No, his party definitely didn't count as a night out.

"Why do we have to go out?" I'd asked Jon.

"It's important for us to get out together."

"No."

"What do you mean, no?"

I'd turned to him, Kayla's sleeper in my hands. "I mean, no. I don't want to go. I don't want to get dressed up and pretend to feel good about it. I just want to have a bath and go to bed."

"Maybe next week?"

There had been hope in his face then. He'd tried. And all I'd said was, "We'll see."

We never went.

"They're called Wood Lilies," Jason said, jarring me from my memory. "They're native to this area."

I released my knees and turned around to find him dressed again. Well, half dressed. He was still naked from the waist up and patting his chest with his t-shirt.

"They're beautiful." I turned back to the cluster of blossoms that had captivated me. "The color is really unique," I said. "Not really orange, not really red. It would be a challenge to recreate."

"You're an artist?"

"No," I said, too quickly. "I mean I was once, but not anymore."

"Well, they are gorgeous." Jason crouched down next to me. "I've always envied artists. If I could, I'd paint them, but with my total lack of skill, I'm sure they'd end up looking like red blobs."

Aware of his proximity, I couldn't control a shiver

that ran through my body.

"Are you cold?"

My body felt about a hundred degrees. "I am a little," I lied. "I should probably get back."

He stood, and his thigh brushed my arm. The rough denim sent a shock through to my core. I desperately wanted to rub the spot he'd touched, but I didn't move.

"Can you find your way back?" Jason asked. "I should get to work." He yanked his t-shirt over his head.

"Of course." I pushed myself up from the ground and tried to pretend I didn't notice the way the dampness made his shirt cling to his chest. "I'll let you get to it," I said, and turned to leave.

I'd only gone a few steps towards the path when he called, "Hey, Becca?"

I stopped, but didn't turn, afraid my face had already given away too much.

"Maybe next time, you'll swim."

CHAPTER FOURTEEN

The next morning, I woke feeling like I did after a bender in college. Only there was no alcohol involved. It was guilt. I knew it. My dreams the night before had been filled with images of the girls. Jordan accusing me of abandoning them, Kayla crying out for me. My head was pounding, my thoughts fuzzy. I needed air.

I grabbed the books sitting on the counter as I made my way to the porch. It was a reflex, a comfort to hold a book, as if it held all the answers I needed.

The morning sun felt good on my skin. I slipped into the rocking chair and tipped my head back. My face soaked up the rays, the feel of the books, their solid weight on my lap, soothed me. I opened my eyes, looking at the first title. *Reenergizing the Connection: Reconnecting with your spouse.*

Reconnecting? Is that all it would take? Marriage shouldn't be so hard. At least, it never used to be.

Jon and I used to be so close, it was like we were two halves of the same person.

It wasn't fair to blame the kids, after all, every relationship changed after children. But when we'd found out we were expecting, even though it was a total surprise, it was exciting. I'd never forget showing Jon the stick with two pink lines on it. I was terrified, but he smiled and swung me around the living room of our little apartment into a dance.

Quitting art school had been tough, but it was made easier by how excited we were. And Jon had been so loving and protective as we watched my stomach grow.

We read the pregnancy books together, marveling every few weeks over the pictures of what the baby looked like. As the months went on, Jon would rub my feet and we'd make plans for the future, talking about what things would be like when the baby came. We'd never been closer.

Then, things changed. After we brought Jordan home from the hospital, the image of the perfect family, the one we'd constructed so carefully, crumbled. Not at first, of course. In the beginning, Jon took time off work and he'd get up in the middle of the night to help me with feedings, he'd bring me tea and keep me company while I tried to nurse. But soon, he had to go back to work and reality set in. It was just me, alone, with the sleepless nights, the endless dirty diapers, and the crying. The crying that never stopped.

Just thinking back to the way I'd wished for Jordan to shut up, just for a minute, caused the ache in my chest to flare up again. I was an awful mother, even from the beginning. She'd cried inconsolably for hours on end. I'd tried everything but I couldn't soothe my colicky little girl. It killed me to watch her, face scrunched up and pink from the effort of her screams.

It was the same again with Kayla. Except with her, Jon only took three days off work. He was needed at the office, he said. And when Kayla cried for hours on end, Jordan would hide in her room, hands over her ears, pretending she didn't have a little sister. And I'd wished I could do the same. Instead, I rocked her endlessly, my own tears falling on my little girl who couldn't be consoled. There were a lot of tears in those early days of motherhood, but somewhere along the way, they'd dried up completely.

Rocking on the porch, with the memories fueling me, a build up of pressure swelled under my ribs, making me breathe deeply, gasping for a solid breath. I didn't cry anymore. Ever.

But it wasn't their fault. And just because I needed a break, didn't mean I could ignore them.

The message light was blinking the minute I turned on the phone. I ignored it and punched in our home number before I could chicken out.

"Hello?"

"Jordan, how are you?"

"Mom? Where the hell are you?"

She wasn't allowed to say hell. I let it go.

"I'm just on a bit of a holiday, how are things there?"

"You're kidding, right?" I could hear her usual sarcasm, but there was an undercurrent of worry too. "Dad is going crazy," she said. "Did you have a fight? Liz's parents got a divorce after they had a fight. Are you getting a divorce?"

"No, Jordan. I told you, I'm just on a holiday." I tried my best to sound cheerful. She probably saw right through it. "Everything's fine."

"Well I don't think it's fine. Dad's making me babysit Kayla tomorrow and I don't think he's going to pay me. He should pay me right?"

"Yes, I'll make sure he pays you," I said. "I know you need to get to school, so I won't keep you. But you can call whenever you want."

"Okay."

"Okay? Is everything alright?"

There was a silence on the line. I held my breath. "Do you want to talk to Kayla?"

"Of course," I said. "But-"

"Hold on," she said. "I'll get her."

I heard the shuffle of Jordan walking down the hall and then the muted sounds of Dora the Explorer as she entered the living room. "Mom's on the phone."

"Mommy?" I heard Kayla's muffled squeal and a second later, "Mommy!"

"Hi, sweetie." My throat clenched at the enthusiasm

in her voice and I swallowed hard. "How are you? Are you having fun with Daddy and Jordan?"

"Yup. We got chicken and fries for dinner. Daddy said we could have pizza tonight."

I smiled. He was struggling without me. "Don't forget to eat some vegetables too, okay?"

"Do I get to play at Auntie Steph's house again?"

"You were at Auntie Steph's?"

"Yup, after school. Are you coming home, Mommy? Pup-Pup came home."

"You got Pup-Pup?" I sent a silent thank you to the teenager at the gas station.

"Yup, Daddy said he took a bus ride. Are you on the bus? Then you can come home."

I could hear the song in the background change to the familiar Scooby-Doo theme music.

"I gotta go, Mommy."

"I love you, Kayla."

"It's me," Jordan said. "She's watching TV."

"I love you too, Jordan," I said, wishing I could wrap my arms around my oldest. I had a feeling she'd let me if I tried.

"Mother, can I..."

"Is that your mother?"

I braced myself.

"Becca?" Jon's voice came on the line. "Where the hell are you?"

"Hi, Jon." I could feel my pulse pounding in my head. "I'm fine."

"Come home, this is crazy."

"I need some time," I heard myself say the words.

"Time?" Jon asked. "Time for what? You can't just run away from your life. You're a grown woman, you can't just leave like this. You have responsibilities."

"I didn't run away." My voice sounded small, even to my own ears. I didn't recognize it.

"Look," Jon said, his voice softening a little. "I get it.

Things can be crazy, and I know you need to look after yourself. I get that. But this isn't the way. This isn't okay, Becca. We need to talk. Where are-"

"I can't." The pain in my temple bloomed. "Not now."

"Becca-"

"I'll call again."

"Becca, don't-"

I powered off the phone and let it fall. Grabbing my head in my hands, I sank to the floor boards and buried my face into my knees as I hugged them to my chest.

The pulsing in my head grew until the roaring was almost unbearable. Jon's voice permeated my brain.

Come home, this is crazy. We need to talk.

Louder and louder. Over and over.

"Shut up," I whispered.

Are you getting a divorce?

Pup-Pup came home.

I needed to scream. To cry. Let it out.

I opened my mouth but no sound came out. Squeezing my eyes tight, I willed the tears to come, to offer some relief. Waves of pain crashed through my head, and the vice in my chest clamped tighter. The voices screaming in my brain reached a crescendo. And still, no tears.

A loud crash from the edge of the trees startled me from my trance. I'd been staring into the field for more time than I cared to think about. I shook my head, trying to clear it and looked towards the noise. Jason was tossing logs into the bed of his truck. I hadn't seen him drive up.

I watched for a moment, letting my thoughts settle and my breathing return to normal. "You're back at it," I called, after a minute.

Jason whipped around to face me, a log in his hands.

"Oh, hi there," he said. "Sorry if I disturbed you."

He smiled, which had the welcome and completely unexpected effect of distracting me from the ache in my chest.

"You didn't bother me at all." Quite the opposite, I wanted to say. He'd saved me from my thoughts, which at that moment, I didn't want anything to do with.

"That's good." He grabbed another log from his wheelbarrow and tossed it into the truck. "I won't be too long, I just need to get enough wood to trade." He wiped the back of his glove across his forehead. The day had heated up, with the sun overhead. I could see he'd worked up a sweat. I tried not to notice the way it made his t-shirt cling to his hard body.

"What do you mean, trade?"

"I trade the logs with some of the locals in town. The ones who like to live off the land, and cook over an open fire, use it for firewood. And yes, before you ask, they do exist. It's hippie land, remember?"

"I remember." I felt my face crack into a smile and I stood from the chair, walking closer to him. "What do they give you for it?"

"All kinds of things." Jason returned to the logs. "The trade system is alive and well in Rainbow Valley. I get cloth for Sheena, fresh baking, meat, whatever really. There's not really a lot of money that changes hands here."

"So, do you ever take a break?" I asked the question and couldn't believe it came out of my mouth.

He turned to face me, a smile playing his lips. "Only if there's a cold drink involved."

A shiver ran through me despite the warm sun. "Absolutely," I heard myself say.

In the kitchen I found some old lemonade powder in the cupboard and filled a jug with cold water. I mixed it up and grabbed a box of cookies I'd bought the day before. I laid it all out on a tray and made my way back to the deck.

Pushing open the screen door with my back, I said, "I hope lemonade is okay, I..."

The second I turned around, I wished I hadn't. That's a lie, I was glad I did, but I wished I'd been prepared. My fingers tightened around the edge of the tray to keep from dropping it. Jason was naked from the waist up, his wet t-shirt draped over a chair to dry. He was sitting on the deck, leaning back on his arms. I tried not to stare at his chest which was gleaming with sweat, and was a great deal closer than it had been the day before. Something about his relaxed pose made his shirtlessness a lot more illicit than it had at Prince's Pond.

I put the tray on a table and occupied myself fussing with the glasses.

"It's pretty hot," I said. "I mean, the weather." I could feel my cheeks burning. "It's only May." I spoke quickly, trying to cover my embarrassment. "And already, it seems to be heating up. It surprises me that it's so warm in the mountains."

"It is surprising," Jason said. I didn't look at him, but there was laughter in his voice, he was likely enjoying my awkwardness. "It's actually quite unusual for it to be so hot at this time of year. But, I'll take it. I like it hot."

His words hung between us as I handed him a glass of lemonade.

"I get the feeling you don't really want to talk about the weather though, am I right?" he asked.

"No, it's fine," I said pouring my own glass. "Don't get me wrong, I'm really enjoying how peaceful it is here, but it's nice to talk to someone else too."

"Are you lonely?"

"No, but honestly? It's nice to have a conversation without a screaming child at my feet." I bit down on my lip. I shouldn't have said that. He didn't know anything about me.

"Oh?"

"Never mind. You're just easy to talk to and I don't usually talk to anyone." Heat rose up my neck and I turned before he could notice. "That sounded so stupid."

"I'm always saying stupid stuff," Jason said. "Don't tell me you didn't notice."

I smiled in response and, foregoing my rocking chair, sat on the floorboards across from him.

"Hey," he said. "Before I forget, Sheena wanted to make sure you got the key."

My thoughts flashed to the small silver key I'd put on the kitchen counter. "Yeah, I found it. Did she drop it in my bag?"

"No, I think she meant it for you."

"For me?" I stopped and looked up. "What's it for?"

Jason shrugged. "She didn't say. Only that you'd figure it out."

"Oh." I looked out over the field. And after a moment, I asked, "So what's your deal?"

He looked shocked for a second, before laughing. "Isn't that supposed to be my question?"

"I thought Sheena told you to leave me alone?" I countered. "Besides, I wouldn't answer anyway."

He took a long drink. "I didn't think you would. But it was worth a shot."

"So talk, what's your deal? Why are you the only person in this town under the age of fifty and not a hippie?"

"Well, you don't really know I'm the only person under fifty, do you?" He raised an eyebrow. "In fact, there's a blossoming population of us young un's escaping the craziness of the real world to commune with nature."

"Is that what you're doing, then? Escaping from the real world?"

Instead of answering me, Jason stared at me. His eyes

locked on mine. He opened his mouth to say something, maybe to challenge me. After all, wasn't that what I was doing? Escaping.

"Okay," I said before he could speak, "why are you the only non-hippie here?"

"What makes you think I'm not a hippie?"

It was my turn to raise an eyebrow.

"Okay," he said. "You're right, I'm not. But I like it here."

"Where did you live before? I mean, what brought you here?"

A shadow fell over his face, a storm darkening his features. "A lot of things," he said. He tipped his head up to the sky. When he looked back down, the storm had cleared, restoring his eyes to their brilliant clarity.

"Why here?"

"I told you, I love it here," he said. "Besides, Sheena needed some help."

I ran my finger around the rim of the glass. "Is Sheena your mom?" I asked, the thought just now occurring to me.

He shook his head. "No, not really. But she took me in when I needed someone. She cares about me."

I nodded, but he must have seen the confusion on my face, because he added, "I don't really have any family of my own."

"I'm sorry," I said, only because I couldn't think of anything better to say.

"Don't be. I'm not." He drained his glass. "So I kind of feel like I owe Sheena and she needs some help with the rental houses and the store. It's not as easy as it looks."

I leaned forward, grabbed the jug and poured him some more lemonade. "Why so many rental houses? I mean, who comes here?"

"You're here."

"Very funny."

"Okay, seriously, we get a lot of artists and writers up

144

here. I mean, look around-"

"It's breathtaking," I finished for him.

Jason nodded. "It is. And it's quiet. Which is also why we get a lot of people who just need to get away." He stared at me pointedly and I didn't pretend not to notice.

"Stop looking at me like that."

He shrugged and grabbed a cookie from the tray. "That's okay, you don't have to tell me. I already know."

My spine stiffened, the smile melted. "You don't know me."

"Nope, you're right. I don't."

I glared at him over the rim of my glass.

"I know you have a kid."

"I told you as much."

"Okay, I also know you have a wedding ring on and your husband isn't here."

I glared at him, trying to shut him up, but he didn't back down.

"I know that you're reading books about broken relationships," he said, and nodded towards the books, still sitting next to my rocking chair. "So I know that much about you." He didn't break his stare. "But I also know there's more."

I was the first to turn away. I put my glass down and picked at the floor board with my finger. "You don't know," I whispered.

"No, I don't," Jason said again. His voice was softer this time, the combative edge, gone.

I looked up into his eyes. The challenge from a moment ago was replaced by concern and something else I couldn't quite read.

"But if you want to tell me about it," he said, "you can."

He wasn't supposed to ask me personal questions. I couldn't even talk about my life with Steph, let alone with a complete stranger. Or could I? He didn't know me, or my history. He didn't know anything. It would be easy to tell him, might even be a relief. I blinked hard and looked down at my feet.

"I get it," Jason said. "You don't have to talk to me. I shouldn't have said anything."

"No." My head jerked up. "No, it's..."

"Honestly, Becca." He reached across the porch and took my hands. "It's okay to talk and sometimes, it's okay just to sit."

My hand felt small in his and I could feel the callouses on his fingers. I wanted to trust him. There was something about the casual way he carried himself, his deep eyes and the way he looked at me. Even the way he touched me.

It felt good. Kind of safe, like I didn't have to worry about anything. Like my troubles would go away if I left them with him.

We sat like that for a few minutes. It was so comfortable just to be holding his hand, that it took me a moment to realize what was happening when Jason's thumb started stroking small circles on the top of my hand. But the sparks that his touch created in me flowed through my body, reaching my core where a long forgotten heat flared up.

I closed my eyes because I couldn't bring myself to look at him. I wasn't sure what was happening. But I was sure I didn't want it to stop.

I was afraid. Afraid of breaking whatever spell bound us. Afraid that what I was letting him do, hold my hands in such a way, was wrong, a betrayal to Jon. But mostly, I was afraid that I didn't care.

"I'm sorry," he whispered, causing me to open my eyes and look at him.

"For what?" I'd enjoyed whatever it was that had just happened. I didn't want him to apologize for it.

"I'm sorry," he repeated. "For this." His grip on my hands tightened and he pulled me towards him, releasing his hold on me only long enough to put one hand on my arm, the other behind my head. His lips were on mine before I could even process what was happening. They felt strange. Foreign. Firm, yet, soft as they gave under the pressure of my own yielding lips.

For a moment I thought I should push him away, stop it before it began. Instead, my mouth opened to him and my body responded with the deep heat. Whatever thoughts I'd had of stopping him vanished as I gave myself to the feeling.

Jason's arms embraced me, wrapping me in a cocoon. Everything else disappeared and nothing mattered as his fingers gently tangled in my hair and we sank deeper into the kiss.

Heat rushed from my core, through my arms and legs, all the way to my fingertips and toes. It felt good. More than good. My head spun from the strange sensation. Desire. It'd been so long, I barely remembered. But my body obviously did.

With a mind of their own, my hands traveled across his back. Jason responded by pulling me tighter into his body, closing the gap between us. The feel of him caused a low groan to come from deep inside. It had been so long, too long, since I'd been kissed like that by Jon.

Jon.

I tried to fight the image of my husband's face from my mind, focusing instead on the minty taste of Jason's mouth. I kissed him harder, trying to push the intruding thoughts out.

Damn it.

Fighting every sensation in my body that told me not to, I pushed against Jason's chest firmly enough to create a slight distance between us. I scooted back and used my sleeve to tentatively wipe my mouth, trying to erase the taste of him, but at the same time, not sure I wanted to.

"Becca?"

"I'm sorry, Jason." Not trusting myself, I dropped my gaze to the floorboards and studied the planks. The desire to reach for him was too strong. "I can't."

"No." His voice was soft. "Like I said before, I'm sorry. I knew I shouldn't have kissed you, but I couldn't help it." I felt his touch on the side of my face. "It was too soon."

Something in his voice made me look up. "Too soon?"

My stomach recoiled and I yanked back from him, letting his hand drop. I jumped to my feet, and said, "What made you think I would kiss you at all?"

"That's not what I meant," he said. "But be honest with yourself, you wanted to. I could feel it."

"You're an asshole."

My body burned from rage, and the lingering effect of him.

He pulled himself to his feet, unfolding his body until he stood only inches away from me. His musky scent, the taste of him still on my lips, it made it hard to focus on my anger.

"Becca, don't be mad."

"Leave."

"Don't," he said.

"Don't what?"

"Don't make me the bad guy."

"Screw you." I put my hands on my hips, hoping I looked stronger than I felt.

"It's okay to let yourself feel, Becca," he said. "Sometimes you have to let yourself go."

"I think you should go."

"Be angry if you need to, but it's not me you should be upset with." He put one finger on my chin, tipping it up to him. "I'll go," he said and then his lips met mine so quickly I didn't have time to fend him off.

I wrenched away, my mouth still sizzling from his kiss. "Good, I hope to never see you again."

I crossed my arms and held myself, willing my body not to move towards him the way it yearned to. I forced myself to be still, not to run to him and return his kiss with one of my own. I tried to focus on my anger as I watched him walk to his truck. He wasn't in a hurry, as if he knew I might break and run to him at any moment.

It was only once he climbed into the cab and drove down the road, that I allowed myself to move. My tongue slid across my lips and my body sang with the memory of his touch.

As the dust settled behind Jason's truck, my body shook with the awareness that we both knew I'd just lied.

Jason's absence had left the porch cold, and empty. I moved inside and a flash of light on the kitchen counter caught my eye.

The key.

I crossed the room, picked it up and spun it slowly between my fingers.

Sheena said it was for me. Does that mean I should have known what to do with it?

"This is stupid," I said. Anger flared through me; at Sheena, at Jason and mostly, at myself. I let the key drop to the counter. "How am I supposed to know what the hell it opens?" I yelled into the cabin. "Maybe everybody else in this weird valley has psychic powers or strange chi, or whatever, but I don't."

I looked down the empty road. "I don't have anything," I whispered into the silence.

CHAPTER FIFTEEN

I woke with a start and sat straight up in bed. My brain barely registered the fact that I was still in my clothes, lying on top of the covers. I couldn't remember going to bed. I'd spent the afternoon walking through the field, replaying the kiss with Jason over and over in my head until I'd driven myself crazy with it. With a need to get out of my head, I'd decided on a nap. I couldn't remember the last time I'd slept in the middle of the day and it must have been a good nap too, because judging by the darkness outside my window, I'd been asleep for awhile.

I listened for the sounds that must have woken me. There were none. I sat in silence for a few moments, waiting for my heart rate to return to normal. Still, no noise.

It was probably my dream that had woken me. Some people were lucky, and never remembered their dreams. I'd tried for years to ignore them, and if it had been possible, I would have stopped dreaming altogether. The thing was, I never had dreams I wanted to remember and relive, they always seemed to be filled with images I wished I couldn't remember. There was a time that I used to share with Steph or Jon. I didn't do that anymore either.

Kayla had only been a few months old when Steph went through a dream interpreting phase. She'd taken a class at the community college, so she was the resident expert. She'd cornered me in my kitchen after a particularly long night with the baby.

"Come on, Becca," she said. "Just tell me. I guarantee that I can tell you exactly what it means."

"I doubt that very much," I said, and cut an apple into slices for Jordan, who was coloring at the table.

"Try me," she said. "I totally aced the class."

"I didn't think they gave out marks in those courses." I gave Steph a look, but she just shrugged. I knew she wouldn't give up until I told her something.

I also knew it was a bad idea to tell her my latest dream, it was too vivid. But I couldn't think of anything else, and I was way too sleep deprived to make anything up.

"Okay," I said before I could stop myself. "Analyze this one, Steph."

She sat at the table with a note pad and pen, looking very official and somewhat comical.

"I dreamed that I was standing in Kayla's room, right next to the crib."

"Go on," she said when I paused.

"I had my easel and paints with me." I didn't look at her when I said that, because it had been years since I'd mentioned painting or even drawing. "I was busy working," I continued. "Mixing colors and attacking the canvas. I was totally focused on my work."

"That's great," Steph said.

"There's more." I waited until she was listening before continuing. "When I turned to see what I was working on, it wasn't there. I was painting Kayla."

"Like drawing her?"

"No, like I was physically painting her." I swallowed hard. "And not in a beautiful way. I was trying to camouflage her into the background of her room. I was trying to cover her. As if she wasn't even there."

It took a minute for Steph to absorb what I'd said. After a moment that went on forever, she let out her breath in a low whistle. "Holy shit, Becca."

"Little ears," I said, jabbing at finger towards Jordan, who hadn't even flinched.

"You know what this means, right?"

I shook my head.

"Clearly your subconscious is trying to tell you that you resent the baby for taking time away from painting."

I took a step back, as if she'd physically hit me. "That doesn't make any sense." I struggled to keep my breathing even.

"Sure it does," she continued, completely oblivious to my distress. "Don't you see? Ever since Kayla was born, you've been wrapped up in baby stuff again. You haven't been able to focus on art."

"I've barely sketched, let alone painted, since before Jordan was born," I whispered.

"Maybe it's your subconscious way of wishing for a time without children when you were free to paint."

A flash went through me. Too close to home.

"What do you know?" I forced a laugh I didn't feel and poured her another cup of coffee. "Your dreams consist of running the Boston marathon, naked, with hot firemen.

Steph laughed along with me, her analysis forgotten.

I hadn't talked about my dreams since. Or made any effort to figure out what they might mean. But there was something about the dream that had woken me. I squeezed my eyes shut and tried to make the memory go away.

Instead the solid image of a silver key formed in my mind. I'd been dreaming about the key.

I reached over and fumbled for the lamp on the nightstand. With a flick, the room filled with a warm purple haze from the scarf draped over the shade. I pushed myself off the bed and retrieved the key from the kitchen. Squeezing it in my palm, the cool metal soothed my hot skin.

In my dream, I'd put the key into a lock. I turned around, rubbed the sleep from my eyes and looked around the living room.

No, it wasn't in here, I thought. It wasn't right.

I tried to concentrate, struggling to remember the details, but all I could manage were fuzzy, hazy images. And colors.

I moved back to the bedroom and stopped short in the doorway.

Purple. Yes, it felt right.

I could feel each beat of my heart in my chest, and the room was all at once unbearably warm, causing a bead of sweat to slip down between my breasts. I looked around the small space, trying to remember. The only image that came to me was the act of slipping the key into the lock and the pressing need to open it. But what lock?

I flung open the wardrobe and tossed the few skirts and blouses I'd hung up into a pile on the floor.

Nothing.

I felt around the back and sides searching for a secret compartment.

Still, nothing. I spun around and stared at the bed. Falling to my knees, I peered underneath.

Empty.

Out of ideas, I pulled myself up and leaned against the bed.

Where could it be?

I looked at the lamp with the purple scarf. The color was right. It felt like the dream.

Maybe that's all it was, a dream.

I let my eyes drift down, coming to rest on the nightstand. But it wasn't a nightstand. It was an antique trunk. The hinges were facing out towards the room, which meant the lock must be facing the wall. I couldn't believe I hadn't seen it before.

I forced myself to stay calm and move slowly. I lifted the lamp and lowered it to the floor, careful to leave the purple scarf in place. Grabbing one corner, I heaved and pulled the heavy trunk around until the lock was exposed. I slid the key into the hole.

A perfect fit.

The key was cool and smooth in my sweaty, nervous hand. I stopped.

"Becca, you're being stupid," I chastised myself. "It's just a trunk."

I turned my hand. The key moved easily, a soft clicking as the lock disengaged. With shaking hands, I lifted the lid.

At first glance, the contents didn't look very exciting. I wasn't sure if I expected gold and jewels, but it certainly wasn't the scarves and books that I found. Even if the contents weren't glamorous, they were still a mystery, so I dug in, removing the tissue thin material. Much like the rest of the cloths scattered around the cabin, they were made of what I assumed was hand dyed, raw silk. The ones in the trunk were definitely more beautiful than the others. Strange that they were the ones hidden away. Carefully folding the silk, I set them to the side and pulled out a large coil bound book that looked too large to be a notebook. On the cover, in small penciled letters, was the name: Vicki.

My mother.

I opened the cover and saw it was a sketch book, much like the ones I used to have. Or more correctly, still had boxed up in the basement at home. Some of the drawings were in pencil, some in charcoal, but most were done in watercolors. The muted colors, blending and bleeding together, filled each page.

The pictures were beautiful. I had no idea my mom had been an artist until Sheena had mentioned it. And she was right, my mother had been very talented. The ideas on the pages were fully conceived and thought out with an artist's skill.

"How come Dad never told me?" I whispered into the silence. I closed the book and stared at the cover for a moment before clutching it to my chest. I sat like that for some time, feeling a connection with my dead mother. One I'd never had.

I'm not sure how much time passed before I set the book aside, ready to see what else the trunk held. I pulled out a small manila envelope full of photos that I dumped on the floor in front of me.

My father's smiling face looked up at me from a picture. Much younger, his hair was down to his shoulders and he sported a mustache and thick side burns. There was a little girl perched on his shoulders. Me. I must've been about two years old. We were standing on the porch of the cabin. Dylan stood next to us, a gangly boy on the edge of a growth spurt. We'd been to the cabin before. As a family. The evidence was in my hand.

My mind whirled, but I continued to go through the images. There weren't many pictures, and most of them were of Dylan as a child, or me as a baby. Some had Dad in them, but there were none of my mother. Dad always said that she hated having her picture taken and the few they had weren't very clear. Looking at the found photos, not one of them a shot of her, it struck me for the first time that I'd never really seen my mother's face. Not that I could remember.

I flipped through the pictures a little faster until I stopped on one of a young woman in the field out front of the cabin. It was Vicki. It had to be. Her face was turned up to the sun, her arms stretched out to encompass the wildflowers she was surrounded by, her long chestnut brown hair fluttered around her head, as if she'd been caught in the middle of spinning. The photographer had caught an expression of complete bliss on her face. I stared at the picture for a long time, before tucking it into the sketch book.

At the bottom of the trunk was a mixture of art supplies. A pouch of brushes, all good quality, a packet a charcoal, a few pencils and a long wooden box. I lifted the box and unhinged the small clasp. I was pretty sure of what I'd find and I wasn't disappointed. Inside were half a dozen tubes of paint. Watercolors. And they were expensive. The inside of the lid was inscribed, the wood burnt with the words: Love Survives.

The tubes looked as if they'd never been touched, let alone used. Something inside me sparked. The familiar itch I used to feel in my fingers when I wanted to create or draw started in my right hand. It had been so long. Too long.

I closed the lid and placed it on the floor next to the trunk. The only other items left were a box of colored pencils and an empty sketch pad.

I stared for a long time at the pile of discoveries. I scooped up the small pile of photos and put them back in the envelope. I felt like there should be something else. Something more.

After awhile, exhaustion took over and I dragged myself back into bed, snapped off the lamp and laid on top of the covers. I slept fitfully, my dreams vivid and haunting.

A young woman stood in a field of flowers. Her head was flung back, her arms outstretched. She was laughing and singing as she began to spin around. Her hair flew around her face, and she spun faster and faster. Her clothing became a blur, until the scene stopped. Caught in a freeze frame, the woman's face was clear. It wasn't Vicki. It was me. Wearing a twisted mask of agony.

"Why did you give me that key?" I asked before I'd

even gotten out of the car.

"Good morning to you too, Sunshine," Sheena said. She lifted her head from the book she was reading and squinted her eyes into the bright sun.

I slammed the car door and stormed up to the bench where Sheena sat in front of the store.

"Good morning," I said, trying to control my voice. "Why did you give me that key?"

"It was your key to have," Sheena said. "I assume you opened the trunk?"

"How could you be sure I'd know what it was for?"

"I knew."

I twisted my fingers around the hem of my blouse. "That's not an answer."

Sheena leveled her gaze and her eyes held me in place, stilling my fidgeting. "That was your key to have. You need everything you find in that trunk."

"That's just it, there's nothing in it. Only some stupid art supplies and old pictures."

"It will help."

"Help with what?"

Sheena didn't answer, but she didn't look away either.

I glared at her for a moment. I knew it wasn't her fault, there was no way Sheena could know about my problems, or that I used to paint once. She couldn't know. Just because Jason presumed to know things, didn't mean this strange hippie lady knew anything either.

"I don't know what you're talking about," I said.

"The energy is strong up at the cabin. It will help."

"You don't even know what you're talking about," I said, my voice shook with every word. "Energy, chi, spirits. Whatever. This is a waste of time. A big fucking waste of time."

I spun on my heel and left her sitting in a cloud of dust, as I tore out of the parking lot. The anger I couldn't explain pulsed hard and heavy in my temple.

I drove fast, but only got as far as the bridge before I pulled the car onto the weed covered shoulder, leaned back against the head rest and let out a guttural scream.

I remembered reading in *Express Yourself*, that releasing pent up emotion could be therapeutic and cleansing. I wasn't sure about cleansing, but at that moment it felt damn good to feel the heat in my throat as I let loose.

I'm not sure how long I sat like that, giving my rage an outlet, but when I finished, I felt better. Damned if it didn't work.

Movement out the window caught my eye and I had only a fraction of a second to compose myself before Jason's truck pulled up beside me.

Fortunately, he didn't unroll his window to talk to me. He gave me a look that said, 'are you okay?', I nodded and he moved on past me up the road. Likely on his way up to clear more logs.

I waited until the truck was out of sight and ran my hands through my hair in an effort to pull myself together. I adjusted the rearview mirror and looked at my reflection.

I looked normal. More than that, I felt normal.

Maybe I was onto something with the screaming?

But I still needed answers. How could I be in those pictures, when I didn't even know Rainbow Valley existed? How come no one told me my mother was an artist? What else didn't I know? Too many questions, and there was only one person who could answer them.

I dug my cell phone out of my purse, powered it up and dialed my brother's number. It was time Dylan told me what he knew.

He picked up on the first ring.

"Dylan, I need to know something."

"Becca? Where on earth are you?"

"You spoke to Jon."

Crap.

"Of course I did. I tried to call you for your birthday, late I know, but when you didn't answer your cell, I tried you at home. He was flipping out, Becca. We're all flipping out."

"I needed a break."

"But you took off? You just left Kayla at school?"

"I didn't just leave her," I said. "Jon was going to pick her up. What version exactly did he tell you?"

"It doesn't matter. What matters is that you're okay. What the hell happened?"

The thought of explaining to my big brother that my husband was oblivious to what was going on around him, our father had totally lost his mind and thought I was our dead mother, and I was definitely in the running for the world's worst mother award, was too much.

"I don't want to talk about it," I said. "But I do need to know something."

"What?"

"What do you know about a place called Rainbow Valley?"

I heard Dylan draw a sharp breath.

When he didn't say anything else, I told him how I discovered the cabin, leaving out the small detail that I was actually staying in it.

When I finished, the silence on the other end of the line was palpable.

"Dylan," I said, forming the words carefully. "What do you know?"

"I didn't know they still had the cabin," he said, finally.

"You knew about it though?"

"Well, yeah. We lived in Rainbow when I was a kid. We moved when you were still a baby. Mom went back a few times on her own. I didn't realize Dad kept the house after, well, after she died."

I looked out the window at the river with the bright flowers dotting the grassy banks. "How could I not know this place existed?" I wondered aloud.

"This place?" Dylan's voice picked up. "Are you in Rainbow right now? Christ, Becca. You are, aren't you?"

"Dylan. Promise me you won't say anything to Jon."

"I don't kn-"

"Please. I just need a little more time to figure things out. To work through some stuff. I can't have him showing up here right now. I need to be alone."

"I don't know," he said. "I'm not sure it's a good idea. What's going on? Talk to me."

"Don't get all brotherly on me now. I haven't seen you in years and now you care."

"Of course I care. What on earth are you talking about? What is going on with you, Becca?"

"Whatever, Dylan." I took a deep breath and tried to compose myself. I needed him. "I really don't want to get into it. But, please just tell me about this place? How come I never knew we lived here? Why was it a secret?"

"I don't think it was a secret so much as something we just didn't talk about. After we left, I remember Mom getting really sad whenever I mentioned it. I think Dad tried to cheer her up and send her back for visits, but she came home even sadder. And then, well, the accident and we moved from Crescent City to Silverdale, which was even further away, and, well you know the rest."

"Why did you leave if she loved it so much?"

"I didn't really know at the time," he said. "I was just a kid. I was excited to move, and go to a school instead of being home taught. But I liked it up there," Dylan's voice turned wistful, "there used to be a swimming pond right outside the house."

"It's not really right outside the house."

"You found Prince's Pond?"

"Yeah." I smiled. "Someone showed me."

"Who?"

"Jason." My heart sped up just saying his name out loud. "He's the guy that looks after the rental houses for the owners. He helps out Sheena."

"Sheena?"

"Do you know her?"

"No, but I was pretty young when we left," he said. "I don't remember everything. She might have been a friend of Mom's. But it was a long time ago. I'm not sure I really remember her."

"Well, she's still here and she remembers you." I experienced a flash of guilt for the way I'd just yelled at the older woman. "Hey," I said, changing the subject. "Do you remember Mom drawing or painting?"

"Painting? All the time. It's what she did," Dylan said. "She used to paint pictures and on weekends we'd visit all the little towns and sell them in the markets. Looking back, I can't imagine it paid very well, but Dad was the valley handyman and Mom painted."

"I never knew that. How come no one ever told me? There's so much I didn't know."

"Becca, you were so little and all of that, Rainbow Valley, it was a lifetime ago. Don't be upset."

I looked out the window again. Don't be upset? There's a whole other life I never knew about, how could I not be upset? I opened my mouth to tell him so, but instead, I said, "Well, I'm here now."

"You should tell Jon."

"Are we back to that? Because I really don't want him to know. Please, Dylan. I need this right now. I need to think."

"I don't know." I could hear the hesitation in his voice.

"Dylan, please."

"Okay," he said after a moment. "I won't tell him, yet."

"Thank you."

"Promise me you'll call again to let me know you're okay."

"I promise."

CHAPTER SIXTEEN

By the time I pulled the car up to the cabin, I'd calmed down. Talking to Dylan had helped, at least a little. I still needed answers, but I no longer felt the intense anger building inside me that I'd woken up with. I knew enough to know it wasn't only anger about the uncertainty of my past. No, there was more to it than that. And when I realized Jason's truck wasn't in the drive like I thought it would be, I knew for sure where the rest of the emotion was coming from.

I'd been so distracted by the trunk, and trying to figure everything out, I hadn't had time to think about Jason, or the kiss. At least, I hadn't had as much time. There was no denying the man got under my skin, but there was something else too. I hadn't kissed another man since I'd met Jon. Jason didn't know what he was talking about, I hadn't wanted to kiss him.

Right?

My insides twisted just thinking about the taste of his lips on mine, the way his hand had stroked my cheek.

With a sigh of frustration, I slammed the car door and went inside. I poured myself a glass of lemonade and my gaze landed on my book, sitting on the counter where I'd abandoned it earlier. It taunted me to read it. But the thought of reading anymore about relationships in trouble, or how I had to accept fault for the destruction of my marriage, made my stomach turn.

I opened a drawer and shoved the book inside.

My thoughts flipped back to Jon and the girls, and for a moment I thought about calling them again. But what would I say? I knew I was being selfish and I didn't care. I couldn't handle the thought of hearing Jon pleading with me to come home. He didn't get it. I needed the break. But for what?

I went to the bedroom and grabbed the sketch book from the pile I'd made the night before and went outside to give it another look.

In the light of the day, I was struck immediately by the first picture. A simple drawing done with colored pencils, each line magnified the beauty of the blossoms on the page. The picture was almost an exact replica of the meadow in front of me. It was as if the artist, my mother, had been sitting in the same chair, sketching the very same flowers that had been enchanting me since I'd arrived.

A chill ran up my spine.

Maybe she had.

The date in the corner of the page read, 07/1965

I stared for a few moments before flipping the pages. There were a few more drawings of the meadow at various stages in the season. According to the dates, the pictures captured most of the summer and early fall. There were a few close up sketches of individual blossoms. Each picture was labeled. Pushing out of the chair, I walked through the meadow, letting the flowers calm me while I explored and discovered which was which.

The mystery of the vibrant red petals was finally revealed. Allegro poppies. The tall blue giants at the back of the field, near the tree line, were wild delphiniums. I didn't even know they could be wild. The white daises were easy, but their yellow and brown counterparts were called Brown Eyed Susans. Flipping the pages, I could see there were wild rose, pink fireweed and delicate blue bells. I couldn't locate all of them, but it was still early in the season; according to the dates, many of the flowers wouldn't be in bloom until much later in the summer.

Returning to the porch, I settled in to take a closer look at the book. Looking at art used to soothe me. Something about losing myself in the brush or pencil stroke of another artist could calm my senses and inspire me at the same time. My mother, Vicki, had captured the intricacy of the petals, the leaves and even details such as a dew drop on the head of a blue cornflower. I ran my fingers along the page, barely skimming the surface. It looked so real.

It was easy to appreciate the artistry in each drawing when I looked at them in the full light, as opposed to the muted glow of the night before. Even in art school, I'd never had considered myself an expert on art. I hated the pretentious people who stuck their noses up at certain pieces because they didn't approve of the media, or the technique the artist used. I knew what I liked, and more importantly, I'd always done my best to create art that held my heart and soul, which translated into pieces people could connect to. At least, I used to.

I hadn't painted in so long I probably couldn't even call myself an artist anymore. There had to be a time limit on such things.

I looked up at the meadow that had obviously been a source of inspiration for my mother, and felt the familiar twitch in my fingers again. When I looked down, they were curved as if I were holding a brush or pencil.

Could I paint again? Or even draw?

What would it feel like to create the pencil strokes? Or turn an empty canvas into a world of color?

My fingers twitched again and my knees bounced. It would feel good. It would feel really good.

I squeezed my fingers tight around the empty air. But what if it didn't? What if I no longer had art in me? Hadn't Dylan said something about our mother putting away her brushes? She'd once created beautiful pictures and then one day, it stopped.

I rocked back in the chair and let out a sigh. There was really only one way to find out.

Before I could change my mind, I ran inside and into the bedroom. I grabbed the empty sketchbook and the box of colored pencils.

Returning to the porch, I dropped to my knees, opened the book to the first page and dumped the box of pencils out in front of me where they rolled across the floorboards.

I froze.

Now what?

It had been too long. This isn't who I am anymore, I tried to tell myself.

"Screw that," I said aloud.

I chose a light gray pencil, and before I could lose my nerve, I touched it to the paper and slowly, lightly, sketched a petal. My strokes were delicate at first, barely leaving a mark, and then bolder as my muscles and my mind remembered what to do.

It wasn't long before the petals were done, and I moved to the center of the flower and then the leaves. Selecting a green pencil, I shaded the stem, looking towards a daisy off the edge of the porch for inspiration. Mesmerized by the process, I alternated between shades of green, trying to get the color just right before moving on to a white pencil and then a yellow one to add a bold splash that made the drawing come to life.

When I was finished, I pushed back on my heels and examined the drawing.

It was good.

More than that, it felt good to draw again.

Really good.

I felt my mouth turn up into a smile that hurt my cheeks. I wanted to scream and shout. I wanted to tell the world that I still had it. I could draw. I tipped my head back to the sky and did just that. "I'm an artist," I hollered. And then looking around at the empty porch, I laughed.

I let the sound ripple through my chest and out of my mouth.

If anyone happened to be watching, I would have looked like a crazy woman. I didn't care.

It felt good. I felt good.

"God, I missed you," I said to the drawing I'd just created and then burst into laughter again.

Why had I waited for so long? At that moment I couldn't remember any reason good enough to keep me from my passion. From the feeling of creating.

I couldn't wait to do it again. But first I had to pull myself together. I smoothed my skirt and reached for my lemonade to cool off. The sun was high, and the heat of the day was starting to press down on me.

The glass was empty.

I put it down and searched the tree line at the far end of the meadow. It didn't take long to spot the break in the foliage that marked the pathway to the pond. There was another way to cool down. And it would feel good to go for a swim.

Buoyed by my artistic accomplishment, I laughed and jumped up. "Why not?" And before I could change my mind, I ran down the stairs, and through the field toward the path in the trees.

My skirt caught on the branches and shrubs as I ran, so I gathered as much of the fabric as I could in one hand and lifted it around my knees. With my feet free from the long hem, I could move faster and the giggles in the back of my throat built until I was sure I sounded like a little girl. Or a crazy woman. But I didn't care.

I used my other hand to push back branches as I moved. I was fairly certain that I sounded like a herd of elephants charging the through the trees. No worries about wildlife then, I thought, and tipped my head back to let the laughter rip from my mouth.

When I broke through the last stand of shrubs and into the clearing of the pond, I collapsed onto the grassy bank. It hadn't been a long run, but my chest heaved with the combination of my growing excitement and the physical strain, no matter how minor.

Before I could over think it, I tugged off my blouse and wiggled out of my skirt. I threw my bra and panties on top of the pile and stood naked in the clearing.

"Let's see if I still remember how to do this," I said, and ran knee deep into the lake, before pointing my hands over my head and diving in.

When I broke the surface, I was in the middle of Prince's Pond. The coolness of the water enveloped my body and tightened my skin. I was right, it felt really good. I took another deep breath and dove under the surface again, kicking hard to propel myself forward. As I moved, the water flowed past, skimming my body and firing my nerve endings.

I kicked harder and arrowed my hands in front of me, pushing to the edge of what my body could handle. When the fire built in my lungs, I had to surface to extinguish it with gulps of fresh air.

After a few more strokes, the excitement of my spontaneity began to dissipate and I relaxed into the swim. I flipped onto my back so I could look up at the vastness of the blue sky. There was nowhere I needed to be, so I took my time, making lazy kicks to move myself along the surface.

It was like I was outside of my body, looking down on someone else. I wasn't so completely uninhibited and free. I hadn't been so unencumbered by insecurity since I was a child. But then again, I hadn't drawn anything in years, either.

It felt amazing. Obviously, a break from my reality

was just what I needed. The freedom to create again, and then, the freedom just to be.

I closed my eyes and lost myself in the sensation of gliding. Moving slower now, I kicked just enough to keep me afloat. The water gently lapped against my exposed chest, licking at my nipples. Every splash and slight wave, caressed me, lighting another fire, this one deeper within.

I let my hands travel down the length on my body. My skin was cool, slippery. I hesitated only a moment before moving up to cup my breasts. My nipples were hard with the cold of the water, and the excitement of my own daring. The touch of my fingers fanned the flames that were building to an unmistakable inferno deep in my belly. It was an unfamiliar, yet not unwelcome sensation. Emboldened by my brazenness, I let my hands inch down my stomach, towards the cleft between my legs. My fingers stopped just shy of their goal.

Go ahead, Becca. Just one touch. Why not? My brain battled with my itself. Reason versus want.

The impetuousness of the afternoon, of the moment, prodded me to break every self imposed boundary I'd ever set. My fingers moved, closing the gap and the shiver that shot through my body had nothing to do with the water. A sigh escaped my lips, as my fingers worked to stoke the flames within me.

A shadow passed over head and seconds later a splash, broke my bliss. I flipped to my stomach, instinctively covering my body under the water. I looked behind me, across the lake where an osprey was emerging from the water, a fish in its talons. Turning again, I looked straight into the gentle dark eyes of a deer, undisturbed by the interruption at her watering hole.

"Shit," I moaned with a laugh. I dunked myself under the surface, the fire inside, now certainly and unceremoniously, extinguished.

I took my time walking back to the cabin. It wasn't like I had anywhere to be. Once the mood was broken, I felt ridiculous floating in the water. Besides, I was ready to draw again. In my rush to leave, I tugged my clothing on without bothering to dry off. I held my bra and panties bunched up in my hand and with my skirt and blouse sticking to my damp skin, I picked my way along the path.

Despite my swim being cut off rather abruptly, I felt refreshed and somehow lighter than I had in the morning. It was amazing how good it made me feel. Or maybe it wasn't the swim at all? Regardless, all of the anger and confusion I'd felt when I woke up, was gone.

As I broke through the tree line and stepped out into the meadow, the sun hit me with full force. It didn't matter how many times I saw the field of flowers, it always had the same effect on me. I stopped and took it in. A rainbow of color dotted through the grasses, making the space come alive. I stopped to pick a daisy and twirled it between my fingers before tucking it into my wet hair and securing it behind my ear.

I was ready to hold the pencil again.

The porch was awash in the afternoon sun. I sat in the rocker and let the sun warm my still cool skin, relishing the heat on my body as I picked up a gray pencil and the sketch pad.

It came quickly, the art flowing through me and into the pencil that moved across the page. I wasn't sure what I was going to sketch until the meadow began to take shape. I switched to green, then red, then blue.

Lost in the process, I didn't notice Jason until he said, "Good afternoon."

A ripple of excitement run through me at sound of

the voice. My mind instantly flew to the memory of his kiss. I took my time turning around, but when I did, I saw Jason standing at the edge of the porch, leaning against the railing. There was something about his casual air that caused the heat inside me to smolder again. I hated myself for the way my body reacted.

"I didn't think you were working up here today," I said, trying to keep my voice cool and neutral.

"Yeah, I saw your car by the bridge when I came up," he said. "I was working, I just parked farther up the road. Easier to haul the logs out that way."

"The logs?"

"By the pond," he said. "I told you I still had more work to do there, didn't I?"

My brain raced and I forced myself to look at him. Making eye contact, I could feel the flush in my cheeks, but I wouldn't let myself look away. "You were there?" I asked. "Today?"

"Sure was." He tucked his hand into his front pocket. "You were swimming."

I flew out of the chair, jumping to my feet. My eyes bored into him. "You were watching me." I jabbed a finger in his direction. "There's something called privacy, you know?"

It was at that moment, that I remembered I wasn't wearing a bra. I crossed my arms protectively in front of my chest and hoped he hadn't noticed.

"Whoa." He pushed away from the porch and held up his hands in defense. "I saw your wet hair," he said. "I guessed."

I brought a hand up to her hair, still damp and tangled. "Oh," I said. But I wasn't sure I believed him.

"I told you." His voice was soft. "Don't be angry with me."

I crossed my arms again and glared down at him. I was angry. But this time it was accompanied by an undeniable arousal, as I thought about the possibility that he could have seen me swimming.

"Come on, Becca. Can we just be friends?" He took a step towards me.

"Friends?"

Friends didn't kiss each other. I almost spoke aloud, but something in his voice made me lower my arms and take a step back.

"I'm sorry about yesterday," Jason said. He stepped closer to me. A shiver ran through me and I hoped he hadn't noticed. He leaned closer, my heart sped up, every nerve ending in my body on alert. I closed my eyes, fighting an internal battle.

"Did you do this? It's really good."

Jason's voice rocketed me out of my trance and I opened my eyes. He was looking past me, at my sketchbook.

"It's nothing," I said, and reached for the book. I grabbed it and clutched it to my chest.

"It didn't look like nothing to me." He turned so his body was only inches from me. "It looked like a beautiful drawing," he said,. His voice was gentle. "I didn't know you were an artist."

I raised an eyebrow. "There's a lot you don't know about me," I said. "Besides, I'm hardly an artist."

Jason held his hand out. "Can I see?"

"Why are you here?" I asked instead. A shadow passed over his face. "That came out wrong," I said quickly. "What I meant was, I thought you weren't coming back. That you were going to leave me alone."

"I am." He made no move to leave. "I mean, I will. If you want me to. But I forgot to tell you earlier that if you bring your milk jug back to the store when you're done, we can get it re-filled."

"You came all the way back here to tell me that?"

"Yes."

His eyes searched mine and I didn't look away. After a moment, Jason broke the stare and asked again, "Can I see?" He held his hand out.

I sighed but passed it to him and sat on the floorboards. I busied myself by gathering the colored pencils that were still, mostly scattered.

I didn't watch him while he examined it. It wasn't my best work, but it was my only work, at least in the last fifteen years.

After a few minutes of silence, he said, "This is really good." Jason sat across from me with his knees almost touching mine. He held out my drawing, which I took from him, placing it next to the pencils.

He watched me as if he expected me to say something in return. I stared past him to the field. I still wanted to draw. But despite, or maybe because of the tension between us, Jason's presence wasn't entirely unwelcome either.

"Look," I said after a moment. "I'm sorry. About earlier, I mean."

Jason shrugged and ran his hand through his shaggy locks. "Forget about it," he said. When he smiled, my breath caught in my throat.

He leaned forward, closing the already small gap between us. "So, do you want me to?"

"Want you to what?" The words came out in a whisper of air.

"Leave you alone." He reached forward and took my hand in his. A jolt of electricity flew up my arm. "I told you I would leave you alone if that's what you wanted," he said. "Is that what you want?"

I looked into his eyes and then down to my hand in his. I shook my head, a slight movement. "No."

CHAPTER SEVENTEEN

After Jason had left the night before, I'd turned my attention back to drawing. The pictures were good, but I was restless. I didn't have to dig deep to realize it was Jason who was distracting me. Or more accurately, it was the way he made me feel that was distracting me. Even so, I kept filling pages of the sketch book with my pencil strokes until finally the dwindling light forced me inside. I'd fallen into bed and directly into a deep sleep. Waking up rested wasn't a feeling I was used to. I liked it.

I'd also woken up with a need to talk to the girls, but after I checked my messages, I decided to drive down the mountain to make the call. I told myself it was because the reception was better, but if I was being honest, it was because I didn't want to share any part of the cabin or my new found happiness. I wasn't ready.

Besides, I had an apology to make. I looked through the windshield, across the parking lot, to the door of Sheena's shop before returning my attention to the ringing phone at my ear.

"Jon?"

"Becca, thank God. Why haven't you been answering the phone? I've been worried sick."

Guilt flashed through me. "I'm sorry," I said. "I don't get the greatest reception here."

That was true.

"Where are you?" Jon asked.

"Just leave it."

"Leave it? How can I just leave it, Becca? Where the

hell are you?"

I sighed and stepped out of the car, gulping in the fresh air. "Jon, I called because I want to, no, I need to talk to the girls."

"They're not here."

"Why not? Where are they?"

"Connie took them to the mall, I have a showing."

"A showing?"

"Yes, Becca." He sounded tired. "I still have to work you know?"

I ignored the implication. "I'll call later then," I said. I leaned back against the car door and kicked at the gravel with my toe.

"No," Jon said. "Let's talk now. Besides, they might not be home till late."

"Where would they be?"

"I can't do this by myself, and it's not fair to have Jordan babysitting all the time. She's going out with friends and Kayla's going over to Denise's."

"Denise?"

Anyone but my meddlesome neighbor. I could just hear her telling the ladies on the playground all about how I'd taken off, abandoning my family, and she had to step in to save the day.

"I told you, Becca. I can't do it alone. I need a break to get some work done."

"A break?" I mumbled under my breath. "Like I ever got a break."

"What did you say?"

"Nothing." I looked up as Jason's truck drove by. It slowed as it passed the store, and me, before speeding away again. My stomach flipped. A jolt of disappointment, and maybe something else, sparked through me as the truck passed. "Who is Jordan going out with? It better not be that boy," I said. "He's too old for her, Jon. You need to put a stop to it before it gets carried away, she's too young-"

"Then come home and do it, Becca."

Anger flared in me. "You need me to come home to handle our children? It wouldn't kill you to step up here, Jon."

"Dammit, Becca," he yelled, and I almost dropped the phone. Jon rarely raised his voice. "I am stepping up. And you'd be able to see that if you came home. You can't just run away from your family and your whole life. You're a grown up, for God's sake, act like it."

"Pardon me?" I whispered. Rage boiled under the surface, but there was more than that, Jon never yelled at me. I needed him to support this, support me. Not get angry.

"I'm done, Becca."

The words felt like a slap. I drew in a sharp breath. "What exactly do you mean?"

Jon let out a sigh and when he spoke again he sounded tired. "I just don't-"

"No." My legs wobbled and I braced myself against the car, afraid they wouldn't hold me up for very long. I couldn't hear what he had to say. I couldn't listen to him tell me that our marriage was over. Not yet.

My stomach rolled and I swallowed hard, afraid I was going to be sick.

"We need to talk about this," he said. For a minute I thought he might cry. I would not be able to deal with that.

I rubbed my hand across my face and willed the feeling to return to my legs. "I can't," I managed to get out, my voice sounded tiny and far away. "There's nothing...I have to go."

"Becca, please." I heard him whisper before I pulled the phone away from my ear.

I closed my eyes and tried to focus on my breathing; on the fresh mountain air filling my lungs.

Was that it, then? My marriage was over? Just like that. My knees gave way and I sank to the gravel. The sharp edges bit into my skin through the thin fabric of my skirt, but I welcomed the pain. Anything but the emptiness inside.

Images spiraled through my head.

Jon. Kayla. Jordan. Jon and I, together.

Jason.

My thoughts landed on Jason, desperate for an island in the storm of chaos. I focused on the way his lips felt against mine. The way he tasted. The way his hands pressed against my back. The way my body responded, wanting more. The unfamiliar, yet inexplicably welcome feelings he'd stirred inside me.

I closed my mind to everything else, forcing myself to focus completely on Jason. His fresh, piney scent. His hands. His lips.

Slowly, I opened my eyes and got to my feet. I straightened my skirt and brushed off the dust. Taking one more deep breath, and with my heart still racing in my chest, I crossed the parking lot to the store.

I opened the door with more force than I'd intended and the screen crashed against the wall, sending the delicate bells that hung from the top, tumbling to the floor.

Sheena popped her head around a display of hand woven baskets. "Holy Mother of Earth, Sunshine. You scared me."

"Sorry, I didn't mean to." I bent to retrieve the bells. I handed them to her, feeling like a chastened child. "Sorry," I said again.

"It's nothing," Sheena said. "You just startled me is all. I'm an old lady, don't forget." She smiled for a moment before her brows knitted into a frown. "You're upset," she said. "Your energy is misaligned. What's wrong?"

Everything.

I almost spoke out loud, but I was pretty sure Sheena

didn't want to hear about all my problems, never mind the fact that I was having inappropriate thoughts about Jason. Besides, she'd probably claim to see into my soul and I already felt weird enough with her.

"I'm fine," I said after a moment. "I did want to apologize to you though. I shouldn't have been so rude to you the other day. You were only trying to help with the key, and well... everything else. And, well, I'm sorry."

Sheena's face flashed and finally settled into a small smile. "Don't give it another thought." She dismissed my apology with a wave of her hand. "Sometimes we need to refocus our internal chi. And if I was the person to help you do that, then I'm honored."

"Still," I said. "Chi or not, I wasn't very nice. You've been very kind to me and it wasn't fair."

"Enough." Sheena waved her hand again. "Now, if you don't want to talk about what's got your aura so out of whack, that's fine. But I'm willing to bet a cup of tea would help."

It wasn't a suggestion, more of a command. The idea of going back to the cabin to be alone to replay my conversation with Jon over again in my head, was the last thing I wanted. Tea sounded great.

I followed Sheena through the store and into the back, beyond the beaded curtain. The cramped storage area looked a lot like the store. Boxes were stacked at random and most looked like they might topple over with even the slightest touch. Cartons lay open, their contents spilling out the top and onto the floor. There were all kinds of goods piled around the room, creating an obstacle course that we picked our way through.

"I'm trying to clean all this up," Sheena said as we stepped over a box of books. "There just never seems to be enough time, now that Jason's back at school. He's a good boy, just not around as much as I'd like anymore."

"School?"

"Oh, I shouldn't have said anything. He doesn't like people to know." Sheena stopped and turned to face me. "I don't know why. I'm sure proud of him, but he must have his reasons for keeping it quiet. And who am I to mess with his cosmic energy? Anyway, I suppose all of this can wait. It's just me here most of the time and the mess doesn't bother me." Her laugh filled the room. I tried to smile along with her, but my attempt was weak. She turned, and continued weaving her way through the space.

We dodged around a pail of fresh-cut flowers before Sheena pushed aside another curtain and led us into a small bright kitchen. I expected to find a room similar to that of my cottage, decorated in scarves and smelling like incense, but her kitchen, was the direct opposite.

It was tiled in crisp white and blue squares. The counter gleamed and held only a few jars filled with flour, sugar and coffee. Instead of incense, it smelled of lemons, fresh and clean. The scent was oddly comforting and when I sank into a chair at the table, I felt instantly at home.

"I'll make you some tea, Sunshine. A good cup of herbal tea always helps to clear the spirit. It will help you refocus your energy."

I nodded and watched Sheena. She placed the kettle on the stove before moving to the counter where she packed what looked like a mixture of dried leaves, berries and flowers into little mesh spoons that she placed in each cup.

"Thank you," I said.

She turned, a mug in her hand. "It's no trouble, Sunshine. No trouble at all."

"No." I shook my head. "For everything. Thank you. You don't even know me and you've gone out of your way to help me, and... well, you've been very helpful."

"Oh, I know you," Sheena said, and turned around again.

"Pardon?" I asked, not sure if I heard her right.

"Of course I know you, you're Vicki's daughter."

I wished I could see her face. "You keep saying that, but you've never met me and I don't even remember her."

"You don't?" Sheena left the mugs on the counter and moved to sit across from me at the table. Her mouth turned down in a tight frown. "You don't remember your mother at all?"

"Connie is my mother," I said. "I'm sure Vicki was great, but I was practically a baby when she died, and Dad and Dylan never liked to talk about her. So, no, I don't know anything about her."

"It's a shame." Sheena cast her eyes down. "She was a magical lady."

For a moment we were both silent. I didn't think I should say anything, it seemed indecent, like Sheena was mourning her. Instead I sat and waited.

"Well, none of that matters," she said after a minute, and reached for my hand. Her strong fingers wrapped around mine and squeezed. "The second I laid eyes on you, I knew you. You're a lot like your mother, you know? In here." Sheena gently pushed my hand back until it rested on my chest, directly over my heart.

"But I haven't even told you anything about me."

"You don't have to tell me your life for me to see the pain. It's in here." She patted my chest again before slowly releasing my hand.

"How can you see that?"

"Sunshine, I can see your aura as clearly as I can see the sun in the sky." She smiled.

"Tell me," I whispered. "Tell me what you see." I surprised myself by caring what she said. And, by believing that she could see anything at all. I didn't normally believe in that type of thing. But for some reason I trusted Sheena, and the desire to know something, anything at all, was too strong to ignore.

Sheena's smile was soft. "You're surrounded by greens and grays." She nodded slowly. "But there are reds in there too. And, even a little pink." She winked.

"What does that mean? What do the colors tell you?"

"Every shade means something different. But you have a strong ring of blue-green that tells me you're going through an emotionally turbulent time. The dark green tells me you have a mental stress of some kind. But I didn't need an aura to tell me that." She raised an eyebrow. "The grays are worrisome though." Her face grew serious again. "The light gray indicates that you feel trapped in your life and the charcoal tells me you suffer deeply from depression or a deep sadness. That's the trouble, Sunshine. The darker gray is strong. It bleeds through all the other colors in your aura."

Depression? That was ridiculous. I couldn't be depressed. Crazy people were depressed.

"What about the other colors?" I didn't want to hear about the gray. "You said there was red and pink."

"Yes," she said. "Just like your mother. You have a ring of crimson."

"What's that mean?"

"It means you've been blessed with creative talents. You've had a chance to look through the items in the trunk, I assume.

I nodded. "I think my creative talent has long since gone," I said. I thought back to my drawings earlier. They were okay, but so far from what I used to produce. I remembered the way Jason had examined the picture. The way my fingers felt when he touched mine. My lips tingled with the memory.

"Ah, that's the pink I see," Sheena said, her smile grew wide.

"What are you talking about?" I could feel a blush beginning its burn across my cheeks.

"The pink in your aura. It's the color of sexual attraction. Desire."

"That's silly," I said. I ran my hands through my hair trying to distract my own thoughts. "I haven't seen my husband in days and even if I did, I wouldn't say that what I feel for him right now is really attraction."

"Perhaps it's not your husband, then."

I looked toward the window. Sheena had to know that Jason had been at the cabin over the last few days. She would know it was Jason making my aura pink.

The whistle of the kettle saved me from saying anything further.

Sheena rose to add the water to the mugs. From the counter she said, "It's not the pink in your aura I'm worried about, Sunshine. It's the gray." She poured the water and steam filled the air. "Just like your mother."

My stomach flipped and twisted into a knot. "My mother?"

"She had a deeply gray aura as well," Sheena said. "But not always, just...well, at the end."

A warm, spicy aroma filled the air and my head grew heavy, full of the weight of the day. I rubbed the bridge of my nose trying to release some of the pressure.

"It's okay to cry." Sheena's voice was gentle.

"I don't cry." I dropped my hand and turned to see Sheena watching me from the counter. "Can't remember the last time."

Sheena smiled a sad smile and turned away. "Another thing in common with your mother. She didn't cry either."

"Ever?"

"No," she said, placing the mug in front of me. "She was a very passionate person, but very troubled as well. I don't think she knew back then how to release the emotions and cleanse herself. Although Lord knows enough people tried to help her."

I wrapped my hands around the mug and absorbed the heat through my palms. I inhaled deeply. The scent of the tea was fruity, with the slightest touch of something spicy. "What do you mean, 'help her'?"

"Like I said, she was a troubled soul. But she wasn't always that way. Her aura used to glow with warmth. There were yellows, oranges, reds and pinks. Oh, the pink."

"Sexual desire?" I asked, not sure if I wanted to hear the answer.

Sheena laughed. "That too. But her aura glowed with a pale pink. The color of true love."

"Dad." I looked into the tea, focusing on the leaves floating around the bottom.

"Yes. I've never seen a purer love than between those two. It was magical. And you and Rayne, you were such blessings from that love."

"Rayne?" I looked up.

"Oh, that's right," she said. "He would go by his given name now."

"Dylan?" I smiled and made a note to tease him about that later. Then my smile faded. "There's so much I don't know," I said. "Maybe you would tell me? About Vicki, I mean."

Sheena took a long time to answer, staring deeply into her own tea mug as if to get answers. When the silence became uncomfortable, she looked up and said, "I don't know why you're here, Sunshine." She held up one hand to ward off my protests. "You don't have to tell me if you're not ready. After all, we all have our own journey to make. But I think before I tell you anything about Vicki, it's important for you to travel your own path."

"What are you talking about?" The pressure built again in the back of my head. "I know why I'm here."

"Do you?"

"Of course." I pushed the mug away. The heat was suddenly too much. I looked up and stared directly into her eyes, and all at once, I wasn't sure. I closed my eyes and visions of Jon, Kayla, Jordan, Dad, Steph and

Connie, flashed through my head, followed by an image of Jason. I shook my head sharply, erasing them all and snapped my eyes open. "I do know why I'm here," I said.

"Really?"

"Yes." I took a deep breath, the roaring in my head increasing in intensity. "I'm sick of it. I'm sick of everything. I'm so damn tired of getting out of bed every day and being a failure at everything I do. I'm supposed to be good at this. Being a mother, a wife. But I'm not. And I'm not me anymore. I don't know even know who I'm supposed to be. Becca the wife? The mother? Or, the artist? I'm certainly not that anymore. I'm nothing. And what's worse, I'm not sure I care."

I pushed my chair back and jumped to my feet. "I'm here because I'm miserable and I don't know who I am. There. I said it." My body vibrated, and my voice shook, but I kept going. "I'm here because I couldn't stand for one more minute to try and be everything to everybody, when all I really wanted to do was close my eyes and make it all go away."

"Good," Sheena said. "Feel it, Becca. That's good."

The roaring in my head grew, threatening to take over my consciousness. I swallowed hard and said. "I'm here, because I'm afraid," I said, much softer.

"Afraid of what?"

I braced my hands on the solid table, bent my head and forced myself to draw the breath I needed to strengthen me. "I'm afraid that...that I hate my life," I managed. "That I might I hate everything I'm supposed to love."

I looked up then and Sheena's eyes were full of tears. "It's okay, Sunshine. It's going to be okay."

"No." I shook my head. "No, it's not."

I hung my head again. It was too much to take.

"You don't hate it all," Sheena said. I could hear her

move around the table and when she placed her hands on my shoulders, the warmth of her touch filled me.

"What if I do?"

"You don't. It's just the natural flow of things," she murmured into my ear. "You'll be okay, Sunshine. You're in the right place. Everything will be okay."

I turned and moved into her waiting arms. They felt good. Secure and comfortable. Letting her hold me, I was reminded of Connie's strong arms when I was a child. "I'm just so scared, Sheena," I mumbled. "Just so scared."

By the time I got back to the cabin, I was too agitated to think straight. The conversation with Sheena had shaken me. Did I really hate everything I was supposed to love? Just because I'd said it out loud, did that make it true? I paced the small rooms, searching my head for answers. But I didn't have to think very hard, I knew there was truth to what I'd said to Sheena. A lot of truth. But still, so many questions.

I walked into the bedroom and my eyes landed on the lavender sachet Sheena had given me. I picked up and inhaled the gentle scent. Sheena's voice rolled through my head.

She didn't cry either. Just like your mother.

I squeezed the pillow, crushing the dried flowers inside.

Somewhere over the last few years, I realized, I'd forgotten to cry. Forgotten how to feel enough. How was that even possible?

I knew I loved my family. But I'd told Sheena I hated everything. That wasn't really true. Was it?

The cabin was too small, too stuffy. I needed to get out. I grabbed the sketch book and retreated to the rocker on the porch.

185

Almost at once I fell into the familiar rhythm of the pencil strokes on the paper. Amazed at how quickly it'd come back to me, I let myself go with it. I didn't focus on anything, except drawing the pictures in my head. It didn't take long for my breathing to slow and my heart rate to return to normal. In only a few minutes, I felt more relaxed.

When I was finished, I sat back and examined the picture. I'd drawn the pond. It was empty. The urge to sketch myself swimming flashed through me. But I didn't draw people. I never had. Not even in art school. There was something about recreating the human form that I could never master. It wasn't just the body, it was the spirit of the person. It wasn't easily captured in art. It took a skill, an insight that I didn't possess.

Instead of dwelling on it, I flipped the page of the sketch book. The sun was disappearing behind the mountains but there were still a few stray streaks of orange and gold left behind in the dusky sky. In the lingering light, I quickly drew a poppy. The flowing lines of the papery petals came easily to me and my hand flew across the page.

When the last of the light faded, there was an easy sense of calm before the deep shadows of night started to creep in. I put the book down and relaxed into the rocker to enjoy the peace. Drawing did that to me. Settled me. It always had. How had I forgotten that?

I stretched back in the chair and closed my eyes. The stress and confusion from earlier was gone; I let my body relax and after a few deep breaths, the sounds of the crickets surrounded me.

CHAPTER EIGHTEEN

I didn't have long to enjoy the quiet of the new dusk before I heard the now familiar rumble of Jason's truck. I didn't move. Even when the engine cut and I heard the slam of the door.

"Hey there," Jason said from the dark. "Am I interrupting something?"

My stomach clenched at the sound of his voice. I could try to fool myself into thinking it was because I'd been alone all afternoon, but my body knew differently and the increase of my heartbeat defied me.

Opening my eyes, I turned to him. "Not really," I said. "I was just enjoying the quiet."

"I'm sorry to disturb that then," he said. "I know how soothing it can be up here. I won't stay long. I just wanted to bring you something." He held up a paper bag. "A peace offering of sorts."

"Peace offering?" I managed.

"Well...yes." He looked away quickly. He didn't seem like the kind of guy to get flustered, and it was kind of cute. "Anyway," he said. "I managed to sweet talk Zeppa into some cheese and a bottle of her homemade wine. I snuck some of Moonbeam's fresh bread too. I thought you might like it."

"Zeppa?"

Jason laughed and the awkwardness of the moment was gone. "Hippies, remember? I couldn't make this stuff up if I tried."

I smiled with him. If felt good.

"Hey, look," he said and his tone became serious. "I'm

sorry about the other day. I can be a real jerk sometimes, I know I came on kind of -"

"Don't." I held up my hand to silence him.

I didn't need or want to hear his apologies, when all I could think of since had been the way his kiss had made me feel. I knew if I closed my eyes at that moment, I'd still be able to feel the thrill his lips had sent through my body. We stared at each other across the porch. His eyes held mine and caused a smoldering to start deep inside. Surprising myself again, I didn't look away.

Jason was the one to finally break the building tension. "So, are you hungry?"

I leaned up against the counter and watched as Jason unloaded his bag. He moved comfortably around the kitchen and it reminded me of the ease which with he'd moved around the cabin on the night we met.

"You've spent a lot of time here," I said.

Jason stopped, the bottle of wine in his hand, hovering. "I have. I rented this place for about a year before I started school. Don't worry," he added. "I know Sheena told you about school. It's fine." He turned back to the fridge. "You okay with something simple for dinner?"

"I'm good with anything," I said. "As long as I'm not making it." It was nice to be served and have dinner prepared for me. "So, why rent this place instead of something in town?"

"I don't need to tell you that it's beautiful here, and peaceful. But mostly I just needed a break from, well, from everything." He stopped moving for a moment, but didn't turn around.

"Can I ask you another question?" I asked, when it was clear he wasn't going to elaborate.

He turned then. "Only if I can ask you one." His voice

teased, but his eyes were serious.

Before I thought about it too much, I agreed, with a courage I didn't know I had. "Deal," I said.

He raised his eyebrows. "Okay. But let's have some wine first." He pulled the cork and poured two glasses. Handing me one, he said, "Ask away."

I took a small sip. The wine was cool and sharp on my tongue. "Why are you going to school?" I asked. "I mean, it seems kind of..."

"Late?" He finished for me. "Because of my age, you mean?"

"Well, it's not that you're old."

"Really?" He grinned.

"Stop it." I snatched a tea towel from the counter and swatted it at him. "You know what I mean."

He laughed and dodged. "I do." He resumed his preparations and reached into a drawer pulling out a knife, he began to slice thin pieces of fresh mozzarella. "I guess I'm not your typical coed."

"Well, no. How old are you?"

"That's two questions."

I eyed him.

"Ok, I'm thirty-one." He watched me for a response.

"What?"

"You just seem shocked that I'm so old."

"You're not old," I said. "I'm older than you. I thought you were younger actually. So now answer my first question, why are you going to school at the ripe old age of thirty-one?"

"Because I can." He grabbed two tomatoes from a bowl on the counter and began slicing them and laying them on a plate next to the cheese.

"You're being awfully cryptic. I don't think that qualifies as a fair answer."

"Okay." He turned to me. "I'll tell you."

I waited while he picked leaves off a small basil plant he'd produced from the bag. "I was married," he said simply. "She was the love of my life, or so I thought. We were childhood sweethearts. I can't remember a time that I didn't love Leila."

It was completely irrational, but I felt a spark of jealousy at the thought of Jason's true love.

"We married too young and we didn't have a plan. All we knew is that we wanted to be together. My parents didn't approve at all and refused to come to the wedding. Mom said I was making a huge mistake not going to school and doing something bigger with my life. Her parents too. They thought we were ruining both our lives."

"That would be hard," I said. "Not a great way to start a life together."

"No," he said. "I wouldn't listen, but my mom knew then what I couldn't see. Leila and I grew up together, we had loved each other since we were kids. Now, looking back, I can see that my love for her ran deeper than hers did. I guess I thought it would be enough. It wasn't." His voice was quiet. "So we married right after graduation and I never went to school. Instead I took on odd jobs for people. You know, landscaping, painting fences, that kind of thing. Leila had always been artistic, so she spent her days making jewelry. On weekends we'd set up at the farmer's markets and spots around town. It was nice. Simple." His face took on a faraway look.

"It does sound nice," I said.

"It was. We were happy. Or I thought we were. Leila wasn't."

"Did she cheat on you?"

Jason jerked, startled from his memory. "Cheat? No." He shook his head.

"She leave you then?" I could feel my anger building at this unknown girl who'd hurt him.

"No."

"Then what?"

"She killed herself."

The air rushed from my lungs. "Oh." I crumpled into a chair. "I'm sorry."

"It's okay," he said. "It was a long time ago. I know now it wasn't because of me. Leila had a lot of sadness in her. Always did. She was a sad child too. I used to think she was just quiet, introspective. I thought I could save her, you know? Cheer her up, make her happy with the sheer power of my love. Even when we were kids. I was always trying to make her smile and laugh. I guess I thought when we got married, that would be enough. Oldest story in the book, right?"

"Jason, I'm so sorry."

He shrugged. "It's in the past now. I blamed myself for a long time. I felt like I'd failed her."

"So, you never knew why? Why she did it, I mean."

He shook his head. "That's the thing. There doesn't have to be a reason with suicide. For some, it's the ultimate selfish act. But for others, the hopelessness inside them just overwhelms them until they really see no other option. The idea of living, it just becomes too much."

"That's so sad."

"It is."

"So what did you do?" I asked.

"I didn't have anyone," he said. "Her parents wouldn't speak to me. I don't think they blamed me. After all, they must have known about her depression. It was just too hard for them."

"What about your parents? What did they say?"

"Nothing. They stopped talking to me after we got married. Even when Leila died, mom sent flowers. But that was it."

"That's awful," I said. I couldn't imagine Dad and Connie cutting me off like that. Abandoning me, especially when I needed them most. They would never do that.

But isn't that what I'd done to them by leaving? I shook my head, unwilling to focus on the thought.

Jason shrugged. "So I left the city. I sold our little house, got rid of everything that reminded me of her, which was everything, and started driving. Eventually I got to Rainbow Valley, and I met Sheena. I guess you could say, I ran away." He looked at me pointedly, like he expected me to say something. When I didn't, he continued. "Sheena kind of adopted me. I guess she could tell I was a lost soul. She let me stay with her for awhile, in exchange for helping her out a bit. I was totally lost in my misery, but after a few months, Sheena made me go talk to someone"

"And that helped?"

"It did. I didn't think it would, but it really did. I pulled myself together, started working more, and moved up to the cabin for a bit. It turned out my parents must have felt some type of loyalty towards me, because I got a letter from the bank telling me about a savings account they'd started in my name when I was a kid. It was almost enough to pay for my tuition. So I decided to get my degree in psychology. Maybe I can help other people like me, people like Leila."

"Do you think you could have saved her?"

He looked at me; the look in his eyes was intense, and it took everything I had not to look away. "Not her, not then," he said. "I loved her so much, but I didn't know enough. But now that I'm learning more about the mind and how it works, maybe I can make a difference. I can save others from going through the pain I did. I'll be able to help people."

"Like me?"

"I didn't say that."

Silence filled the kitchen, but it wasn't uncomfortable. Jason stacked the tomatoes and cheese with the basil and drizzled olive oil over it all. He filled a basket with fresh bread and grabbed both plates.

"Let's eat outside."

"There is nothing better than fresh tomatoes and cheese," Jason said between mouthfuls.

"I couldn't agree more. This is fantastic."

I'd spread out a large piece of batik cloth that I'd found in the cupboard, and we were eating picnic style in the middle of the porch. Stars were beginning to appear in the night sky, but the only real light came from the window and the few lamps we'd left on in the kitchen.

The somber mood from inside had been replaced with a lighter tone, that good food and wine only helped along.

Jason swirled a piece of bread through the oil before popping it in his mouth. "So, now you can answer a question for me."

"Go for it."

"Feeling brave are you?" Jason laughed.

"It must be the wine." I raised my glass, and he refilled it.

"Ok, I'm going to ask the obvious question."

"Why am I here?"

"Actually, I was going to ask what you're running away from."

I swirled my wine, studying it through the glass. "What makes you think I'm running away from someone?"

"I didn't say someone."

I picked up another piece of tomato, and inhaled the fresh basil before putting the whole piece in my mouth. "Good, cause I'm not," I mumbled.

Jason raised an eyebrow.

I swallowed hard. "I'm not. Running away from someone, I mean."

"Could've fooled me."

"I'm not."

"If you insist." He smirked behind his wineglass.

"Why should I be running away from someone?" I pushed up from the floor with the need to put space between us. "Why would you even think that? Just because a woman comes up to the mountains, alone, to get away from everything, you assume she must be running away from someone. Maybe you should take a few more classes, because I just needed to get away. A vacation. That's all." I walked to the edge of the porch and stared out into the building darkness. I inhaled the clean air, letting it fill my lungs and settle me. I didn't know what was worse; that he'd hit a nerve, or that he surely knew it.

"Get away from what?" he asked. I didn't look but I heard the creak of the boards as he stood.

"I couldn't stand the thought of going home and looking at him. Looking at all of them." The words came out in a rush before I could stop them. "Dealing with the latest drama, the next tantrum, seeing how I'd failed. But now...I've made everything worse."

I could sense him standing behind me, the warmth of his body radiated into my back. "I left," I whispered, as Jason's arms slid around my waist and pulled me towards him.

The desire to lean into him, to let him hold me and make me feel better, was strong. It would be easy to give into my body, to stop over thinking things. And why not? Why shouldn't I?

I tensed and turned away from him.

"Becca."

"I can't."

"I'm not asking for anything." He moved towards me again, his hand came to rest on my shoulder. Through the thin blouse, my skin warmed under his touch, but I shivered from the sensation. "You're cold."

His hand slid down my arm and wrapped around me. This time I didn't fight him. He circled my body with his other arm and pulled me in to him. The heat from his body filled me. I leaned back and let him support me.

Together, we stared into the darkness. Despite my emotions running wild, my mind wandered and floated again to my children.

"I'm an awful mother."

"No, you're not."

"You don't even know," I said, choking on the words.

"I know you can't be that terrible." His breath was warm on my ear. "Look." He unwound one arm and pointed to the sky.

I followed the direction of his hand. "What am I looking at?"

"Andromeda. Do you see? Just to the west of the Milky Way. It looks like a V."

"I do. I see it." I spun to see Jason's small smile before settling back into the comfort of him.

"Not many people pay attention to Andromeda."

"I've never heard of it." I turned and returned my focus to the stars.

"You may have heard of her mother, Queen Cassiopeia?"

I nodded.

"Well, the Queen would brag to the sea nymphs about how beautiful the two of them were. Finally, the nymphs had enough of listening to her boasting. In order to save her kingdom from the angry sea nymphs, the Queen was ordered to sacrifice her daughter by chaining her to a cliff for the hungry sea monster as a sacrifice."

"That's awful." I turned around, out of Jason's arms.

"See? Cassiopeia. Now that was an awful mother." His smile lit up his face and I couldn't help it, I burst into laughter.

When I caught my breath again, I asked, "What happened to her? Andromeda?"

"She was rescued of course." Jason pulled me close again. "Perseus, swooped in on his winged horse right before the sea monster could attack. They were married on the spot and lived happily ever after."

"The damsel in distress, rescued by the dashing prince routine, huh?" He was so close, I could feel his chest rise and fall with every breath. Was the beating I felt, Jason's heart? Or my own?

"It seems to be a common theme." He spun me, so I faced him. "Don't you think?" His breath was warm on my lips. It came in small puffs with every word.

"I'm not -"

He cut off my protests with a kiss. This time, his lips felt familiar, and my body responded just as it had before. When he pulled me tighter, I didn't push him away but sank deeper into his embrace, losing myself. Too quickly, the kiss ended and Jason pulled away, sucking on my lower lip as we parted.

"Just for the record," he said, his voice deep and rough. "I'm not trying to rescue you."

I closed my eyes and tried to squeeze out the images of my family. It was only after their faces grew blurry, that I opened my eyes again and looked directly at Jason. "Good," I whispered. "Because I don't want to be saved." I wound my arm up around his head and pulled him down, his lips locking firmly onto my own.

CHAPTER NINETEEN

We made our way inside. Like teenagers, stopping every few steps to lose ourselves in another kiss and a quick exploration of each others bodies. The bedroom was dark and when Jason turned on the bedside lamp, the room filled with the soft purple glow I'd come to enjoy. I didn't protest about the light, as I normally would. Instead, I took a step back, watching Jason.

He reached for me, but I held a hand up. "Let me do this," I said.

With his eyes fixed on me, I slowly lifted my blouse over my head and pulled it off. My breath caught in my throat. The awareness of what I was doing mingled with my unfamiliar boldness and scared and thrilled me at the same time. I swallowed hard and let the top flutter to the floor. I reached up to pull the elastic from my hair. Released, it came to rest on my bare shoulders, tickling my skin.

"God, Becca," Jason breathed the words but didn't make any move to touch me. His eyes traveled my body, and with his smile for encouragement, I undid the string of my peasant skirt, letting it fall to the floor in a puddle around my feet. I paused for only a moment before reaching behind me with both hands. When the clasp of my bra unclipped, I had a moment of insecurity. After all, I had stretch marks, extra pounds. Mine was not the body of a twenty year old. I'd been touched by child birth and age.

"Becca," Jason said from the bed. "You're beautiful. I want to see you. All of you."

I met Jason's eyes, and was shocked by the intensity there. It had been so long since a man had looked at me with such blatant desire in his eyes. Even Jon. After awhile, the passion had faded. My mind flitted to Jon. Could I do this to him? The thought flashed through my head before I could stop it. "No," I said. My voice was barely a whisper. I turned so Jason couldn't see the confusion on my face.

"Becca?" I heard him ask behind me, but I ignored him, caught up in my own conflict.

It wasn't Jon I was doing this to, I reasoned. It was different here. I was different. I couldn't be that Becca anymore. I couldn't be the Becca he wanted me to be. Besides, I thought, hadn't he all but told me our marriage wasn't working? I shook my head clear and turned around.

Jason was waiting, watching. He raised an eyebrow in question. I offered a small smile and slid my bra straps from my shoulders in response.

He took a step forward and my body tingled with the need for him to touch me. But I stopped him with a slight shake of my head. "Not yet."

He waited and I hooked both my thumbs in the elastic of my panties. With a slight bend at the waist I pushed them over my thighs and to the floor. I straightened up and stepped free of the pile of clothing. I was no longer insecure bathed in the glow from the lamp. With Jason's hot gaze roaming my body.

I couldn't remember the last time I'd stood naked in front of a man. I should have felt exposed, vulnerable. But somehow, I didn't. All I could think of was the man in front of me, how it made me feel when he kissed me. How my body would sing from the first touch of him on my naked skin. I ached with anticipation.

"Now?" he asked.

With a slight grin and a nod, I beckoned him.

He crossed the floor to me, and stopped only inches

away. I could feel the heat of him against my bare skin. I yearned to reach forward and close the gap between us. My breath came in short, shallow puffs.

"Let me look at you," he said, his voice heavy with desire.

I did. His eyes roamed over me, and I didn't cover my body. I didn't turn, or cower, or try to distract him. I didn't want to. The bold need blazing in his eyes, as his gaze worked over me, was enough to send my heart racing. I stood still, shaking from the excitement of his eyes drinking in every inch of me. Finally, when I thought I'd explode from the need for him to touch me, he reached out and brushed the hair off my shoulder exposing my neck. He ran his thumb along my cheek, sliding it behind my ear and down to my neck.

When I closed my eyes, my knees started to quiver and a low moan escaped my lips. The gentle pressure of Jason's thumb was replaced by his mouth, and he alternated between kisses and nibbles down to the swell of my breast. The sensation he caused sent an electrical storm raging through my body. I moaned, louder this time, and arched my head away to give him better access. One hand found the small of my back and pulled me so I was pressed up tight against him. The rough denim of his jeans felt foreign against my skin. The heat between my legs continued to build and I refused to think about anything besides the sensations overtaking my body.

His other hand wound through my hair and tugged my head further to one side. His mouth continued its work across my breasts and up the other side of my neck. He moved so slowly and with such precision, I thought I would scream from the pleasure and urgency building within me. I let my own hands grip his back through his t-shirt to keep myself from falling to my knees.

Just when I thought I wouldn't be able to take one

more second of his teasing kisses on my skin, he switched from nibbling to a gentle sucking with subtle but determined pressure. It reminded me of being a teenager, and I almost giggled before a sharp pain so exquisite it nearly made me climax on the spot, stopped me.

I opened my eyes and pulled back a little. "You bit me."

"You loved it," he said, and flashed me a wicked smile.

I returned his smile and reached for him. I found his mouth with my own and kissed him with a fervor I didn't know I possessed. My hands grasped at his clothes until they pulled his t-shirt free. Breaking our kiss, I pulled it over his head and revealed his stomach. From the first moment I'd seen him take his shirt off, I'd wanted to run my hands down his body. I spread both hands wide and placed each palm flat on his chest. Working my way down, I took my time feeling every ripple of hard muscle until I was stopped by the waistband of his jeans. My fingers found the belt buckle, and paused for a second before sliding the leather through.

My hands took on a life of their own as I tugged at the button and slowly undid the zipper. It was Jason's turn to let out a low moan when I tugged his jeans and boxers down in one move, releasing him.

"Enough," he said, and took my hands pulling me against him again. Despite myself, I gasped when I felt him press against me. Wanting me. Needing me. "From the moment I met you, I -"

"No more talking," I said, and pressed my mouth against his, silencing him.

Without breaking our connection, Jason moved us back towards the bed and lowered us to the mattress.

This, I thought as we came together, this, is who I am.

###

"Becca?"

"Umm?"

I was nestled in the crook of Jason's arm enjoying the heat of him, the total relaxation of my own body. His other arm was wrapped around me, lazily stroking my hair.

"You're okay?"

"Umm hmm." I nodded gently, barely moving my head. I was better than okay. I couldn't remember ever feeling so physically satisfied. So spent, yet totally rejuvenated.

"I'm glad," he said. "But, I can't be your solution."

"Uh, huh," I murmured. "I know." My eyes were closed, my body relaxed, heavy and detached. The muted light gave me the feeling of being underwater. Like I was floating in a dream.

"No," he said. "Really, Becca."

"Umm hmm." His touch felt blissful in my hair, I willed him to shut up and never stop moving his hand.

"Are you listening?" His fingers paused in their delicate dance.

Sighing, I propped myself up and let the sheet fall away. "Yes. I'm listening. What would you like me to say? Can't I just enjoy this?"

"Yes, of course." He pushed himself up so we were facing each other. "I want you to enjoy it. God knows I did." He smiled and reached for me.

His touch on my bare arm made my pulse race again. "Then you need to be quiet and let me enjoy it." I relaxed into him and let myself sink back into the pillow.

"I don't know exactly what's going on with you," he said. He ran his fingers up and down my arm, relighting the fire within me. "But I do know that it wouldn't be fair to you if I didn't say what I need to say."

My body tensed, the fire inside dying. He needed to stop talking.

"Becca, I-"

"Please don't." I pushed his hand away, his touch suddenly irritating me. I sat up, and said, "Just. Stop. Talking, Jason. I don't really care what you need to say."

"It's just that I feel like we shouldn't have done that."

"What?"

"Don't get me wrong. I'm happy we did. Lord knows I wanted to." His small smile made my stomach flip despite the growing annoyance with the conversation. "But I can't be the solution to your problems. I'm sorry, Becca."

"You're sorry?"

"That didn't come out right."

"Then by all means, try again." I glared at him, but he didn't seem to notice.

"All I'm saying is, I'm sorry if I made things worse for you. You probably don't need any more complications right now."

I looked away when he smiled. I refused to be affected by him.

"I'm a big girl," I said. "I'm sure I can decide what complications I can and cannot handle."

"Don't get mad."

All at once I became aware of my nakedness and tried to pull the sheet up to cover myself, but Jason grabbed my hand.

"You're laying here, in my bed, after we...after we did what we just did, and you're telling me we shouldn't have just done it. How can I not get mad?"

"I can't help it. It's the classes I'm taking. They get me thinking. I analyze everyone." He pulled me closer and used his free hand to cup my cheek. "It's annoying, isn't it?"

"Yes," I said. "It is extremely annoying." Despite myself, I closed my eyes when his hand moved and his thumb began stroking the sensitive skin behind my ear.

"Can I just say one more thing?" Jason asked. The hand he had on my arm began massaging the bare skin, working its way up. The combined effect was almost hypnotic. "Then I promise, no more talking." He brought his lips to my neck, leaving a trail of kisses.

I sighed in agreement. How could I not?

"All I wanted to say is that right now you're exhibiting classic signs of-"

"Enough," I cut him off, the spell broken. I slid out from under his hands and off the bed. I yanked the sheet from him and wrapped it around my nakedness. "I can't sit here and listen to this. I can't remember the last time I felt so...well... that I felt so damn good."

"Becca."

"No," I yelled. My voice filled the small room, but I didn't care. Anger boiled through me, it needed to get it out. "Don't ruin this. Don't you get it? I don't need to analyze this, I just need to feel it. I just need to *feel*, Jason. I don't want to know why I'm doing what I'm doing, or why it's probably wrong. At this moment, I don't care, because I finally feel good." I tightened the sheet and started to leave but spun around again. "And, for the record. You're not a psychologist. You're only a student. So you can save your psychobabble for the classroom." With that, I turned, and stormed from the room before he could say another word.

The night air was a relief on my hot skin, and my mood. I sat in my rocking chair and took deep breaths of the sharp air. Despite the chill, it felt warmer than the last few nights. Probably a sign that the season was moving deeper into summer.

I heard the screen door open and shut softly behind me. Then, footsteps. "Becca?"

"He wants to leave me." I didn't turn around but continued rocking and staring out into the dark night.

"Your husband? He told you that?" Jason moved in front of me, blocking my view of nothingness.

"Not in so many words," I said. "I didn't give him a chance. I didn't want to hear it."

"That's why you're here?"

"No." I looked at him then, bringing my eyes into focus on his bare chest that I'd so recently run my hands down. To keep myself from reaching out, I wrapped the sheet around me and clenched the rocker with my free hand. "I mean, yes. I guess so."

"You don't sound so sure," he said. He crouched down, so we were at eye level. "Which is it?"

"Both, I guess. I feel real here. At home, with all the other shitty stuff going on, well... I don't even know who I am anymore."

"Talk to me."

I narrowed my eyes at him. I didn't need a repeat of his psychoanalysis.

"I promise," he said, and held his hands up in mock surrender. "I'll do my best to stop with the whole...what did you call it?"

"Psychobabble."

"Right," he said and the smile in his eyes softened me. "Let me listen."

I sighed, and started talking. "My fourteen year old is dating a much older boy, my best friend is gearing up to travel the world and leave me behind, my father is totally losing it and thinks I'm my mother, who's been dead for more than twenty years, my step-mother should have him committed, but can't bring herself to do it, my youngest daughter is one sonic tantrum, I'm totally failing as a mom, my husband more or less announced on my birthday that he wants a separation, and to top it all off, I'm not sure if I care." I exhaled.

Jason blinked but didn't say anything for a moment.

Finally, he let out a low whistle, and said, "Wow. That's a lot for anyone."

"You want to know the worst part?" I rocked the chair hard so I was sitting straight up. "I don't cry." I looked at him, trying to gauge his reaction. "Not once. I haven't cried in years. My whole life is crumbling around me and I haven't shed one tear. What does that say about me?" I turned back to Jason, challenging him with my eyes.

"Becca, you've been through a lot."

"Shouldn't I cry?"

"Everyone handles stress differently."

"It's like I'm dead inside."

"It's a coping mechanism."

"Did you learn that in class too?"

He grabbed the rocking chair with both hands bringing it to a jarring halt. "Becca, stop."

"I don't cry, Jason." I spoke each word slowly and carefully. "What do your books say about that?"

He ignored my question. "Earlier, you said you felt something. That what we did, it made you feel good."

"Jason." My voice softened. I wanted to look away, but something in his eyes held me.

"See? You did feel something," he said. "You're not dead inside, Becca. You're lost inside."

I closed my eyes, breaking his intense stare. I could still feel his hands on my skin, his kisses on my neck, his body moving on top of me, inside me. I opened my eyes and looked directly into his again.

"Yes," I whispered. "You made me feel. I haven't felt like that, not with Jon, not with anyone...not for a long time. But that was sex." All at once everything was too much. "Oh my God." I pushed past him and stood at the edge of the deck looking out into the darkness. "What does that say about me? What does any of this say about me? I cheated on my husband. Isn't that something that's supposed to make you feel terrible? I did an awful thing, but it made me feel good. For the first time in years, I feel like myself again. What does that say about my marriage? My whole life? This is so fucked up."

"Hey," Jason said. He put his arm on my shoulder and turned me until I was facing him. "Look at me. Lots of people cheat and have affairs. That doesn't make you a bad person."

I laughed a bitter laugh. "But it doesn't make it right."

"No," he said. "It doesn't. But it happens."

"Not to me." I shook my head. "I'm not this person. I'm not-"

"Aren't you? You just said that you finally feel like yourself again."

"This is stupid." I pushed away from him, stumbling over the bed sheet as I moved. "I can't believe I'm sitting here talking about what an awful person I may or not be, with the man I just...you should go."

"You don't really-"

I looked at him then, really looked at him. His face wore a mixture of pity and concern. Neither of which I wanted. "Go home, Jason."

For a moment he didn't speak. Then finally, he took one step towards me and said, "Okay. If you really want me to, I'll go. But promise me something."

I nodded. He took another step and stood inches from me. I could feel the heat of his chest through the thin sheet. A shiver ran through me. He placed his palm against my cheek and I leaned into him, drinking in the simple pleasure of his touch. It was too easy to lose myself in him.

"I may be only a student," he said. "But I do know one thing. Even if what happened between us wasn't the best choice, you felt something. And all that crazy stuff that's going on with you right now, if you don't starting feeling something, anything, it won't ever get better."

"Jason-"
"You need to find you, Becca."

.

CHAPTER TWENTY

The ring of my cell phone jarred me from sleep.

I tucked my head under my pillow, willing it to go to voice mail. I snuggled deeper under the covers. It rang again and I cursed myself for not turning it off. Why did the stupid thing have service first thing in the morning anyway?

The ringing stopped and I relaxed into bed, trying to sink back into slumber.

I recalled my dream. It was the same one I'd been having the last few nights. I was in the field, just like the woman in the photo. Spinning faster and faster, emotions flashing through me. Every time, the dream was different, but this time, the pain I usually felt as I spun was gone, replaced by pleasure. It was euphoric. Only it didn't last. As I'd continued to spin, the good feelings flew out of me one, by one, until all I felt was an overwhelming sense of emptiness.

I groaned and flipped over to my back. Sleep eluded me. The dream didn't disturb me as it usually did in the morning. It felt different. I felt different.

Jason.

My thoughts started to drift back to Jason and the night before. But before I could get too lost in my fantasy or attempt to justify what'd happened, my phone started ringing again.

"Really?" I threw back the covers and pushed myself out of bed. "It better be important."

As soon as the words left my mouth, panic filled me. The girls. What if something was wrong with the girls?

The familiar weight of guilt crashed down. If something had happened to the girls while I lounged in bed, miles away thinking of my lover...oh God, I couldn't bear it.

Still naked, I ran into the living room to grab the phone before the caller gave up. I pushed the power button without looking at the number on the display.

"Hello?"

"It's about time."

"Steph?" She sounded pissed. "Is everything okay?" My thoughts flashed to the girls again. "Kayla? Jordan? Are they okay?"

"What? Of course they're fine," Steph said.

Relief flooded through me. "Thank goodness everything's fine."

"No, everything is not fine, Becca."

I took a breath and forced myself to stay calm.

"Steph? What's wrong?"

"Really, Becca? Really? You run away from your family, leave me to pick up the pieces and then have the nerve to ask me what's wrong?"

I took a step backwards as if I'd been slapped. "Pick up the pieces? Why would you-"

"Who did you think would do it, Becca?" I'd never heard such venom in her voice. It scared me. We'd been friends for longer than I could remember and never had Steph been angry with me. "Jon is scrambling, he doesn't know what to do," she said. "Of course I'd help." Her voice softened. "Of course," she said again.

"I'm sorry," I whispered. "I didn't realize."

"Of course you didn't," she said, her voice returning to normal. "I'm your best friend, you know there's no where else I'd be. Now, will you please tell me what's going on?"

I sighed and looked around the cabin. "I don't know where to begin," I said.

"How about by telling me where you are?"

I shook my head even though she couldn't see me. "I can't, Steph. I don't know how to explain it, but I'm not ready to share." I looked out the window. The sun was starting to come up, sending beams of light over the meadow. "This place is magical. I feel so different here."

"You sound different," Steph said. "Hey, I need to...hold on..." I could hear her murmuring to someone for a second before she came back on the line. "Do you think you could talk to Kayla?"

"Kayla?" My heart leapt in my chest at the thought. "Of course. Why is she-"

"Mommy?"

"Kayla? Hi, honey. How are you?"

"Good. I got to sleep at Auntie Steph's last night. And we're going to have a tea party, with cupcakes and everything."

I swallowed hard and forced some cheer into my voice even though my heart had shattered at the sound of her voice. "That's great. It sounds like fun."

"It is," she said. "I got to play yesterday too."

"It sounds like you've been having a good time. I'm happy to hear that."

"Mommy?" Kayla's voice went soft and I had to strain to hear her. "I'm trying my best to be good. I'm sorry."

My chest constricted. "Sorry for what?"

"I'm sorry I was so bad that you went away."

My hand flew to my mouth. It took a moment before I trusted myself to speak again.

"Kayla," I said slowly. "Mommy didn't leave because of you. Don't ever think that, okay?"

"Then why did you go away?"

"Sometimes mommies just need to take a little vacation," I said. "But I'll be back."

"Ms. Steely says Kindergarten is almost over. We're gradudating soon."

"You mean, graduating," I said with a smile. "You're going to graduate from kindergarten."

"Yup. There's going to be cake too. And we get to wear hats." Kayla's voice brightened. "Will you come?"

"Of course, sweetie. I wouldn't miss it for anything."

Would I be there? Did I just lie to her?

"I love you, Mommy."

"I love you too," I whispered into the phone.

"Becca?" Steph's voice came on the line. "It's me again. Kayla went to play."

"Oh." I ran my hand through my hair. "Why is she with you?"

"Jon had to work, and Jordan had a date last night, or something like that. When Jon called, he was all stressed out and I told him that she could use some Auntie Steph time and she could stay with me for a few days. Don't worry, I'll get her to school."

"That's not what I'm worried about," I said. Jon was pawning off our children? And who was watching Jordan? My stomach churned and for a moment I thought I might be sick. Was she with that man-boy? He was too old, and- I forced myself to stop the thoughts flying around my head. Hadn't I chosen not to worry, when I left? I'd made my choice. Hadn't I?"

"Guess what," I said to Steph, forcing my brain to change channels. "I'm drawing again. Can you believe it?"

"I can't." She laughed. "I mean, I can. It's just been so long."

"I know, right?" A shiver ran through me and I remembered I was still naked. "It surprised me too. But it feels so good."

"Despite everything," Steph said. "You actually sound good." Her anger was melting. I could feel her enthusiasm through the phone and I soaked it in, greedy for our closeness to return. I'd missed it.

"I know, it's crazy. But everything here is... you just wouldn't believe this place, the people."

"You haven't even told me where you are."

"I know. I'm sorry, but I'm not quite ready to share that yet. But, I will tell you one thing."

"What?"

"Promise you won't say anything."

"Becca, we're not sixteen anymore. Of course I won't say anything. What is it?"

"I had sex," I said. My skin tingled with the memory of Jason's touch, his hands on fire over my skin. "I mean, real sex."

"Sex? What do you mean, real sex? With who?" Steph's questions tripped over themselves and I laughed.

"I mean, of course I've had sex before. But this was different, it was so powerful. It stirred something inside me." I giggled, feeling like I was in fact, a teenager again. "That sounds so stupid, but I can't think of any other way to explain it."

"I don't really know what to say." She wasn't laughing with me. "What about Jon? Becca, you're married."

My euphoria vanished. "What about him?" I asked. "I can't think about Jon right now." I remembered what he'd said to me the last time we'd spoken. He didn't want to be with me. He was going to ask for a divorce. I'd failed. At everything. "He doesn't seem too concerned with me right now, anyway." I tried to push my anger away, unwilling to let it cloud my mood. "With Jason, I feel something. And Steph? I can't remember the last time I felt anything at all."

"Jason? Well, I'll admit you sound like a completely different person. There's something to be said for that. But, whatever's going on, it's not real life, is it? You have to come home. You have to figure out things with Jon either way, and there's Jordan and Kayla too of course."

"I can't think about it right now." I focused my attention on the field. The bursts of color from the flowers. I knew she was right. I didn't want her to be right. "I finally feel like me again, Steph. Is that crazy?"

I heard her sigh on the other end. "Yes. Yes, it is."

"What?" She wasn't supposed to say that. She was supposed to agree with me.

"It is crazy, Becca," she said. "Who are you? Who is it that you feel like? You're a wife and a mother. That's who you are. And even if you want to, you can't stop being that. Not ever."

"I'm not doing that."

"That's exactly what you're doing, and you know it." Her voice raised. Steph never yelled. Ever. Especially not at me. "I'm glad that you're drawing again. I am. But you can't be that art student anymore. You can't be that person anymore, Becca. It's just that simple. Your life is changed, you've changed, you-"

I pushed the power button on the phone before she could tell me one more time what I couldn't be. I placed it deliberately on the counter. For a moment I stared at it. Daring it to ring again. For her to call me back. Or better yet, for it to be Jon on the line.

I couldn't feel my hands. My whole body went numb. I continued my showdown with the phone.

I was more than a wife and a mother. Much more. There was nothing wrong with that.

Rage began to seep in, replacing the numbness with every heartbeat.

Who was Steph to tell me I couldn't be more? Who was Jon? He'd tried to keep me back for years. Prevent me from being who I really was so I'd fit into his mould. Hadn't he?

"Bastard!" I swung out and sent the phone flying from the counter.

"That seems a little harsh."

I spun around at the sound of Jason's voice.

He stood on the porch looking through the screen at me. "That's what I like to see first thing in the morning," he said, and gestured towards me with the paper bag he held in has hand. A tray with two coffee cups balanced in the other.

I grabbed a batik sheet from the back of the couch and wrapped it around my nakedness.

I turned my rage on him. "What do you think you're doing?" I barked. "Just barging in here whenever you feel like it?" I tightened the sheet in an effort to keep my body from shaking.

"For the record, I didn't barge in. I'm on the porch," he said, and offered me a smile. "And I was hoping you would talk to me. I don't like the way we left things last night. I'm sorry, I didn't expect you to be...well, so exposed this morning."

We stared at each other through the screen.

"Can I come in?" he asked after a moment. "I brought breakfast."

I nodded but didn't make a move to open the door. Instead I watched as he balanced the tray and maneuvered his way into the kitchen.

Hot anger continued to boil through my veins, seeping into every inch of me.

For years I'd been subdued, kept down. Forced into a life that wasn't mine. I didn't even know who I was anymore.

But in Rainbow Valley, with Jason...

I looked at the man in my kitchen, opening cupboards and arranging muffins on a plate.

I could be real. I could be me finally.

Too many thoughts bounced through my head. Jason was talking, "...fresh baked this morning..." I couldn't concentrate on his voice. "...I thought you might-"

"I don't want to talk," I said abruptly.

He stopped what he was doing and looked at me.

I shook my head, trying in vain to clear the swirl of confusion. I forced myself to focus on him. His eyes, his hands. His kisses.

I let the anger fuel me and released the grip I held on

the sheet, letting it fall to the floor. In three strides I crossed the room and closed the gap between us.

"Becca-"

"I told you," I said, my voice deep, unrecognizable. "I don't want to talk."

I reached up, grabbed his head and pulled his mouth to mine. His hands found my back and drew me in close. His clothing scratched my naked skin but I tugged him closer, needing to deepen the kiss.

My body burned under his touch as he responded to my need. His kisses were rough as he worked his way down my neck and to my chest. He moved his hands to my breasts and squeezed with a pressure that matched the intensity in his lips as they moved first to one nipple and then the next.

I groaned and clawed my way down his back and into the waist of his jeans. I yanked at his shirt before my hands flew up to cup his head, pulling him even closer. I needed to be everywhere at once. I needed him. I twined my fingers into his hair and tugged, wanting to taste him again.

The heat built within me. The need to forget about Jon. About my life. About who I might or might not be. I bit greedily on his lip and tore at his belt. Jason pulled way, breaking the kiss. His hands moved to still mine.

"As much as I'm enjoying this," he said. "I'm confused. "

"Stop talking," I whispered, my voice cracking with desire.

"I don't know if we should be doing this."

I struggled against him trying to free my hands from his grip. "Really?" I challenged. "Because it seems to me that your body is saying something different." I looked down to the bulge in his jeans.

"It's just that after last night, I didn't think that-"

"You're the one that said I need to keep feeling," I said. I yanked back and broke his hold on me. I lunged for him again. My eyes hot with anger and passion, burned into him and I could see the conflict raging on his face.

Without breaking my stare I pressed myself up against him. "Don't tell me you don't want this."

He let out a low moan as I reached into his jeans. "Becca, I-"

"Make me feel, Jason," I pleaded. "I need to feel like me again."

He groaned, his desire winning the battle. He pulled me close, drawing me into a deep and hungry kiss before lowering me onto the floor boards, where he indeed answered my plea.

By the time we made it to breakfast, the coffee Jason brought with him was cold, which was too bad because I still hadn't figured out how to work the coffee press. I dumped it down the sink and poured us each a glass of milk. I took the muffins, put everything onto a tray and went out to the porch where Jason was waiting.

"You don't have to serve me, you know?"

"It's the least I can do."

He gave me a knowing look.

"That's not what I meant," I said, and put the tray down on the table. "You brought breakfast, the least I could do is bring it outside. But you're out of luck with the coffee, I hope you're okay with milk."

I chose a glass and sat in the rocker across from him.

Jason reached for a muffin and took a large bite. "Worked up an appetite, did you?" he mumbled through a mouthful.

"Something like that." I took a sip and let the cool milk soothe me from the inside.

"Want to tell me what that was all about?" he asked as he wiped crumbs from his jeans.

I didn't answer. Instead I busied myself with a blueberry muffin, picking off small pieces and popping them into my mouth, one at a time.

"Well?"

"It doesn't matter," I said, after a moment.

"Oh, I think it does. I'm not an idiot, Becca. I know angry sex. Especially when I'm involved." He finished the muffin and took a long drink of milk before continuing. "What's going on?"

I put a berry in my mouth instead of answering him.

He watched me for a moment before grabbing another muffin. "Well, you seem more relaxed now anyway."

"I am." I smiled. "Thanks to you."

"So, you're feeling better then?"

"I am."

"About everything?"

"No." My smile faltered. "Not everything." My thoughts flashed to Jon and the girls. Steph's words echoed in my head. *You can't be that person, Becca. Because you aren't that person.* I looked over at Jason. Was she right?

"You're in control here," Jason said, shaking me from my thoughts. "Whatever you left behind, you get to decide what happens next."

I nodded.

"You like it here." It wasn't a question. Jason reached across the table and took my hand. "You feel good here."

"I do."

"Because of me? I mean, I'm not trying to sound egotistical, but..."

"I know." I smiled. "And yes, obviously that's part of it. But it's more than that." I put my milk down and stood up. Walking to the edge of the porch, I looked past the field and into the trees. "Maybe it's this place?"

"It is amazing here."

"But it's more than that."

"I'm helping?"

"You're infuriating," I said, and turned back to him.

Jason stood, a smile on his face. He moved towards me and took my hands in his. "Maybe so," he said. "But you don't seem to want to get rid of me very badly."

CHAPTER TWENTY-ONE

After Jason left, I'd grown restless in the cabin again. I was ready to move from my carefully constructed comfort zone and explore more of what Rainbow Valley had to offer.

I drove down the mountain road and pulled my car onto the weedy shoulder next to the river. I grabbed the bag I'd packed up at the cabin, from the front seat and ventured down the banks. The river wasn't moving fast enough to be intimidating, but the steady flow of the rapids danced over the rocks, stirring up a froth before settling into a smoother flow. Close to the edge, the water was clear enough to see the rocky bed below, but further out it turned to a deeper green, almost teal, and the rocks vanished in the depths. I dipped my fingers into the water and yanked them out again. The water was as frigid as if it'd just come off a glacier, which it likely had.

I found a grassy spot hidden from the road with an unobstructed view of the river, settled in and pulled my sketch book from the bag. Within moments I was lost in the rhythm of the pencil strokes and soon I had a rough outline of the bank across from me. Moving to the colored pencils, I shaded the water, focusing on blending the blues and greens to create the perfect hue that would capture the flow. I worked methodically, entranced by the process, and it wasn't until the water was complete that I sat back and stretched my neck.

The newness and fear of drawing again after so many years had worn off. Looking at my work again filled me with, what? Peace? A sense of pride? I couldn't pin point it, but whatever it was, it was a welcome feeling.

I dug through the bag and pulled out the long wooden box of watercolors I'd thrown in on a whim before leaving. In college, my medium of choice was oils and acrylics. I favored them over the subtle, almost delicate look of the watercolors. I had a need for bold and dramatic back then.

I unclasped the box and examined the small tubes. The idea of the softer colors intrigued me. The blending and feathering that would create the froth of the water, the flow of the rapids over the boulders.

So many choices. Every one resulting in a different outcome.

I let my fingers slide across the tubes and shut my eyes. My fingers twitched to hold a brush again instead of a pencil. Painting had always been my true love. I knew I could capture the fragility of the flowers in the meadow better with paints. The blossoms would be so much more vibrant. They would come alive. But could I do it again? Would I remember how?

I could do more. I knew it. If only I took the chance.

My eyes popped open, I ran my fingers across the tubes one last time and clicked the box shut.

It was time to pay Sheena a visit.

The little store was busy when I arrived. I was used to finding Sheena's empty, and for a moment I considered not going in. But my fingers opened and closed, eager to hold a brush. The desire to try paints won out over my need to be alone; I left my car and went inside.

There were a handful of people doing their shopping and visiting with each other. Deciding to wait until some of the shoppers left, I moved to the back of the store and started browsing the handicrafts. I was examining a brown crocheted purse when a large woman, her basket overflowing with fresh vegetables, turned into the aisle. She wore a tie-dyed robe, secured at the waist with a thick macrame belt, that gave her the look of an overstuffed throw cushion. Her long gray hair was twisted into two thick braids like tassels, that fell on either side of her puffy face.

"Pretty purse," the woman said, stopping next to me.

"It is. Not really my style though."

"Not good enough for you?"

The edge in her voice startled me into dropping the purse. It swung on the rack. I turned and was confronted by angry eyes, narrowed into slits that were almost swallowed by the swollen folds of her face.

When she spoke again, I was assaulted by the sour stench of the woman's breath. "You think you can force yourself into our world, and insult our goods? We're very proud of our handicrafts here," the woman ranted, her volume increasing with every word. "Just because you come from a big city someplace with all your money, doesn't mean you're any better than us."

"Pardon me?" I bristled with her words and stood taller. "That's not what I said at all. What I said was-"

"That she prefers her purses to be a little more colorful," Sheena said. She came up behind me and stood at my side. "Her personality is far too bright for a brown purse." Sheena took my hand and gave it a squeeze.

"Is that what you meant?" The woman spat the question.

"Yes." I nodded. "That's exactly what I meant. It's a beautiful bag, the craftsmanship is impeccable, but I like them a little brighter." I gestured to the bright canvas bag I'd found at the cabin, thankful I'd left my own black purse behind.

"See now? No one is saying they're better than anyone else," Sheena said. "Are you just about done with your shopping, Crystal? Go on up to the front and

I'll get you taken care of so you can be on your way."

Crystal nodded once, her eyes burning into me, before turning and making her way up the aisle. Her basket bounced against her heavy leg with every step.

"Don't you worry about Crystal," Sheena said. "She just gets a little protective about her work."

"You mean, she made it?"

"That's right and now she'll probably make you one with the brightest yarn she can dig up," Sheena said. Her voice crackled with laughter. "Now, what brings you down to the store today? You're looking better." She looked me up and down and nodded with satisfaction. "Yes, much better. What have you been doing with yourself? I like this change in you."

My mind flew to Jason. His hands, his lips, his touch. I tucked the images to the back of my mind, but allowed my mouth to curl into a smile. I pulled out my sketch book and opened it to the picture I'd just finished. "I've been drawing."

Sheena's face flashed with something unreadable before taking the book from my hands. Just as quickly as it'd appeared, the strange look was gone and she said, "This is lovely. You're very talented."

"It's been so long. But it feels right, you know?"

Sheena nodded slowly. There was a sadness about the movement. "I do," she said. "But I don't think it's just the drawing that's caused such a dramatic shift in your aura. Am I right?"

I recalled how I'd spent my morning. No. It was definitely not just the drawing. "Well, actually-"

"Sheena!" a voice, presumably Crystal's, called from the other side of the store.

"Sorry, Sunshine. I should take care of that. Will you be here for a few minutes?"

"Of course. I need to pick up a few things. Go. Take care of your customers."

Sheena disappeared in a swirl of skirts and shawls. I

picked my way up and down the aisles in search of the supplies I needed. The store was remarkably well equipped for such a small place. Of course, Jason had mentioned that the primary visitors to the valley were artists and writers. Sheena knew her market well.

I remembered there were brushes in the the trunk, but I picked up a few new ones anyway. I couldn't resist. If I was going to do it, I wanted to do it right. I chose a few canvases in varying sizes, grabbed a wooden palate to mix the colors on and started to work my way to the front of the store. Only an aisle away, my eyes landed on a small doll made from rags, clearly handcrafted.

Kayla.

I shifted my items to one arm and picked up the doll. It was well made and reminded me of the easy innocence of childhood. I took the doll, and remembering Jordan, went back to the rack of purses and choose a pretty blue bag with small gemstones sewn into the front.

At the front desk, as I waited for Sheena to finish up with her last customer, I pulled out my sketch book and tore out the first picture I'd drawn. The white daisy.

On the back of the page I wrote:

Girls,

I miss you very much and think about you both every day. I saw these and thought of you. Kayla, I gave the dolly hugs and kisses to give to you. Please share them with Jordan.

I'll be home soon.

Love, Mommy

Would I be home soon? I refused to dwell on the question. I needed to focus on the present.

"Sorry about that, Sunshine." Sheena came around the corner and slid out from behind the desk. "It's not usually so busy in the middle of the week. Anyway, I have a few minutes now. What have you got there?" She pointed to the doll and purse.

"I just saw them and thought of..."

"Your girls?" Sheena took my hand.

There was no longer any point to deny it. I nodded. It would have been so easy to sink into the guilt, but I straightened my shoulders and shook off the sad heaviness that threatened to weigh me down. "Do you think you could send another package for me?"

"Of course. I'm actually sending a parcel of fresh jellies to a customer in the city this afternoon. So we can send it by courier."

"Really?"

"It'll get there tomorrow morning." Sheena patted my hand before releasing it and reaching for the pile of art supplies. "It looks like you're going to do some painting."

I picked up a brush and absently swiped it back and forth across my hand. "I'm going to try. It's been so long since I've touched paint of any kind and I've never used watercolors at all. But, it feels right. So, why not?"

"Why not indeed. You'll be using the ones in the wooden box, I assume?"

I nodded. "Those are the ones. They've never been opened."

"No. Your father gave them to Vicki. But she never used them. Couldn't bring herself to paint with them. They've been locked away in the trunk all this time."

"Do you think I should use them? I mean, if she didn't-"

"No," Sheena interrupted. "I don't think there's anything your mother would like more. You go ahead and use those paints." Sheena's eyes took on a faraway look, but it didn't last long. After a second, she snapped back to her usual self and said, "You know. I have something in the back that you might find useful. Wait here."

She disappeared behind the beaded curtain,

returning a few minutes later with a folded, wooden easel that she dragged across the floor and propped up against the desk next to me.

"This was your mother's. After she...well, after, when your father decided to rent out the cabin, he didn't want anything that was left, so everything was packed up. You've already seen what was in the trunk. The easel was too big to fit, but it didn't seem right to get rid of it. I've had it in the storage room ever since. I think you should have it."

"It's beautiful." I touched the easel and let my fingers travel down the smooth wood. I was already visualizing where I'd set it up. "Why didn't she have it with her?" I asked. "Why did she leave all her art supplies here instead of taking them home?"

Sheena bent her head and reached for the pouch around her neck. After a moment, she said, "Your mother had a hard time in the city. It was lifeless, dead. There was no inspiration there. She would come back for visits though. By herself. She'd try then to paint, but it wasn't the same. It was never the same after the move." Sheena tucked the pouch back into her blouse. "But that was a long time ago. And now, I think you should have it. It belongs to you."

"Thank you." My voice sounded far away to my own ears. I stared at it, trying to picture the woman who once stood before it. Was I like her? Was there something wrong with me too? A reason I couldn't paint for so long?

"Now, that's enough talk of the past." Sheena's voice brightened, breaking away the heaviness of the moment. "Let's talk about something happier, like why all of a sudden your aura is so much brighter."

I did want to talk about the past. I wanted to learn more about my mother, but it was clear that subject was closed.

"Do I need to guess, or are you going to tell me?"

Sheena prodded.

"Guess what?" I tried to focus on the conversation.

"What's created such a shift in you? You look different. Freer somehow. If I didn't know better, and I think I do, I'd say you were in love."

Love? I almost laughed out loud. Lust maybe, but love?

I grabbed a sachet of lavender, held it to my face and inhaled deeply. She couldn't know about Jason. And if she did, would she be angry? After all, they were close. Jason said she'd all but adopted him.

"No, not love," Sheena mused. "But there's definitely something going on. The pinks in your aura are vibrant. Have you spoken to your husband?"

I tossed the sachet down. "Oh, I've spoken to him alright."

"Not good?"

"No."

Her eyes questioned me, but she didn't push. "Well, I don't know what it is, but I'd swear that you have the look of a woman who's had a good roll in a field of flowers, if you know what I mean?" She winked. "Maybe, you've discovered yourself?"

I didn't turn away fast enough to hide the flush that filled my face.

"Don't be bashful, Sunshine. A satisfied life is nothing to be ashamed of. Look at me." Sheena gripped my shoulders gently, but firmly enough to spin me so we were face to face again. "But there's more. The pinks and reds emanating from you are pulsating with sex, passion and..." Her eyes locked on mine.

I saw the moment of realization in her eyes.

She knew.

The silence built between us. I couldn't read the look in her eyes, but I knew enough not to say anything. Jason was like a son to her. She wasn't going to like to hear that something had happened between us.

Not that there was anything at all between us. It was just sex. Wasn't it?

My mind raced as we stared at each other. Finally, Sheena broke the silence. "You should stay away from him," she said, and busied herself by stacking the art supplies.

"Excuse me?

"It's not a good situation."

"It's not like that. He's helping me." As soon as the words came out of my mouth, I wanted to reach out and pull them back.

Sheena looked up and gave me a wry smile. "Is he now?"

"That's not what I meant. It's just..." I let the words trail away, unsure of how to finish the thought.

Sheena didn't say anything else but she didn't look away either.

I tried again. "Don't be mad." The urge to rewind time was strong. I needed this strange friendship with Sheena. I needed the comfort from someone who didn't judge me. "Sheena, please."

"Mad?" Sheena burst into laughter.

Whatever I'd expected her to say, it hadn't been that. I took a step back from the counter and crossed my arms in front of me. "Is it so funny that I don't want you to be angry with me?"

Sheena wiped her eyes and put a hand to her chest. "Oh, Sunshine. You make me laugh."

"Do I?"

"You really thought I'd be mad at you?" Sheena asked, and swallowed hard to keep her laughter from bubbling up again. "For sex? Goodness, no."

"It's just that...with Jason..."

Sheena waved. "Jason's a big boy and I'm not blind, he's a very sexual being."

"So, you're not mad?"

"No," Sheena said. "Sex is a powerful thing. Our bodies have the ability to promote energy flow to all areas of our lives if they're treated properly. Physical love isn't the solution to internal harmony, but it's certainly part of the journey."

"I can't believe I'm having this conversation," I muttered.

Her smile grew wider. "Did you say something?"

"Nothing." I shook my head. "But if you're not mad, then why did you say that you didn't think it was a good idea?"

Sheena turned serious, her forehead wrinkled in concern and concentration. "I don't think it's a good idea for you. Some of us believe in the freedom of love, but I have a feeling that you're more of a traditional soul. You said your husband hurt you, something he said. Is that what this is about? Getting back at him?"

Sheena's voice was gentle, but her words stung.

I looked at the doll I'd picked out for Kayla. "He did hurt me." My voice was quiet. "But there's so much more going on than just that. And I know it doesn't make what I'm doing with Jason okay, but," I looked up, "it feels good somehow."

Sheena's smile was warm. "Of course it does."

"I'm changing here, Sheena. It's this place." I gestured to the pile of art supplies. "I feel like me again. I thought I'd forgotten who I was. But drawing again after all this time, the fresh air, the flowers, and..."

"Jason?"

Becca blushed and nodded. "Yes, and Jason. I don't want it to be, but I can't help it. Just being with him has awakened something in me. It's like all of a sudden I'm aware of things again. Aware of myself. Does that sound crazy?"

"No. But, I do want you to be careful. Don't invest more into a relationship with someone else until you've settled your own soul. Before you can give yourself to another, or fix things with your husband, you need to know who you are. And you don't need Jason for that."

"What if I'm not sure anymore if I want to fix things with Jon?"

Sheena smiled. "You may not know right now, but you will. In the meantime, be careful that you don't lose Becca just when you're starting to find her."

I shook her head. "What does that even mean?"

She gestured for me to come closer, and when I did, Sheena took my hand and opened my fingers to expose my palm.

"The answers you're seeking." Sheena's finger traced a circle in my palm as she spoke. "You won't find them in Jason. You won't find them in this place. Or even in your art. You'll find them within you." Her finger stopped moving and she closed my hand giving it a squeeze. "Only you."

I hauled my new supplies up to the porch and dumped them on the floor, eager to get back to the car and retrieve my new easel. I couldn't drive fast enough. The need to try out my new brushes, and leave the conversation with Sheena behind, was strong. I was anxious to paint.

I set up the easel close to the railing and dragged a chair over so I had a place to arrange the paints and brushes. When everything else was ready, I selected the biggest canvas in my pile. I propped it up on the easel and stared at it.

There was nothing left to do but get started. I picked up a brush and held it, poised over the tubes.

Nothing.

I wanted to paint. I wanted to capture the field, the flowers, the feelings bursting from within me. But I couldn't. My thoughts kept swirling from Jason, to Jon, to the girls.

Was Sheena right? Was I making a mistake?

I stood back and took a deep breath to focus my thoughts. The air was hot and it filled my lungs with a warmth that pushed out my confusion as I exhaled.

Calmer, I picked up the wooden box, unclasped it and opened the lid. The photo of my mother slipped out and fell to the floor. I retrieved it and leaned it up in the lid of the box next to the burnt words.

'Love Survives'

I ran my finger over the words, feeling their delicate grooves.

"What did your love have to survive?" I asked the photograph. "Why did you stop painting? What were you running away from when you came here?"

I couldn't see her face in the photo, but her body language didn't look sad. She didn't seem to be running away from anything at all, she looked blissful. Happy even. Dylan said she loved it in Rainbow Valley. That it was the happiest he could remember seeing her. But Sheena made it sound different. Like something had changed somewhere along the way.

I looked away and let my fingers slide across the paints. A green tube caught my eye. I lifted it from its resting place and carefully punctured the top. I squeezed a glob onto the pallet and repeated the process with a tube of white. Picking up the brush again, I swirled the colors together and created a paler shade. Gingerly, I touched the brush to the canvas, unsure of what to do next.

I looked down at the picture and back to the easel. Moving my hand quickly upwards, I left behind a stroke of green. Before I could over think it, I did it again. Putting more paint on my brush, I repeated the motion again and again creating the grassy meadow.

Soon, I was lost in the process, mixing and blending colors to create the right hues and shades of the blossoms in the meadow. I worked without stopping, without thinking. An urgent need to capture the scene filled me and I let the art and the process of creating, take over. I paused only long enough to tie my hair back away from my face.

Finally, I stepped back and examined my work. It wasn't bad. In fact, it was beautiful.

I'd captured the flowers and the pines in the background. Even the grass of the meadow and the sparkling sky above seemed to come alive. But there was still something missing. My gaze landed on the photo of my mother.

I'd never painted a person before.

But there was something about the picture that I couldn't look away from. Something drew me.

Before I could over think it, I picked up a narrow brush and dipped it in paint. With tiny, delicate strokes I began to create the outline of a woman in the middle of the wildflowers.

Like the dream.

When I got to the face, I stopped. I couldn't see her face in the photo and in the dream it was always different. I looked between the picture and my painting. I dabbed the brush in the paint and poised it over the canvas but put it down again.

It wasn't right.

Leaving the face for later, I went back to work on her skirt. I worked hard to capture the flow of the fabric, making it seem as if she was in mid-spin, like she could come right out of the painting.

I lost myself once again, breaking concentration only when I heard Jason's truck coming up the road.

A moment later, I turned and said, "Hi."

"No, don't stop. I love watching you."

He crossed the porch and stood next to me. My hand trembled from his closeness. He ran a finger along a smudge of paint on my cheek. "You're beautiful when you paint. You look completely at peace. It's really something to see."

I pulled away, just enough to create a slight distance between us. But I didn't miss the change in his eyes.

For a moment he looked like he was going to ask me something, instead he said, "You've been busy."

"I'm not quite finished, but I like it." I turned to look at the painting.

He moved closer to the easel, his arm barely brushing mine when he moved and my skin burned from the proximity. Sheena's words rang in my ears and I clasped my hands together to keep from reaching out to him.

"It's really good, Becca," he said. "You have a natural talent. Who is it?" He pointed to the woman in the painting.

"I'm not sure yet." My eyes slid from the faceless form to the photo still propped up against the canvas.

Jason followed my eyes."You look just like her."

"How can you tell?" I asked, but then added, "I'm beginning to think I'm more like her than I ever knew."

"Becca, I need-"

I cut him off by moving out of his reach again.

"I saw Sheena today," I said, still not looking at him.

"And? Did you tell her about us?"

"I didn't have to. She knew."

"She would," Jason mused. "I don't suppose your visit has anything to do with the fact that you won't let me touch you?"

"No." I turned to face him. "Well, yes. She told me to be careful."

"With me?"

"With everything. She told me not to lose myself."

"She's right," he said simply.

"What if by being with you, I'm losing myself before I really know what I've found?"

Jason stepped closer and took my hand. This time I

didn't pull away. His skin was warm and his grip around me comforted and excited all at once. "What if," he said, "by being with me, you're discovering yourself?"

"I don't see how-"

He silenced me with a kiss. His lips were gentle as they worked, parting mine.

Jon never kissed me like that.

I tried to pull away. To give myself a little distance to think.

"Don't, Becca," Jason whispered. He held me so close that I could feel his breath on my face. "Don't shut yourself off. It's okay."

"No, it's not okay." I closed my eyes against his intense stare.

"It is. Look at you, you're changing, discovering yourself a little more every day. I see it in you. I see it in your painting. I know you can see it too."

I took a deep breath. "I do," I said. "I do see it. When I think about my life, and who I was only a short time ago... I feel so different."

"You're finding yourself." He smiled, then said, "I told you once that I'm not your solution. And I'm not."

I opened my eyes and looked into his.

"I'm not, Becca," he said answering my unspoken question. "But it doesn't mean that I don't want to be part of it."

"What does that mean? That you like me, but not enough?"

"I do like you. But I'm not going to fool myself into thinking that this is something it's not. You have a life apart from here, and when you're ready, you'll figure it all out."

"What if-"

"No," he interrupted. "Let's not play the 'what if' game." He pulled me tighter and placed a kiss on my neck.

"I think..." he said between kisses, "that we should..." he traveled down my neck towards the collar of my blouse, "just worry about today."

My eyes snapped open and I put a hand to my chest, trying to settle my heart's frantic beating. Next to me, Jason slept, one arm draped over my waist.

It was the dream again.

I knew how to finish the picture.

I slipped from the bed, pulled Jason's t-shirt over my head and left the room. The night sky was black, with almost no moon, so I flipped the switch in the kitchen to give me some light on the porch.

It didn't take me long to work out the details for the figure's face and when I was finished, I put the brush down on the easel, and picked up the photo.

I looked back and forth between the picture in my hand and my painting. "I think I might be figuring it out," I said aloud.

My work done, exhaustion settled over me. I put the picture in its place on the easel and padded back into the bedroom where I tucked myself under Jason's arm again. He groaned in his sleep and pulled me closer.

CHAPTER TWENTY-TWO

"Just go outside to the porch and I'll bring something out," I said and swatted Jason's hand away from the fruit bowl. I gave him a gentle shove towards the door. I knew if he didn't give me some space, we'd end up back in the bedroom and I needed to eat something.

"How do I know you can cook anything?" he asked. "I think I've always been the one doing the cooking." He grabbed me and pulled me in for a kiss.

"I'd hardly call cutting up tomatoes and cheese 'cooking'. I'm perfectly capable. Now go." I unwound his hands from my waist and pushed him away.

After my middle of the night painting session, I'd slept deep. Waking up with Jason's arm still draped over me, made me smile. It'd been years since I'd cuddled all night. Jon and I usually pushed as far to each side of our king sized bed as possible.

From the moment I'd woken up, I'd let myself relax into the easy familiarity of things with Jason. There was no room for negative thoughts in my mind. I'd read years ago in *Positive Perfection: Ten easy steps to a positively perfect life*, that when you felt good about something, you should do your best to banish any and all negativity and let the good feelings take over. It was about time I took that little piece of advice. I was determined not to let my good mood slip.

"Okay, I'll go," Jason said. "But only because I want to enjoy the morning sun before the clouds come in." He lifted the scarf off the window and peered out. "Looks like we might be in for a storm finally. When the clouds start to build like that, it means the valley will be socked in. Could be cozy," he added, as he dropped the scarf and leaned in for another kiss.

"I told you to get out." I gave him another push and then flicked him with the dishtowel.

"I'm going, I'm going," he said, as he rubbed his backside. He crossed the room, laughing as he went and pushed open the screen door.

I smiled as I watched him go. It was nice, the ease between us. Maybe something I could get used to? Before I could dwell on that thought, I turned my attention to making breakfast.

"So," I called out, "I'm thinking eggs." I peeked into the fridge. "Are you okay with that?"

"Eggs are great," came the reply from the porch.

I put the basket on the counter and opened the cupboards searching for a frying pan. After a bit of rummaging, I finally located one among a pile of pots I hadn't used yet.

"How do you like them? Fried or scrambled? I make awesome scrambled eggs. Just don't ask me to make pancakes. Pancakes are definitely not my speciality."

It seemed like forever ago that I'd burned breakfast. The memory crystalized in my mind and I stopped what I was doing. It was a call from Dad that had caused the ruin of breakfast.

How was Dad?

I hadn't given him so much as a thought since the last time I'd seen him, and I certainly hadn't phoned to check on him or Connie. I'd have to call them later. After Jason left. I hadn't been a very good daughter. Something else I'd failed at.

I forced the negativity from my mind. *Positive Perfection* had also said that by distracting yourself with a task, you could block unhappy thoughts from intruding. I got back to work on breakfast.

"Jason, do you want orange juice or milk?" I called

outside again. "I'm not good with this coffee press thing." I turned towards the door and waited for the answer. When it didn't come, I muttered, "Orange juice it is." And poured us each a glass.

Where was he?"

I took the juice with me and headed to the porch, using my back to open the screen door.

"Jason, I can't start cooking if I don't know how you want your eggs." I turned around. "Jason?"

The porch was empty.

He couldn't have left. Not after everything.

I crossed the porch and stepped down onto the gravel pathway that led around to the drive. When I turned the corner of the house, I froze and dropped both glasses. They shattered in the stones, covering my legs in sticky juice.

"What the hell are you doing?" I yelled and jumped over the broken glass. I ran towards Jason, who had wrestled a man down to the ground, wrenched his arms behind his back and was kneeling on him, having pinned the man's face into the gravel.

"Stay back," Jason said. "I found this creep skulking around the cabin."

"I wasn't-"

"Shut it." Jason increased his force on the man's back, effectively shutting him up. "I tried to call to you, to tell you to stay in the house." Jason turned his head towards me.

"I didn't hear you," I said. "I was getting...it's not important." I shook my head and focused on the man. "Who is he?"

"Becca," the voice on the ground said.

"I told you to shut-"

"No. Wait," I said, stopping Jason before he could smash the man's face into the ground again. "He said my name. Let him up."

"I don't know if that's a good idea."

"Let me up, you asshole," the man mumbled, having gained a bit of leverage.

"Dylan?" I fell to my knees next to him. "Jason get off him. It's Dylan."

"Who's Dylan?" he asked, but reluctantly shifted his weight, allowing my brother to push up into a sitting position. Dylan touched his cheek and pulled his fingers away looking for blood.

"Are you okay?" I asked him.

"I'll be fine," he said. "No thanks to him." Dylan jerked his head towards Jason who was shifting from foot to foot, still ready for a fight.

"What are you doing here?" I asked.

"I tried to call," he said. "But it kept going to voice mail. I need to talk to you."

Avoidance, I remembered. Step six in *Positive Perfection,* had been avoidance. It was okay to put off unpleasantness for the sake of a positive day.

I pulled him to his feet, and said, "Can I have a hug?"

"Of course."

It'd been years since I'd seen my big brother, but he still felt the same. Ever since we were kids, Dylan had been a solid presence I could rely on. That hadn't changed, and I relaxed into his embrace.

"How are you?" he asked. "Really?"

"I'm okay," I said into his shoulder. "I really think I am."

He pulled back and examined me at arm's length. I used the opportunity to do the same. His chestnut hair was streaked with gray and the lines around his eyes had deepened, but he was still the same Dylan.

"I missed you," I said. "It's been way too long."

"I'm sorry-"

The sound of rocks clattering interrupted our reunion. We both turned in the direction of the noise to find Jason, not very subtly, kicking rocks against a stump at the edge of the lane. In all the excitement, I'd totally forgotten we weren't alone.

"Oh, Jason."

He picked up a rock and tossed it from hand to hand as he walked over to us. "This is your..." He let the question trail off.

"My brother," I said. "This is Dylan, my brother."

They nodded at each other. "I'd say it was nice to meet you," Dylan said, "but under the circumstances I don't think that would be very accurate."

"Sorry about that," Jason said. "I didn't know who you were."

"And I still don't know who you are." Dylan looked up to me.

"Oh, sorry. Dylan, this is Jason. He lives in the valley and works for Sheena."

Dylan accepted Jason's outstretched hand. "Sheena? You mentioned her before, right?"

"You'll meet her, I promise."

The men shook hands somewhat awkwardly and then took as step away from each other. I stood between them and looked from one man to the other. After a few seconds, I broke the silence. "Dylan, you must be hungry. How about some breakfast? I was just about to make eggs." I grabbed my brother's hand and pulled him to the porch. Before I rounded the corner I took a look back at Jason, who had returned to kicking rocks.

"Go ahead," I said to Dylan. "I'll be right there."

Dylan glanced between me and Jason before nodding. He stepped over the broken glass, and disappeared onto the porch.

"I'll get this," Jason said and bent to pick up the glass. "I'll give you two some time."

"This is kind of awkward, isn't it?" I said.

"Well, it's not really the way I thought we'd be spending our morning. Awkward is definitely one word I can think of."

"I'm sorry. I didn't know he was coming."

He rose and touched my cheek. "It's fine," he said. "I'll get rid of this mess and make myself scarce. I should probably get some work done before it rains anyway. Those clouds are getting darker."

He bent and kissed me quickly. It felt wrong. Forced somehow.

"Go. Spend some time with your brother. I'll see you later."

So much for *Positive Perfection*. I made a mental note to throw those books out.

I walked across he porch where Dylan stood, his back to me, staring out over the meadow.

"Is it like you remember?" I asked, when I got close.

"It hasn't changed a bit. It's exactly the same." He turned to face me; his smile reflected his memories.

The air around us was thick, but cool with the impending storm. The clouds overhead continued to build and darken, but the sky didn't look like it was ready to release yet.

I reached for Dylan's hand and said, "I really missed you. It's been way too long."

He squeezed me in his grip. "I know. I missed you too. I'm sorry I've stayed away."

I smiled, letting him off the hook. "You're here now. And I'm starving. Let's go inside and I'll make you some breakfast."

I led him towards the house but he stopped when we approached the easel.

"Are you painting again?"

"I am. It feels so good."

"It's beautiful."

"Thanks. It really does feel unbelievable to paint again. Freeing somehow."

"It's so much like mom's work." Dylan stared at the painting. He brought his fingers up to touch it, but at the last moment pulled away. He turned to me, his brown eyes shone with unshed tears. "You're just like her, Becca."

"I don't know about that. I didn't even know her. I didn't even know she painted. Not until a few days ago."

We stared at each other for a few seconds and I tried to read the expression in his eyes. He looked like he wanted to tell me something. When he didn't, I grabbed his arm. "Come on." I pulled him away from the easel. "I think we have a lot to talk about."

I placed a basket of fresh bread on the table and sat down across from Dylan and the two plates of steaming scrambled eggs. I still couldn't believe he was in front of me. It'd been so long since we'd been together, and it was great to see him, but I couldn't help thinking of the way the morning might have gone had he not shown up.

As if he read my mind, Dylan asked, "Will security be joining us for breakfast?" He took a bite and watched me as he chewed.

"I don't think so." I examined my eggs and pushed them around the plate with my fork.

"Not on my account, I hope?"

"No, I'm sure he had work to do." I took a bite.

"Is that what he was doing here? Working? Kind of early in the morning to be doing maintenance, don't you think?"

I met his gaze, and the challenge in his voice. "What are you saying, Dylan?"

"Becca." His tone softened. "I don't know what's going on with you. I don't know why you ran away-"

"I didn't run away."

"Okay. Well, I don't know why you're here. And I don't know what the maintenance slash security guy has to do with it."

"Jason. His name is Jason."

"Right, Jason." Dylan took a slice of bread from the basket and tore it in half. "Becca, I'm not going to get all big brotherly on you, isn't that how you put it on the phone?" I narrowed my eyes at him. "Anyway," he continued, "I know I'm not in a place to comment on your life or your choices."

"Then don't." I went back to pushing my food around, my appetite vanished.

"It's just, you and Jon-"

"What about me and Jon?" I dropped my fork, letting it clatter onto the plate.

"You've been together forever, Becca. You guys have always had the perfect life. You have everything."

"I had enough. I don't know if I want it anymore."

As I spoke the words, something inside me released. Was that all there was to it? It was so simple. A sense of calm and acceptance filled me. I'd had enough.

"I'm sure that whatever happened, you can fix it." Dylan said. His voice brought me back to the conversation.

"Whatever happened?" I repeated.

"Yes, whatever happened to make you run away."

"I told you, I didn't run away. I just had enough. Of everything. Do you know it's been years since I've done anything for myself? And even if I did have a chance, I wouldn't know what to do, because I have no idea who I am anymore."

"C'mon, Becca. What happened?"

I let out a deep breath and spoke as calmly as I could manage. "Dylan, all I've had for years is non-stop tantrums and attitude from children who don't appreciate my existence, a closet full of clothes that don't fit, a workaholic husband who's never home, a father who can't remember who I am, a brother who can't be bothered to visit and a best friend whose life is so God damned easy and free, that every time I talk to her, I feel a little bit more like a failure. That's my life. That's what my days are filled with. So, perfect? I don't think so." I shoved my chair back and stood, staring out the window. "But here," I continued, "here I can just be me, and figure out who that really is. For so long I've been trying to keep everything together, it's exhausting keeping up the act. But now, right now, it's just about me. And I think I like that."

"I had no idea," Dylan said after a moment.

"Of course you didn't."

"I'm sorry." He came up beside me. "But this Jason, he's not the answer, Becca. Doing this to Jon-"

"I'm not doing anything to Jon. I'm doing this for me."

"But that's why, right?" His voice was gentle, but his words bit into me. "Because it's your way out, your point of no return."

"My point of no return," I repeated the words under my breath and as I spoke, I knew there was a spark of truth in what he said. Jon would never forgive an affair. Was that what Jason was? My way out?

I let my eyes drift over the meadow, around the tree line to the break in the woods where the path to Prince's Pond lay. The past few days rolled through my mind.

"Are you happy now?" he asked. "Are you happy here?"

My memories returned to each moment with Jason, my drawings and paintings, Sheena, the phone calls with Jon, missing the girls. Finally, I turned and looked my brother in the eyes. "I don't know," I answered truthfully. "I can't explain it, Dylan, but I just don't know."

CHAPTER TWENTY-THREE

"Come on. Let's go out before it rains," Dylan said as soon as I emerged from the bedroom. A shower and a clean set of clothes had refreshed me, but the time alone hadn't given me anymore clarity into his question.

Was I happy here? Could I leave everything behind? What about Kayla and Jordan? Could I fix things with Jon? Did I even want to? The questions circulating through my brain were making my head throb. Fresh air would be good.

"Sounds like a plan." I slipped on my shoes.

The clouds had settled thick into the valley, heavy with the promised rain. The air had grown even cooler which offered a welcome respite from the heat of the last few days.

"Do you mind if we go for a walk?" Dylan asked. "I'd kind of like to see the pond. I don't know when I'll get another chance."

"Sure." I followed him across the field. Dylan didn't seem to have any trouble picking out the break in the tree line. "How long do you plan on staying?" I asked his back.

"I can't stay long. I'll stop in and see Dad and Connie in the city before I fly out, but I should get back to work in a few days."

"Ah yes, the fast paced life of a travel writer. Where are you off to next? Somewhere much more exotic than this I presume?" I looked down at my feet as we walked. "You know, Dylan, you could think about settling down and finding a wife, having a family."

He laughed and spun around. "Cause that's working out so well for you?"

"Low blow." I frowned and looked down at my feet.

"It was. I'm sorry." He smiled apologetically. "Really, I haven't seen a whole lot of relationships work out. I'm not in a big hurry. Besides, we're here to talk about you. Come on."

He took my hand and led me down the path.

We didn't say another word until we reached the lake. "Well?" I asked him. "What do you think?"

"I think it's been way too long since I've been here." He turned to face me, a smile lit up his face and his eyes sparkled. "Becca, I grew up here. This was my backyard. I swam all summer and skated all winter."

"It *is* great." I didn't want to ruin the light moment we were sharing, but there were still so many things I didn't know. "Why didn't you come back? If this was so important to you, such an amazing place, why didn't I ever hear about it? How did I go my whole life not even knowing that Rainbow Valley existed?" The questions spilled from me. "I have so many questions. And I need answers, Dylan."

The smile slid off his face and the light in his eyes dimmed. He sat on a large flat rock that jutted into the water. "I know you do. And I promise, I'll do my best to answer them. But first let me talk and then you can ask me anything you need to."

I nodded and sat next to him, letting my feet splash in the water.

"I probably should have told you about all of this years ago," he said. "I used to try, but when we moved, Mom would get so sad every time I asked about it, and then Dad would get upset, so I stopped. By the time you were old enough to talk about it and understand, our old life was never mentioned. Do you remember how Mom would go away once in awhile?"

I shook my head. "Not really."

"Well, she would," he said. "First she'd get 'sick' and start sleeping a lot during the day. Then the next thing we knew, she was gone. Dad always said she was going to visit friends. She was coming here."

"Here?"

Dylan nodded. "Dad would send her here to try and cheer her up."

I moved my feet back and forth letting the cool water slide over my feet. "I didn't realize she was so unhappy."

"Becca," Dylan said. His voice changed and I looked up at him. "It was more than that. I know you were just little and you probably don't remember very well, but Mom hated living in the city. She was a totally different person after we moved there."

I didn't remember. She was my mom and the little I did recall, was magical. Like when we made sun tea on a hot summer day, or went to hunt for the perfect rocks to paint and turn into pets, since Dad wouldn't let me have a dog.

"Why did we move?" I asked after a minute. "I mean, why leave this place if it made Mom so happy?" I turned away from him, and scanned my surroundings.

"I told you on the phone. Dad was trying to do the responsible thing. Everything was fine when it was just the three of us, but then you came along and when we got older, I guess he decided it was time to move to the city and get a real job, provide for his family."

"So I was the reason?"

"Not entirely." Dylan scraped up a handful of stones and began throwing them one by one into the water. "I was getting older, I needed more education. Home schooling was okay, but Dad wanted more for me too. It was just time to go."

"But Mom hated it." I watched the ripples caused by the stones expand and grow larger until they disappeared. The air was thick with the heavy scent of ozone. The rain was coming closer.

"She did. Everything changed. I know Dad thought he could fix it by sending her back here for visits, but it just made it worse and then..." he drifted off.

"What?" I turned to him again. "Then it was too late? He couldn't fix it because she died?"

"Well, yes." Dylan's voice was quiet. He stopped throwing the stones. "That's what I need to talk to you about."

"What?" My body went cold and a breath caught in my throat.

"You need to know the truth about Mom."

I pulled my feet from the water and massaged them trying to bring the heat back. I rubbed harder but the coldness persisted. Ice slid down my spine.

"Becca?" Dylan's hand on my arm burned my icy skin but I couldn't shake it off. "Mom didn't die in a car crash. She wasn't hit by a drunk driver."

The ice crawled from my spine across my back. It circled around to my chest, squeezing tighter.

"I think I know the truth," I said. It was a thought that had been building for the last few days. The more I learned about her, the more her death didn't make sense.

"You do?"

"She killed herself, didn't she?" I heard myself say. "She was so unhappy that she couldn't bear it, and she killed herself."

The ice crept up my throat. Somewhere in the back of my head the familiar roaring began to build.

"Becca-"

"I know I'm right."

Part of me had known. I'd always known. But to say it out loud. That was different.

"Becca?" My brother's voice penetrated the ice and battled with the building storm in my brain.

"How?"

"That's what I need to tell you," Dylan said. "Mom didn't kill herself. She's not dead."

I shook my head. "What?" The roaring increased. I hadn't heard him correctly. "What did you say?"

"At least, I don't think she is," he said. "The truth is, I don't know. But she didn't die in a car accident. She left us, Becca."

"She left?" I hadn't heard right. I couldn't have.

"She hated her life. She hated the city. Everything. I don't think anybody knew how unhappy she was, maybe not even her. And then one day, she was gone."

"What do you mean, gone?" My brain spun and twisted. None of it made sense.

"She was really sad," he said. "Worse than usual, so Dad told her to go to the cabin for a visit. He told her to find her spirit again. At first when she didn't come home, we thought she'd stayed for a few extra days. Finally Dad came to get her, but she was gone. There was just a note telling him that she couldn't do it anymore. She couldn't take one more minute. That was it."

"Where is she, then?"

"I don't know. Dad kept the house here, renting it out, just in case she came back. She never did."

"You told me she died. You all told me she died."

He threw a large stone, heaving it further than the rest into the middle of the lake. I watched the ripples, focusing on the spreading rings traveling the water's surface.

"Dad thought it would be easier for you than to think she'd left you."

"Why now?" My voice didn't sound like my own. "Why tell me now?"

"I should have told you years ago. Dad should have. It wasn't right, I know. But you were just a kid. We didn't want you to blame yourself, or have that stigma. That's why we moved again. Dad didn't want us growing up with people knowing our mother had abandoned us." He gently turned me to face him on the rock. "I'm telling you now because you are so much like her. You're so unhappy."

"I'm not."

"Becca." The sharp edge in his voice cut through the fuzz in my brain. "Look at you. What are you doing? You ran away from your husband, your children. You can't tell me you're happy."

"I am now."

"No." Dylan's voice softened again. "Becca, you're not."

The sky rumbled above, and at the same moment, I felt the first drops hit the side of my face and roll down my cheek.

"I think you're lost. Just like Mom was. I think you-"

I yanked away from him and pulled myself to my feet. "I'm not her."

"Don't let history repeat itself." He rose to face me.

The rain started falling harder and it didn't take long for it to soak through my thin clothes. I stared into the water, the surface was broken and churned by the constant hammering of drops.

"Where is she?" I asked the water. "I need to know why she left. I need to know where she is."

"I told you, we don't know."

You're Vicki's girl. It's the gray aura. Just like your mother. Sheena's voice came back to me.

"But someone does," I said. "Sheena."

"I don't know Sheena," Dylan said.

"She knows." As soon as I said it, I was sure. Sheena knew more than she'd told me.

The roaring in my head competed with the howling wind and sharp claps of thunder overhead as the storm took hold. I struggled to maintain one coherent thought. "She knows," I said again.

"Becca-"

"No," I yelled at Dylan and pushed past him, almost knocking him into the lake in my hurry to go.

I didn't bother to grab my shoes before I turned and ran through the woods. Rain pelted my face, stinging my skin. My bare feet splashed through the mud. Sticks and rocks cut my soles as I ran. I barely noticed. Dylan's voice calling after me faded into the growing storm as I ran. I needed to see Sheena. I needed the truth.

I pushed my way through the brush, letting the branches snap, tear at clothes and slap me in the face.The short path seemed to go on indefinitely as I thrashed through the bush. Maybe I got lost. I don't know. The rumbling thunder in the skies paired with the roaring in my head to create a wild symphony that threatened to take over my consciousness, but I kept moving. Eventually, I emerged in the meadow. Without the protection of the trees, I was exposed and the rain fell harder. Like pebbles on my skin, each drop hit with a stinging force.

I took a few fumbling steps and stumbled in the tall grass and flowers where I fell to my knees.

"Becca?"

"You didn't tell me. All this time and you let me believe a lie. And Dad too. What about Connie? Did everyone know but me?"

Rain streaked down my face and I swiped at the drops, trying in vain to clear my vision.

"I'm sorry, Becca, I am. It was wrong and if I could take it back, I would." He wiped at my cheeks. "Don't cry."

"Cry?" Anger fueled me again. "I don't cry, Dylan." I shook his hands off and pushed up to my feet. I faced him. "There's something wrong with me and you know what, there was with her too. She didn't cry either. Did you know that too and not tell me?"

"Calm down." He reached for my arm but I pulled away. "Let's go inside. We're getting soaked."

"You don't get it, Dylan. You knew. You all knew this awful secret about me. I don't care if you were trying to protect me. This whole thing, it's shaped me. My whole life. It's who I am, but you never said anything. You just watched me self destruct. I left my family. Oh, God. I left the girls." My chest twisted in pain, the guilt almost dropped me to my knees again. "Jordan. Kayla."

Dylan tried again to move closer, to touch me. "Becca."

"Don't," I warned. "Does Jon know? He must know."

"No." He shook his head. "I don't think he knows."

"How could he not?"

"Who would have told him, Becca? Besides, he would've said something."

I pushed past him and started thrashing through the tall grass again, crushing the flowers in my path.

"Where are you going?"

"I have to know." I called over my shoulder. "I have to know everything."

251

CHAPTER TWENTY-FOUR

When I flung open the door to Sheena's shop, the bells sounded their familiar chime and I had to fight the urge to reach up and rip them down.

Before I could act, Sheena's voice sang out from the back of the store. "Sunshine, for heaven's sake, child. You're soaked to the skin. What are you thinking going out in this storm? Come in, come in, I'll get you some dry clothes."

I stood, rooted to the spot.

What did she know?

"Well, don't just stand there. Come dry off." Sheena walked closer, her arm outstretched. She almost took my hand but stopped short, pulling back. "What's going on? Your energy is all wrong."

"My mother," I said. "Tell me about my mother." The words came out in gasps of breath as I struggled to control myself. "I need to know everything."

Her eyes flickered and she opened her mouth to say something. Before she could, the bells over the door rang again and Sheena's gaze shifted over my shoulder.

"Rayne?" Sheena mouthed so softly I barely heard her. "Bless my soul, is it really you?"

I watched as her expression morphed. The concern that had lined her face moments earlier had vanished into a mixture of terror and elation.

I turned to see Dylan standing in the doorway. He'd followed me in his car, down the mountain. His face bore a mask of shock.

"Dylan," I said. "This is-"

"Mom."

"Rayne."

"No." I shook my head. "Dylan, this is Sheena. The woman I was telling you about."

I looked between them. Into my brother's bright blue eyes, clouded with disbelief. Back to Sheena's own blue eyes so much like...like ours.

"No," I said again.

"What are you doing here?" Dylan asked her. "Have you always been here? All this time?"

"Why don't you both come in, dry off," Sheena said. "You're soaking wet. Once everyone's dry we can talk."

"Mom?" I asked, staring at the woman I'd come to care about in the last few days. I'd let her comfort me, guide me, counsel me. Like a mother would. But... no.

"Becca." She reached for me and I took a step back. "There's so much I need to tell you. That we need to-"

"No."

I turned, ready to run. I needed to get out. The roaring continued to build in my head. The pain threatened to overtake me. But the pressure wasn't just in my head. It was in my chest. My heart. Everywhere. I needed to go somewhere. Anywhere. Away from the horror that was unfolding in front of me.

Dylan caught me in his arms. "Becca," he said softly. "Don't run."

"Dylan, I can't." I closed my eyes, willing my body to take me away. "I can't do this. She's dead. She's not here. This isn't happening."

"It is." His voice was low, his arms were safe and I rested my head on his chest letting him hold me and protect me. Just like when we were kids.

"Please." Sheena's voice cut through the chaos in my brain. "Can we sit and talk? Can I explain?"

I looked up from Dylan's chest. I was still mad a him for keeping such an awful secret, but at that moment he was the only thing holding me to reality. I turned to look at her, and said, "You let me sit in your kitchen and talked to me as if you were someone else. You told me about Vicki like she was, like you were, dead. Why?"

"Vicki is dead," Sheena said. "I'm not that person anymore. I don't think of myself as her. She was a complete and separate being. I'm not that woman anymore. I'm Sheena."

"That doesn't make sense," Dylan said.

But it did. To me.

"Let me explain," Sheena said.

"No," he answered. "I don't think we have anything to say to you."

"Rayne, please. You don't understand. I had to leave."

"What you had to do was be a mother," he said. I'd never heard such anger in his voice. It scared me. "You didn't. You ran away instead. You left us. And for what? This? It was worth giving up everything, to live here, alone?"

I stood straight and stepped away from him. I watched Sheena carefully for her answer. Was it worth it? She'd run away. Just like I had. I needed to hear her answer.

"You don't understand." She looked old all of a sudden. As if she'd aged ten years in the last five minutes. "I was dying there. Suffocating a little more each day. What kind of mother could I be when I hated my life? I was afraid I'd hate you too." She added the last part and looked directly at me.

Our eyes met. I knew exactly how she felt. And she knew it.

"That's not an excuse," Dylan said.

"Wait," I said quietly, my eyes not leaving hers. "What do you mean, you were afraid you'd hate me?"

"Not just you, Sunshine. Both of you. I was afraid if I stayed, I'd end up resenting you both, blaming you for my unhappiness. And it wasn't your fault. It wasn't fair to you that I couldn't be happy with myself."

"It was the city," I said. "Dylan told me you hated being in the city. So why didn't you just move back? Why didn't you tell Dad how unhappy you were and move back here. You could have made it work."

"No," she said and grabbed the counter for support. "It wasn't just the city. It was everything. I couldn't stand waking up every day and doing the same thing, day in and day out. I wasn't made for that life. I didn't know who I was anymore. I'd lost my spirit. I tried. But I couldn't do it."

"You didn't try hard enough," Dylan snapped.

"Rayne-"

"Dylan."

"I did try. You, both of you, you were everything to me," Sheena said. I thought she might cry. Something I remember her telling me popped into my head.

"Wait," I said. "You told me I was just like my mother. That she didn't cry either. You sat across from me and talked to me about her, about you, like she really was dead."

My body started a slow shake. I was cold, but it was more than that. I clenched my teeth to keep them from clattering and rubbed my arms with my hands.

Sheena stepped back. "Like I said, she is dead, Sunshine. The woman who was your mother, Vicki, she's gone. I'm not that woman anymore. I'm Sheena now. Vicki died a spiritual death long ago. It was like a rebirth for me. I'm different. I'm-"

"Full of crap," Dylan interrupted.

"Please," Sheena said again. "Let's sit down, have a cup of tea and talk."

"Wait," he said. "Have you been here the whole time? So close to us?"

Sheena closed her eyes for a moment. "Not the whole time, no." She shook her head. "I knew he'd look for me. I knew he'd look here. I loved him, your father, so much. And I knew if he came after me, I'd go with him.

And I'd be miserable again. I couldn't do it, so I went South. I picked fruit in California for a long time. I moved around a lot and didn't stay in the same place very long. I managed to save a bit of money, but no matter where I went, the call to come home, to Rainbow Valley was strong."

"You had to return," I said. "Like a force, pulling you back."

"Exactly." She smiled at me. I tried to return it, but it didn't quite reach my lips.

"When I came back, I stayed with Johnson, do you remember him?" she asked Dylan. He didn't answer, only looked away. "He ran the store," she said to me. "He took me in and I worked for him. It was through him that I learned your dad had kept the house. Johnson said he'd kept it hoping I'd come back. But by then your dad was remarried, and from what I could tell, happy. I didn't want to interrupt your lives. I knew I still couldn't be a mother to you both. Not the way you deserved."

"And you didn't want to be," I said.

"No. I didn't," she said. "That's the truth and that's what you both deserve right now. So I stayed and worked for Johnson. When he passed, he left the store to me. This is my home. It's where my soul belongs."

"But you were so close all this time," Dylan said. His eyes shone with tears.

"I'm sorry," Sheena said. "I can't make up for what I did. I'm so sorry."

She held out her arms and I watched as my big, strong brother went to her. She held him like a child and rocked him gently while he cried. He knew her. Dylan had always felt more of a loss when it came to Mom. She was part of him. But for me, she was gone too young. You can't feel the loss you're detached from, can you?

I watched the scene as a bystander. An intruder on a

private moment between mother and son. It was my fault she'd left. Dylan was older, it was my arrival that pushed her over the edge. Was I difficult like Kayla? Had Kayla pushed me over the edge? I'd always thought it was strange that Jordan and Kayla were almost the same age split as Dylan and I. Mom was an artist. She didn't cry. So much the same, but so many differences too.

I took a step back trying to distance myself from them. A shudder ran through me and my headache intensified.

What else did we share?

She'd abandoned her children. I'd abandon-

"No!" I yelled, and turned around crashing into a barrel of fishing rods. It clattered to the ground, scattering the rods.

"Becca."

"Sunshine."

They spoke at the same time, detaching themselves from their embrace. Tears streaked down both of their faces, identical masks of pain.

"No," I said again. "I'm not like you. I'm not a-"

Before I could finish the thought, the bells over the door announced the arrival of another customer. Aware of how I looked, my clothes stuck to my body, my hair plastered to my face, I instinctively turned away. I tried to shift behind a row of shelves, so I could maneuver to the back of the store and away from everything, but the voice rooted my feet to their spot on the floor.

"Becca? What on earth's happened?"

I stood, frozen. With every thump of my heart, my pulse pounded in my head, fueling the throbbing in my temple. I didn't turn to look in the direction of the voice. I didn't need to. A hand slid over my shoulder and the easy familiarity sent a thrill through me, despite the storm of emotions raging inside my body.

"Becca," Jason said. "You must be frozen. Are you okay?"

I let him spin me around and take me in his arms. It felt good to be held and the warmth radiating through his t-shirt penetrated to my chilled skin. I clung to him like an anchor. Closed my eyes and tried to remember being alone with him. Anything to take me from the hell of the moment I was in.

I breathed in his clean, woodsy scent and tried to regulate my breathing. When I opened my eyes, I looked over Jason's shoulder and saw Dylan and Sheena standing together. Despite his own confusion, Dylan didn't even try to mask the disproval on his face as he watched me. But Sheena, I refused to think of her as Mom, wore an expression of sadness and regret. Like a child, I hid behind Jason. Out of everyone in the room, the man I'd just met seemed to know me better than anyone. All everyone else had done was lied.

Sheena attempted a small smile in my direction and looked as if she was going to say something. But it was Jason's voice that reached me. It took me a moment to realize he'd been speaking to me.

"What?" I asked.

"I asked you what you were doing," he said. "You're totally soaked. What were you doing out in this downpour?"

"I was-"

"She's fine," Dylan interrupted. "The last thing Becca needs right now is some guy complicating things even more for her. So why don't you just leave her alone?"

Jason stood tall and squared his shoulders. "I'm not complicating anything, buddy. I think your sister can make her own decisions just fine." He turned to me and his voice softened. "We should get you into some dry clothes before you get sick."

"I think that's a good idea." Sheena spoke up. "I have some clothes in the back. Why don't you come get changed? Then we can talk some more."

"What else is there to know?" I asked. The need to get away from the store and all the secrets and lies was intense. "Is there more?"

"Wait a minute," Jason said, his glance darted between us. "What are we talking about? Will someone tell me what's going on here?"

"Jason," I started. "Let's just go-"

"She knows," Sheena said, cutting me off. My eyes were on Jason while she spoke so I didn't miss his split second reaction when Sheena said, "Becca knows the truth. It was time."

I saw his face flash with a look of worry. Or was it guilt? I couldn't be sure, but it was clear that even without details, Jason knew exactly what Sheena was talking about.

I took two steps back at the same moment he reached for me. His fingers brushed my arm and my skin prickled with the touch. "You knew," I said.

"Becca, I-"

"You knew," I said again. I tried to fight the anger from rising in my voice. I failed. "And what's worse, is you pretended to care about me."

"I do care about you."

"No. You don't." I let my anger loose. "None of you do." I whirled around, meeting all of their eyes in succession. Facing Jason again, I said. "I trusted you. I let you...damn it." I couldn't bear to look at him. My stomach revolted at the thought of the trust I gave him and the whole time he could have helped me. He knew that history was repeating itself, and he did nothing but watch it all happen. To help it happen.

"Sunshine, please." I could smell the familiar scent of patchouli as Sheena approached and stood behind me. "You have to understand. It wasn't my place to tell you.

How could I come to you after all these years and tell you I was your mother? Especially when you were hurting so much yourself. The best thing I could do for you, was to be there. To let you talk. Give you a shoulder. Please understand."

I slowly turned to face her.

"I was wrong," Sheena said. "You deserved to know the truth. I'm so sorry."

For a moment, looking at the woman who was so much like me, I felt my anger melt a little. I had an urge that was almost unbearable, to go to her and let her hold me. For her to give me the comfort I'd needed from her all these years. I leaned towards her, drawn in.

Jason's voice snapped me back into place. "I don't think you were ready to hear it. You're still too fragile, too-"

"What do you know?" I whipped around to face him. "What do you really know about anything? You think I'm a God damned psychology experiment. Go read another textbook."

"I told you that I couldn't be your solution, that was fair."

"No," I said. "You took advantage of me."

"I helped you."

"With what?" I spat.

"I helped you find yourself." He spoke so calmly, with so much self assuredness, I had to fight the urge to slap him. "Because of me, our relationship, you opened up to yourself, to what you really want."

A ringing noise filled the room and my head. It battled with the storm that was still raging in my brain. "Becca." Dylan's voice came from somewhere behind me. I half registered the sound, but I couldn't focus on him.

"No." I shook my head. The anger dissipating as I realized the truth. "You're wrong," I said to Jason. "It wasn't because of you." As I spoke, the realization crystalized in my mind. "I didn't need you to help me find myself. I did that all on my own." I glanced over to Sheena who was smiling through a curtain of tears. I looked away quickly. I didn't need her approval.

"I opened you up to feeling again," Jason said. "You were finally able to-"

"No." I cut him off.

"I don't know what kind of psychology classes you're taking, and I'm sorry if-"

"Becca." Dylan's voice again.

"I care about you," Jason said. He reached forward, placing his hands on my arms.

"You care about me?" I narrowed my eyes at him. "You don't know the first thing about caring. Any of you." I yanked away and he released me, just as Dylan grabbed my shoulder.

"Becca," Dylan said, his voice firm.

"What?" I turned and snapped at him before I noticed the look in his eyes. A nugget of fear formed in my belly. "What's wrong?"

He held up my cell phone. "I think you should take this."

The tone of his voice chilled me. My whole body shuddered and I forgot about Jason standing right behind me. The room and everyone in it, fell away as I reached for the phone.

CHAPTER TWENTY-FIVE

In slow motion I took the phone from Dylan and put it to my ear.

Jon's voice. "Becca, thank God I got you."

"What's wrong?"

"There's been an accident."

There's been an accident. The words reverberated in my skull. The room started to spin. I reached out for something, anything to ground me.

"You need to come home."

"Kayla?" No. I took a deep breath. "It's Jordan, isn't it?" As soon as I said the words, I knew. My heart knew. "Jon, you're scaring me. What's going on?"

"I had a showing." His voice sounded wrong. Scared. "She said Mac would pick her up. They were going to a movie."

"Mac?" The man-child. My breath quickened, I couldn't focus.

"The roads were slick...the car..."

"Jon?" I didn't recognize my voice. "Jordan? She's okay?"

He couldn't hide the quiver in his voice when he said, "She's in surgery. I'm here, we're...oh God, Becca." I could picture him on the other end of the line, rubbing his face, trying to hold back tears. Trying to be strong.

The vice on my heart squeezed, sending waves of hot guilty pain through my body. "I'm coming," I whispered.

I pushed the button on the phone, cutting off the connection. I stood rooted to the spot, unable to move.

"Becca?" Dylan's voice reached me.

"I have to go," I said.

I looked up then. All three of them stood staring at me. I focused on Sheena. Tears glistened in her eyes. "My baby," I said. "Jordan needs me."

Sheena nodded.

"I'll take you," Jason said, sliding up beside me. He put his arm around my shoulders and I shrank away from his touch.

"No." I ducked away and turned on him. "I don't need you."

"Becca-"

"I never needed you," I said. I pulled myself tall. "It was a mistake." I met his gaze, challenging him to say otherwise. After a moment, I shifted and locked eyes with Sheena. "It was all a mistake," I said. "All of it."

I took a deep breath, letting the air fill my lungs, giving me strength. Finally, I turned and said to Dylan, "Will you take me please?"

"Of course."

My big brother wrapped me in his warm coat and ushered me out the door, leaving Sheena and Jason behind.

We drove in silence. Dylan navigated the car as quickly as he dared down the slick mountain highway. The rain continued its drum beat on the windshield and I focused my concentration on the droplets that formed on the window. Each drop slid backward with the movement of the car and I traced the water tracks with my eye, focusing intently on the patterns they created. The phone conversation replayed its continual loop through my head.

"Can't you drive faster?" I asked, not for the first time.

Dylan spared me a quick glance. Worry clouded his eyes. "I'm doing my best. The roads are awful."

I nodded and went back to tracing the rain tracks on the glass.

The drive was excruciatingly slow, which gave me far too long to think about what might be waiting for me at the hospital. I tried to take deep breaths and relax. But every time I inhaled, fresh flashes of pain pierced my chest. All I could think about was Jordan, caught in the twisted wreckage of the crash. Alone, hurt and scared.

I should have been there.

"Do you think she's still in surgery?" I asked Dylan.

"That was a few hours ago, it's hard to say."

"I need to be there when she wakes up."

"I know," he said. "I'm doing my best."

I nodded. "Why did you answer my cell?" The question just occurred to me.

"What do you mean?"

"You answered my phone, back at the store. If you hadn't..."

He shrugged. "I don't know. It was in your purse and it just kept ringing. It was one of those things, you know? Sometimes you just get a feeling that you should look. So I answered it and it was Jon."

"Well, thank you."

Numb and exhausted, I looked out the window at the landscape that was beginning to change. The mountains and trees were giving way to fields with the occasional ranch or farm house. It wouldn't be too much longer until the city began to spill out into the countryside.

"Do you want to talk?" Dylan asked. "About something else I mean. It might help to get your mind off things for a bit."

I didn't turn from the window. The images outside were a blur.

Was there anything else?

"I'm serious," he said reading my brain. "Tell me about Dad."

"Dylan."

"I mean it. Tell me. How are Dad and Connie doing these days?"

"You could go visit and see for yourself."

"I will."

"Really?" I stared at him then.

"Sure. It's not that I don't want to see them. I do care, Becca."

"Then why don't you ever visit? Or pick up the phone?"

"It's hard," Dylan said. He didn't take his eyes off the road.

"Hard? Do you want to know what's hard? Being the only one around to help Connie when Dad's having a really bad day. That's hard. Or having your dad look at you and see your dead...or not so dead mother. That's hard." When Dylan still didn't look at me, I turned back to the window. The rain had stopped. The fields looked fresh and clean.

"I'm sorry, Becca. I am. But you were always closer with Connie than I was. I barely even know her. It's weird for me."

"That's not my fault." I struggled to keep my voice even.

"You're right. I'm sorry. I guess I just thought you guys always had things covered," he said. "I was wrong."

"She's the only mother I ever had." I didn't acknowledge him. "I barely remember Vicki, Sheena, whoever she is. I needed a mother, Dylan, and you guys wouldn't even talk about her. I guess now I know why."

"I'm sorry," he said. "It hurt too much."

"It hurt? Did you ever think that I hurt too? I was just a little girl, Dylan. I lost my mother and nobody would even talk about her. I needed to talk. I needed to know.

But it was like she didn't even exist. God, do you have any idea how that screwed me up?"

"I don't know what else to say. It was Dad's idea. He didn't want you to think it was your fault, because it wasn't. But I was only a kid too. Don't forget that. I lost my mother too. She left me too, Becca."

"I know." I softened my voice. "It couldn't have been easy."

"It wasn't," he said. He swiped at his face. I didn't want him to cry.

"Are you okay?" It just occurred to me that I hadn't asked him. But seeing her after all that time would have been intense for him too. "I'm sorry, Dylan. I didn't even think about what it's been like for you today."

"It's okay," he said, and turned briefly to smile at me. "I think part of me always knew she was back in Rainbow Valley."

"Why didn't you go look for her?"

"Why would I? She didn't want to be found. She didn't want me. Us. I know it sounds crazy, Becca. But after awhile, I started to believe that she really was dead. She might as well have been."

We sat in silence, letting the road go by. After a moment, I said, "Do you really think I'm like her?"

"In lots of ways, you're a lot like her. But so different too."

I swallowed hard and looked out the window. The trees, blurred by the water still on the glass, looked like green smears as we rushed past.

"I think maybe you should talk to someone," he said. "Get some help. The way Mom should have."

"I can't think about that right now."

"You need to think about it right now. You need to be there for Jordan and Kayla the way Mom wasn't there for you. It can't happen again, Becca."

I flipped in my seat to confront him. "It won't happen again. It would never... I would never."

"We didn't think she would either," he said.

"Dylan."

"I'm serious, Becca. We knew she was unhappy. Dad said it happened after I was born too. Mom fell into a 'deep funk', he called it. Why do you think there are so many years between us? It took her along time to snap out of it. I remember her spending a lot of my childhood sad and in bed. Even in Rainbow Valley."

"Really?"

"Yes. It wasn't until I was about six that she came around a bit. I have no idea what it was that did it. But the same thing happened after you were born. Only it was worse."

"So you think it's hereditary?"

He nodded. "What's the age difference between the girls?"

He knew the answer.

"That's not why," I said. "Kayla wasn't planned. I was going to stop at one."

He raised his eyebrow at me.

"The thing is, Becca, it's pretty clear that history's repeating itself. I see it. We all see it."

"I told you. I would never do what she did. I would never leave my children like that."

"But don't you see?" He spoke slowly. "You already did."

CHAPTER TWENTY-SIX

We didn't say another word for the rest of the drive. As we entered the city limits, I started to get edgy. My legs bounced and my fingers tapped on the door. The sky was still gray and overcast. It was an ominous way to herald my return.

Dylan pulled up to the hospital doors and I jumped from the car before he even had it in park. I ran into the lobby and straight to the information desk.

"Jordan Thompson," I barked at the clerk. She looked up painfully slowly from her magazine. Her finger still posed to flip the page.

"Who?"

"I'm looking for Jordan Thompson. My daughter."

The clerk, who couldn't have been much older than Jordan herself, turned the magazine over and punched Jordan's name into her computer.

"Fifth floor," she said, and went back to her reading. "Check with the nurses, they'll tell you what room."

"She's not in surgery? I was told she was in surgery."

"Guess not," she said, without looking up. "All I know is fifth floor."

I resisted the urge to grab the girl and tell her that there were kids in an accident. Kids around her age. Maybe she knew them? Or went to school with them? And maybe, she should show a little compassion if she was going to work at the front desk.

I turned and sprinted to the elevator bank.

I pushed the up arrow on the wall. None of the four doors opened. I pushed it again. And again.

"Come on, come on," I muttered under my breath. I needed to get there before Jordan woke up. I needed her to know she wasn't alone. I would never leave her.

Finally, a ding, and the door of the elevator furthest away creaked open with excruciating slowness. I jumped in and jabbed at the buttons.

Circling the small box, I paced like a caged tiger as the elevator creaked and lurched upwards. When the doors finally opened on the fifth floor, I launched out and dashed to the nurses' station.

"Jordan Thompson," I said to the first nurse I met. "Where is she?"

"Are you family?" the young nurse asked. She hardly looked old enough to be out of high school. Was the entire staff made up of children?

"I'm her mother."

"Becca?" said a voice behind me.

I abandoned the nurse, turned and ran down the hall to Jon. It was a reflex of the heart to run to the man I'd loved so long, who'd comforted me so many times before. I stopped short and held myself back from going to him, seeking strength from his arms. I clenched my hands together instead.

"Where is she?"

Jon pointed to the room next to him. "She's sleeping now."

"And Kayla?"

"Steph took her to Connie's for the night."

I nodded. "I need to see Jordan." I'd deal with everything else later.

Jon nodded and I pushed past him into the tiny room where I stopped short. She looked so small, fragile. Wires led to monitors that beeped and flashed next to her head.

I dropped my purse and tiptoed my way to the bed. I fell into a chair that had been pulled close and gently lifted her hand off the sheets. It was so light, even with the IV needle sticking from it.

"Jordan," I whispered. "Mommy's here." I brought her hand to my mouth and placed a gentle kiss on it.

I turned towards the door and looked at Jon. He'd followed me in. "What happened? What's wrong?" I turned away and scanned Jordan for injuries. She looked fine. Besides a large plaster cast on her left leg, she looked to be sleeping.

"She's going to be okay," Jon said. He crossed the room in two steps and stood next to me. "Her femur was broken pretty bad. But it was a clean break and they put a rod in it. The surgeon said because she's young and healthy, it'll heal fine."

"What else?"

"She has a concussion," he said. "She was conscious at the accident site but by the time they got her here, she'd lost consciousness again."

"But, she'll be fine?"

"The doctors think so."

"They think so?" I fought to keep my voice level, to keep from screaming in the quiet room. How could he be so calm? Our baby was broken, laying in the hospital.

"Becca," he said softly, and reached to touch my arm. His touch burned and I pulled away. Hurt flashed through his eyes, but he said, "She'll be fine. I know she will. We were lucky."

I nodded then turned back to Jordan. She looked like an angel. There was no sign of her teenage attitude, her snappy comebacks when I asked her a question. She was my baby. She had to wake up.

"We were lucky," Jon said again. I could feel him move behind me and the heat from his body as he got close. I thought he might put his arms around me. But then, he was gone, moving past me to the chair on the other side of the bed. I let out a breath and swallowed hard.

"She was with Mac," he said.

"You told me on the phone. Why did you let her go with him? You knew I don't like her driving with those kids."

"He wasn't driving."

"It doesn't matter," I said, trying not to raise my voice. I kept smoothing Jordan's hair from her face, hoping the action would wake her. "I think he's too old for her. A fourteen year old has no business hanging out with a boy so much older, it's nothing but-"

"He's dead, Becca."

My hand froze over Jordan's brow. "What?"

"He died in the crash," Jon whispered. "One other girl is in intensive care. The driver's fine. Just a broken arm. It wasn't their fault. A pick-up ran a red and hit them on the passenger side. Jordan was on the...we're so lucky." A sob escaped him but still I couldn't look at him.

I didn't say anything. I couldn't. The only thing I could think of was how grateful I was that it was some other child and not mine. Some other mother that had to receive the phone call that would destroy their life. Another parent that wouldn't be taking their child home. It was an awful thought. What was that poor woman going through? What was she doing? Whose hand was she holding now that her son was dead? I gripped Jordan's hand tighter. The only sound in the room was Jon's weeping and then after a few moments, it too was gone.

Finally, I said, "She doesn't know."

"No," he said. "I don't know how I'll tell her."

"How we'll tell her," I said, and looked at him. Our eyes met and locked. "I should have been here," I said.

My throat tightened with the words and my eyes burned.

"Becca." Jon shifted to the edge of his chair and reached for my free hand. I let him take it and his touch instantly calmed me. "Can we talk?"

I didn't answer him. Instead, I looked at my daughter's delicate face. Part woman, part child. She looked impossibly tiny in the big bed. Despite the purple bruise that was beginning to form over her left temple, her slightly tanned skin made her look healthy with a smatter of freckles across her nose. There would be more by the end of summer.

There would be a summer. The sting of unshed tears, burned my eyes.

"Becca?"

I bent low over Jordan's face and whispered, "I'm so sorry, baby." I placed a gentle kiss on her cheek and said, "I'll make it better."

I kept my face close, inhaling her scent. A mixture of the strawberry shampoo she used every morning along with the unfamiliar, harsh smells of the hospital. And, was that a hint of lavender too? I could feel the gentle puff of air as she exhaled. "I promise, sweetie. I won't ever leave you."

A single tear fell and landed on Jordan's cheek. "I promise," I said again and kissed it away, tasting the hot saltiness on my lips.

I straightened and turned to Jon. More tears, unshed, blurred my vision. "Yes," I said. "Let's talk."

Once the tears started, I couldn't stop them. And what was more, I didn't want to. It was like a rusty tap had finally been cranked opened inside me, and with the flowing tears came the emotion. I let them snake down my cheeks and I tasted each drop as it reached the corners of my mouth.

Standing in the corridor, I hung my head and let my long hair fall around me like a curtain. My sobs shook my body and I let loose into a messy sort of cry. In the past, I might have stopped myself, self consciously aware of who was watching, but at that moment I didn't care. The feeling of letting my body shake, experiencing every vibration through my limbs, was foreign, but totally welcome.

When I felt Jon's familiar arms come around me, I closed my eyes and let him hold me. It was like home. He was safe. I snorted and sobbed, soaking his shirt, but he didn't release his grip. As my tears began to subside, I noticed the rise and fall of his chest, in time with mine. And his scent. Clean, like the soap I bought.

I breathed it in.

When I felt ready, I pulled away slightly and he released me.

"I'm sorry," I said, and swiped at my eyes. "I don't really know where that came from."

"Christ, Becca. Don't apologize. I've done some crying myself. That's our baby in there."

"I know, but...I..."

"You don't cry," Jon finished for me. "I can't remember the last time." His voice was gentle and he reached for me again, but I sidestepped him.

"We need to let this go," he said. "Especially now. We need to move on."

"Move on?" I pulled back.

"That was the wrong word." He moved closer, trying to bridge the gap. "What I mean is, what we have, it's too strong, too important to throw away." He reached for me again. "Becca, please. We can fix this."

I looked at him. Really looked at him. I took in his face, twisted with pain. His hand outstretched for me. I could take it. I could take it and forget everything that had happened. It was within my power to make everything better. Just like I'd told Jordan I would.

But, I still had to tell him about Jason. How would he feel then?

In slow motion, I lifted my hand and moved towards him. I watched as the pain in his eyes morphed.

So much had happened. Maybe too much.

Jon held my hands tightly in his own before I could pull away again.

"The best part of me has always been you," he said. "For the girls, for us, we can figure this out."

The desperation in his eyes was too much. I looked down at the hem of my skirt, swaying over my feet. I thought of the cabin. The meadow. Jason, and the feelings he'd ignited in me. The painting I'd left on the porch. Sheena, my mother, alive all this time.

When I looked up at Jon's familiar face, I saw the new lines that were etched into the skin next to his eyes. They hadn't been there when I'd left. Had they? His weariness and worry displayed for all to see. Or maybe I just hadn't looked.

We had a lifetime together. Jordan. Kayla. Everything.

I felt his pulse beat through his hands, into me, connecting us. I took a step towards him and let him pull me close. He released my hands just long enough to wrap his arms around me and I lost myself once again in the familiarity of his embrace.

It could all go away. I knew in that moment that if I wanted it to, everything that happened between us would go away and we could go back to what we were. Rainbow Valley, Jason, none of it mattered, because Jon was here with me, and I could have my life back.

If I wanted it.

"Jon," I said and stepped back. "I have something to-"

"Becca?"

We both turned in the direction of the voice to see Dylan running down the hall.

"Dylan?" Jon asked. He looked between us. "You answered Becca's phone." Jon looked to me. "You've been with your brother?"

I shook my head.

"Is she okay?" Dylan asked.

Thankful to have something else to focus on, I filled Dylan in on Jordan's status.

"Thank God," he said. Then to Jon, "I got her here as soon as I could."

Jon nodded. But his eyes locked to mine. "Are you ready to tell me where you've been?"

Dylan glanced between us. "You have a lot to talk about, I know." He reached over and gave me a hug. "It's going to be okay, Becca. It will," he whispered into my ear.

Before he released me, I looked up and stiffened. Over his shoulder, I saw Sheena walking towards us.

"What is-" Dylan broke off when he turned and saw her.

Her eyes, red from crying, highlighted the creases on her face. She'd gone from a young hippie to an old woman.

"I'm sorry to interrupt," she said, "but I brought your things and I wanted to, no, I needed to see how your little girl was doing. And you too." Turning to Jon she said, "You must be Jon."

Ever the gentleman, Jon offered his hand, which Sheena took in her own and squeezed. "My name is Sheena. I'm..." she trailed off and looked at me.

"She's my mother," I finished. It was the truth. Sheena smiled and turned back to Jon, who looked as confused as I'd been.

"I'm their mother," Sheena said.

Jon looked at me for an explanation.

"I'll tell you about it later." I shook my head. "It's too much right now."

"Your wife is very special," Sheena said to him. "I can see how much you love her. And she loves you too. Trust me, I know. But she's troubled right now."

"I don't under-"

"Jon," Dylan broke in. "Why don't we go get a coffee? I think they need some time." His gaze slid over Sheena.

I knew he was hurting. I knew he needed time with her too. My heart swelled for the sacrifices my big brother had made for me.

We waited while Jon and Dylan disappeared down the hallway.

When they were gone, I turned to Sheena. I opened my mouth to tell her to leave. That I didn't need her and I wanted her to go. I opened my mouth but nothing came out. A tear slid down my cheek and when Sheena opened her arms, I surprised myself and went to her. I knew she would never and could never take Connie's place, but I couldn't ignore who she was. She was part of me.

I let myself cry for a few minutes and when I was ready, I pulled back and looked at her. Her face was streaked with tears of her own. "There's so much to say, isn't there, Sunshine?"

I nodded.

"We'll have time," she said.

"Sheena, I-"

She held up a finger. "Please. We'll talk later. You need your energy for your family right now. I just need you to know one thing." I let her take my hand. "You are not like me."

I opened my mouth to protest. Hadn't I just spent the last few days learning just how much like my mother I actually was?

Before I could say anything, Sheena said, "No. You're much stronger than me. I was weak and I took the easy way out. By the time I realized what I'd given up, it was too late. Don't make the same mistakes I did."

"I won't," I said, and as I spoke, I realized it was true. I wouldn't do the same thing. "My family is my heart," I said. "I could never leave them. I know that now."

Sheena squeezed my hand tight before releasing it. Her smile was small and sad. "Love yourself, Sunshine and everything will be okay." Before I could say anything else, she was gone in a whirl of skirts, and leaving the now familiar scent of patchouli in her wake. As I stood there, watching as she walked down the corridor and out the double doors. A strange sense of calm settled over me. I still didn't know how, but I felt in my heart that Sheena was right. Everything would be okay.

CHAPTER TWENTY-SEVEN

After Sheena left, I'd phoned and talked to Kayla. I told her I was with Jordan and I'd come get her soon and take her home. She sounded tired, and scared. I didn't know how much she knew about what had happened to her sister, but she was a smart, sensitive girl, and her world had been turned around in the last week. I was proud of how well she was handling everything.

Speaking to Connie after, I filled her in on Jordan's condition the best I could. "I'll come and get her," I said, referring to Kayla. "She should be in her own bed tonight."

"You just take your time, Becca. Jordan needs you too."

"I know. I'm headed back to her room right away," I said. I took a deep breath and added, "Dylan's here."

"Dylan? What's he doing there?"

"It's a long story. I'm sure he'll fill you in." I didn't have the energy to tell her about Sheena right then. "But, Connie?"

"Yes?"

"When he tells you everything." I swallowed hard before continuing. "Please know that you're the best mom I could have had."

A tear slid down my cheek.

"Oh, Becca," she said. "I'm sorry."

I knew in that moment, that Connie knew the truth. Instead of being angry, the way I thought I would, I nodded to myself. Of course she'd known the truth.

"I love you, Connie."

"I love you too. Everything will be okay."

I smiled through my tears. "Yes," I said. "It will be."

Jon still wasn't back when I got off the phone, so I went to take up my post next to Jordan's bed. I refused to close my eyes, despite the exhaustion that had settled into every fiber of my body. My muscles were so relaxed into the chair, I couldn't even feel my legs. But I wouldn't take my eyes of my daughter.

I'd been watching for any sign of movement. Even the slightest indication that Jordan knew I was with her. I refused to miss it when she woke up. I'd missed too much already.

I was losing the battle to stay awake when Jordan's hand twitched. My eyes popped open and I scanned her.

There was no more movement. No change.

Maybe I'd imagined it?

But then it happened again.

"Mom?" Jordan moaned so quietly I wasn't sure I heard it.

"Jordan?" I dared to let myself believe it was true. I scooted to the front of my chair. "Baby? Mommy's here. I'm here." I reached out and brushed her soft brown hair off her forehead. As my hand swept over her brow, Jordan opened her eyes and I thought my heart might break from the exquisite sight of her blue eyes.

"I'm here," I said again.

"Mom?" Jordan's voice cracked. She sounded impossibly small. "My leg hurts, Mom."

"I know, baby. There was an accident," I said, doing my best to keep my voice level. "But you're going to be fine."

"I remember," she said. "Mac picked me up from school."

"Ssh, don't try to remember now," I said. I wanted to

protect her as long as I could. "Just rest."

"We were in Bruce's car. I remember the truck. It came through the light. I rememb-"

"Ssh." I brushed my hand over her brow again. "Baby, don't worry about that right now."

Jordan looked at me and when her eyes locked on me, I could see in her eyes that she knew there was something I wasn't saying. For a moment I thought she might ask about it, but when she opened her mouth, she said, "I missed you, Mom."

Her eyelids fluttered closed, exhausted from the effort of talking.

"I missed you too." I blinked hard against my tears. "Rest now, everything is going to be okay, I promise."

I watched while Jordan's chest rose and fell with every breath. She'd learn about her friends, and her boyfriend, soon enough. But for that moment, she could rest easy.

After a few minutes, I slipped from the room. Dylan was slumped against the wall directly across from the door. He jumped up when he saw me.

"How is she?"

"She woke up," I said. "She's going to be okay." He grabbed me into another hug.

"That's awesome news." After a moment, Dylan pulled away, and asked, "And you? Are you going to be okay?"

I nodded. "I have a lot to think about. A lot to fix. But, yes. I think I'll be just fine."

Dylan smiled. "Of course you will. You're not her, you know that right?"

"I know," I said, and then added. "Don't hate her, Dylan. She made some bad choices, but you can't hate her."

He fiddled with the zipper on his jacket before answering. "Know what's strange? I don't think I do. I'm angry, yes. But after you, and...well, everything with you, I think I can see it a little differently. We have a lot of talking to do though."

"We all do," I agreed. Thinking about all of the talking I still had to do, I looked up and down the hall. "Where's Jon?"

"I sent him home. He didn't want to leave, but I think even he knew he needed the rest."

"You told him? About Sheena, I mean."

He nodded. "I did. Of course he was surprised and tried to get a lot more out of me. But I couldn't answer the questions he was asking," Dylan said. "Only you can."

I looked at my feet. "I know." I was no longer scared of talking to Jon, of telling him the truth. I was tired of all the secrets and misunderstandings. I looked up, into my brother's eyes. "And I will. I'll tell him everything. But first I think there's one more thing I have to do."

I knew she'd be there. There was no where else she'd be. She was my best friend, and she loved my girls like they were her own. When I stepped into the hospital cafeteria, I scanned the room before seeing the back of her blond head bent over the table.

I slipped into the seat across from her.

"Thank you for being here," I said.

Steph looked up. She looked tired and I knew that not only had she been there, she hadn't slept.

"Where else would I be?" she asked. "You know I'll always be here for you and the girls. No matter what."

"I know," I whispered, and took her hand.

"They...you, you're my heart," she said.

"I know."

She didn't say anything else. Instead she just looked at me.

"You should have been here," Steph said. Her voice

was quiet, but I knew I'd heard her properly. "If you hadn't gone, this wouldn't have happened."

The words were a slap, and I felt it acutely.

I wanted to yell at her. I wanted to scream and tell her it wasn't my fault, that it could have happened even if I had been there. I didn't. Tears blurred my eyes as I reached for her hands. I didn't know if she would accept the gesture, or me. But she pulled me across the table into a hug and we held on tight. Together we cried tears of forgiveness and fear.

"I'm back," was all I said.

"How is she?" Steph asked fifteen minutes later. We were sitting outside in the meagre garden area the hospital provided. There were a few benches placed under the scraggly trees and a couple of pots of geraniums that looked like they'd been used more as ashtrays than for growing flowers.

"She woke up. That's a huge relief. Of course she has a broken leg, but she'll heal. At least her body will," I said. I couldn't help thinking about the boy who wouldn't heal. Her boyfriend.

"Her heart will heal too," Steph said. "It'll sting for awhile. But she's a strong girl. She'll be okay."

We sat in silence for a few moments.

"I'm glad you're back," she said.

I took a deep breath and kicked at the ground with my toe. "I should have been here and-"

"No. I didn't mean to say that earlier, you needed to go."

I turned on the bench so I could look at her. "What do you mean?"

"Becca, you needed a break. The accident could have happened if you were here. But whatever happened to you," she said, and waved her hand in my direction. "That couldn't have happened if you were here. You needed to go."

I nodded. I knew she was right.

"Do you want to know something?" I asked.

"Of course. I want to know everything."

"Today was the first time I cried, since...well, I can't remember. And when I started, I couldn't stop."

"It's been a hard day."

"It has. But it was more than that. I don't know if I can explain it, or if I should even try. But when I saw Jordan lying there, I just realized that everything that's important to me, everything that matters in the whole world, it's right here. The girls. They're everything."

"And Jon?"

I looked down at my hands and twisted the fabric of my skirt around them. "I need to talk to him. And he's not going to like what I have to say." I thought of Jason and what had happened between us. Jon wasn't going to like it, but he needed to hear it. "We need to figure a few things out. Then I guess we'll go from there."

"You're going to tell him about the guy, then?"

I nodded. "I have to, Steph. Jason was part of everything. And I'm tired of hiding from the truth. I need to be honest."

"That's a good way to be," she said. "Honest I mean. With Jon and with yourself."

I looked up to the sky. Blue patches had started to break through the clouds, but the sun was starting to set. My memories flashed back to the magnificent mountain sunsets in Rainbow Valley.

"It is a good way to be," I said, and looked back to her. "I guess it took leaving to learn that everything I really wanted, was right here." I took a deep breath. "I can't imagine going again, but when I think about the way things were, well I can't imagine that either."

"So, you're stuck?"

"Not stuck." I shook my head. "Definitely not stuck." I stood and stretched my hands over my head. "It took me awhile, but now I know exactly what I need."

Steph smiled up at me. "And what's that? A trip to Europe with your best friend?"

I laughed. "I still don't think that's going to happen." I rolled my shoulders, releasing some of the tension there. "No," I said, "what I need to do is be true to myself. Did you know I've spent the last fifteen years thinking that I couldn't be Becca anymore?"

Steph nodded. "Actually, I've noticed."

"I know. You tried to tell me that. You all did." I sat again and looked Steph in the eyes. "I was so stuck on being what I thought I should be, that I couldn't be who I needed to be."

"And you know the difference now?"

I closed my eyes and remembered the mountains, Prince's Pond, swimming, painting, Jason, Sheena. I let the feelings flow through me unchecked. I wouldn't stifle them again. I couldn't. Finally, I opened my eyes, and said, "Yes. I definitely know the difference."

CHAPTER TWENTY-EIGHT

After checking in with the doctors, Steph offered to stay with Jordan and lend me her car, so I could go get Kayla before stopping at home to shower and change. It was almost nine when I pulled up at Connie and Dad's house. Dylan's car was parked on the road out front.

"She's sleeping," Connie said, after answering the door and pulling me into a hug. "Come, we should talk."

"I'll be right there."

Before following Connie into the kitchen, I made my down the hall and into the spare room where Kayla was tucked in. She was curled up on her side, Pup-Pup snugged up tight in her arms. I bent and kissed my baby on the forehead. "I'm home, baby," I whispered. "I love you so much."

I didn't want to wake her, so I backed out of the room slowly and eased the door shut.

"It's so quiet in here," I said, when I joined Connie in the kitchen. "Where's Dylan? And Dad?"

She nodded and I noticed how tired she looked.

"They're talking in the den." She managed a small smile. "It's been nice to see Dylan."

"Did he tell you then? About my mother being in Rainbow Valley?" My stomach flipped and I reached for Connie's arm. "What I said on the phone, I meant it. You're the best mother I could ever have wished for."

A tear slid from Connie's eye and her hand moved to cover mine. She pointed to a seat at the table. "Why don't you sit down, dear?"

I did as I was told. I sat and waited. After a moment she spoke. "I need you to know that I couldn't tell you about your mother. It wasn't my secret to tell. Your father told me the truth before we married. He had his reasons for not telling you. Even if I didn't agree with them, please know, I didn't ever mean to hurt you. Your dad didn't like to speak of her. And Dylan, he was always so distant." Her eyes drifted over my head as she recalled a memory. "I know now there's so much I should have done. So much I could have done to help you deal with things. This news, that you've found her, it doesn't change how I feel about you. I hope you know that you're every bit as much my daughter as you were before all this."

I swiped at the tears in my eyes and reached across the table for her hands. The hands that had taken care of me and comforted me for most of my life. She was right, Sheena's existence wouldn't change anything between us. "I love you, Connie."

She squeezed me tight in her grip. "I know it, Becca. And I love you. So much." We sat for a few minutes, tears rolling down both our cheeks, our hands clasped tightly. Finally, it was Connie who released me.

"How's Dad taking the news?" I asked. "Does he understand? I mean, is he..."

Connie nodded. "I think he knows. It's interesting, because for the last little while, as he's gotten worse, he's mentioned her more. Your mother, I mean."

I thought back to all the times he confused me with her. It'd been awkward for sure, but now that I knew the truth, it made a little more sense. "Maybe it was his way of trying to tell the truth? I don't know, but do you think it's possible that his subconscious was trying to let go of the lie?"

"There's so much about it that we'll never know," Connie said with a sad smile. "I don't think we should even try to figure it out. Dylan's doing his best to talk to him, but I know he's finding it difficult. Becca, I should tell you..." Connie stopped to blow her nose and wipe her eyes. I waited while she pulled herself together. I knew what she was going to say. "I think it's time we put your father in a nursing home. I just, I just can't anymore. I'm so sorry." Connie dissolved into sobs, her shoulders folded in on herself and her whole body shook.

I pushed up from my chair and took her in my arms. It was my turn to offer comfort. I held her while she exhausted her tears. "I know," I said. "And it's okay. We'll be here to help."

"Oh, Becca," Connie said and pulled away. "I feel terrible. I shouldn't have dumped this on you right now." She wiped at her tears and all at once was the strong and in control woman I'd always known. "You have enough to take care of right now. Don't even give this one more thought until Jordan is out of the hospital."

"Connie, it's-"

"Nonsense." She stood from the table. "You just leave Kayla here for the night. She's asleep and comfortable. You can get her in the morning," she said. "Besides, I'm sure you have something you need to take care of tonight." She looked at me knowingly, but before I could say anything, she added, "You don't need to tell me the details." She waved her hand in the air. "Just tell me that you're okay. I need to know that you're okay now."

I nodded and smiled at her intensity. "I'm fine now, Connie. I swear." She tilted her head and narrowed her eyes. "Well," I added, "I will be." I laughed. "I promise. I know now what I need to do."

For a second she didn't say anything, and just when I thought I'd have to try harder to convince her, she straightened and smiled. "I knew it. You're a strong woman, Becca. Even if you don't always see it. And you can have it all. You just need to decide what that looks like for you."

She walked me to the door, where I gave her another hug.

"You can do this," she said. "Be true to you and everything else will fall into place." I didn't have to ask what she was talking about.

Her words replayed in my head as I navigated the car though the familiar streets towards home, and my husband.

The house looked bigger somehow. I pulled into the driveway and went in the front. The door was unlocked, as I knew it would be. Only one lamp burned in the living room. Jon sat, head slumped in his hand, fast asleep. I sat in the chair across from him and watched him for a minute. Even in his sleep he looked troubled. His hair was still wet from his shower, but the worry etched into his face, combined with the stubble that was beginning to turn into the makings of a beard on his chin, made him look much older than he was. I didn't want to wake him from his much needed sleep, but I needed to talk to him. It couldn't wait any longer.

I stood and went to him. Kneeling in front of him, I put my hand lightly on his knee. The gentle touch woke him. He didn't startle. Jon opened his eyes slowly and a slow, sad smile worked across his face.

"You're home," he said.

I nodded and sat on the chair across from him.

Jon shook his head, clearing it of sleep and focused on me. "Jordan? Is she-"

"She's fine," I said before he could panic. "She woke up, but she's sleeping again. The doctor said she would be fine."

He sat back in his seat. "I knew she'd wake up for

you. She wanted to see you."

I laughed. "She never wants to see me," I said. "A teenage girl never wants her mother."

"That's not true. She's asked about you every day since you left."

"She has?"

"Of course she has, Becca." Jon ran his hands thorough his hair making it stand out at odd angles. "You're her mother. She missed you."

"Point taken." I pulled my legs up and hugged them tight to my chest.

"You look good," Jon said. "Different. But good."

"Thanks. They're not my clothes." I smoothed the skirt over my knees.

"I figured." Jon let out a tight controlled laugh.

It wasn't much, but I took it as a sign that he was open to talking things through. I took a deep breath, and said, "A lot has happened."

He nodded. "And, I'm not going to like what you have to say, am I?"

I looked away. I wouldn't lie to him.

"That's what I thought," Jon said without malice. "So, this is it then?"

My stomach flipped. I didn't want to think about our marriage being over, but I knew it was a very real possibility, once he learned the truth. I had to accept that.

I swallowed my fear. "I'm not going to apologize for leaving. I needed to do it. I admit, it wasn't the best way to handle things." I watched Jon try to smile as he agreed with me. "But I didn't know what else to do," I said. "I was lost, totally numb and completely confused about who I was or what I wanted. And then I found Rainbow Valley and Sheena."

"Dylan tried to tell me about her," he said. "But I still don't understand it all."

"Neither do I," I said with a little laugh. "But she's my

mother. Sheena used to be just like me." I absorbed that. We were very much alike, but very different too. I needed to remember that. "She ran away from us when I was little, just like I did."

"But you-"

"I came back."

"Because of Jordan?" he asked. I could see the hurt in his eyes but I didn't look away again. I needed to feel it.

"Of course," I admitted. "I couldn't sit there while my baby was in the hospital." He looked at his feet. "But it was more than that. I would have come home anyway. It took a bit, but I realized what I should have known years ago." I waited until he met my gaze again. "For so long, I've been caught up in what I thought I should be. But I totally forgot about who I was. Now I know that the person I should be, is me. I've been going through the motions for so long, that I didn't even remember who Becca really was or is. Up until a few days ago, I couldn't tell you what I was feeling at all. I was numb."

"And now?"

His eyes were tired and full of sadness. But when he looked at me, I could still see the love he held for me. After everything, there was still love. "Now I know more. And I know that I have a lot more work to do on myself. I started painting again."

Jon's face lit up. "You did? That's excellent."

"It is. It feels so good and it's not too bad."

"I bet it's amazing," he said. "You're good at everything you do."

"That's not true."

"It is, Becca. I know there've been some hard times, and I agree with you that the Becca I knew years ago has kind of been in hiding for awhile. But even through it all, you've always been a great wife and a fantastic mother."

"Now I know you're lying to me." I grabbed the hem of my skirt between my thumb and forefinger. "I'm not a good mother. And I haven't been a very good wife lately either."

"What do you mean?" I didn't answer right away and I could see it in his eyes when he realized the truth of what I wasn't saying. He made a sound that was a painful combination of a laugh and a cry. "Becca?"

"I'm sorry, Jon," I said softly. "It wasn't about you. It was about me. I thought it was over. I thought it was all over. This," I said with a gesture around the house. "Us. Everything. It doesn't make it okay. But I was totally lost. You'd told me you wanted to separate, I thought the girls hated me, I was failing at everything and then Jason-"

"Don't," he interrupted. "Don't tell me his name."

I resisted the urge to look away from his anger. "I'm sorry," I continued. "I wasn't looking for it to happen. It just did. And I can't remember the last time I felt the way I felt with him. It was like I was living a whole different life. Maybe I was. I'm sorry if it hurts you. Like I said, I never intended for it to happen. But I'm not sorry for the way he made me feel. He was part of this whole thing, like it or not. And if it had to happen to help me realize what was missing, then I'm glad it did. I don't want to be like my mother and run away from everything and everyone I love. Because I do love you, Jon. So much. And I realize that you may not want anything to do with me after all this. I won't blame you if you want to go through with a separation or even a divorce. But I need to tell you that whatever happened to me in Rainbow Valley, all of it, I'm glad it did. Because if it hadn't happened, I wouldn't be able to sit across from you right now and tell you that I know now what I want."

"And what's that?" The anger I'd seen in Jon a moment earlier, was gone. "What do you want, Becca?"

"I want to be, no, I need to be, true to me." I smiled as a tear fell. "It's like a dam has released, Jon. I can't even explain it. A long time ago I thought I could be happy just by being the wife and mother you wanted me to be. But I need more."

Jon hung his head between his knees and used one hand to rub at the back of his neck.

"Jon?"

"I really screwed things up, didn't I?" he asked when he looked up.

It took me a moment to realize what he'd said. It was me that screwed things up. Not him. "What do you mean? It wasn't you, Jon. It was me."

He shook his head. "No, Becca. You don't understand. It was me that pushed the wedding when we got pregnant. I wanted us to move, I let you give up everything. Your art, your passion. All of it. I knew it wasn't you, that you wouldn't be happy. But I let it happen because it was easier that way. It was easier to have you at home with Jordan and then Kayla, instead of following your own dreams." I tried to interrupt, to disagree with him, but he held up his hand. "No," he continued, "please let me finish. I saw it, Becca. I've seen for years that you've been unhappy. I should have done more. I blame myself. And I have blamed myself. I just didn't know what to do. I was losing you. In many ways, I'd already lost you. We're so far apart, Becca. I just didn't know what to do to reach you." He covered his face with his hands and rubbed his eyes.

I moved to the couch, the cushions sinking under my weight as I sat next to him. "I'm sorry," I whispered. I put my hand on his leg and waited until I was sure he was listening. "I'm sorry if you feel responsible. But I won't let you bear the weight of this. I'm not a child. I am, and have always been, responsible for my own happiness. It just took me awhile to figure it out."

He looked at me. "What does this all mean, Becca? I mean for us. Where does this leave us?"

I looked over his shoulder and my eyes caught sight

of a picture, framed on the mantle. It wasn't a formal portrait, or even a portrait at all. It was a photo taken the summer before in Dad's garden. We were playing a game of lawn darts and were actually all smiling and having fun together. Nobody was fighting. It had been a great day. We could have that again. I looked back to Jon and decided to lay my heart out. "I want us back. I still have a lot to figure out about myself, but I'd like to do it with you, Jon. I understand if you can't get past what happened. And if you choose to go through with the separation, it'll hurt, but I'll be okay."

Jon turned to me and took my hands in his. "It was never about a separation, Becca. I never wanted to end things with you. Not ever."

"But you said-"

"I know what I said, and it was stupid. It was me being frustrated and scared. It was stupid. I didn't know how else to reach you. It kills me to think of you with another man, Becca." My breath caught in my throat, but I didn't say anything. "I'm not going to lie to you and tell you that I'll be able to forget about it. I'm not sure if I can."

I looked down at my hands, still clasped in his. I squeezed tighter, not wanting to break our bond. I looked then at my husband. Really looked at him. I saw all the years we'd shared. Our first date at a dingy cafe that served the best clubhouse sandwiches. The first time we'd made love. How I knew I wanted to wake up in his arms every day. Our wedding day, surrounded by friends and family. I told him then that I'd love him forever. Could that change? The day Jordan was born when he took her in his arms, so gentle but so unsure of how to be a father. Years later when Kayla was born, and he was more confident. How he called us his perfect girls.

Looking at him, there was no doubt in mind. No doubt about what we shared.

"I love you, Jon," I said. My voice was soft, barely more than a whisper.

"I love you, too. You're my heart."

"And everything that's happened?"

I felt the tears come to my eyes again. The sensation was still so new. My eyes felt wet and awkward and I swiped at them.

"We can't change it," he said. "But we can change the future." He wiped away my tears with his thumb, as his own eyes filled. "You are and always have been the best part of me, Becca. Without you-"

I silenced him with a kiss. It took a moment as my lips found their place again with his, but then Jon's mouth moved against mine in a way that was both familiar and new at the same time. I let myself relax into his embrace as we remembered each other.

Much later, lying in bed next to my husband, my head rested on his chest while his hand gently drew circles on my back. My body was heavy, yet weightless at the same time, and I soaked up the heat radiating from Jon. His movements slowed and I knew he was falling asleep. I placed a soft kiss on his bare skin and snuggled closer.

"Becca?"

"I thought you were asleep," I said, and lifted my head to look at him.

His eyes were closed, a half smile fixed on his lips. "I'm glad you're back, Becca."

In response, I pushed up on the bed and kissed his lips, wearing his smile as my own.

I cuddled next to him and waited until I could hear the gentle rhythm of his breathing. When I was sure he was asleep, I slipped from bed, wrapping myself in my house coat.

Dylan had given Jon my art supplies to bring home from the hospital, they sat in the living room waiting for me. It didn't take me long to set up my easel with a fresh canvas and lay out the paints.

My fingers gripped the brush and I got to work, painting fast and feverishly, fueled by the emotions from the last forty eight hours. I started with the flowers, recreating the vibrant colors, the bursts of blossoms that filled the space. Then I added my family. One at at time. Jon first, then Jordan standing next to him. I put Kayla sitting cross legged on the grass in front. I waited until last to paint myself. I positioned myself next to Jon, hand in his, smiling down at the girls.

Finished, I took a step back and examined my work. I smiled. It wasn't perfect, but neither was my family, or the future we faced together. I didn't yet know how we were going to get through the coming challenges, but in that moment, I knew we could.

I dipped my brush in the green, just a shade darker than I'd been using. Working slowly, I painted the words carefully, so they almost blended in with the grass under Kayla's feet.

I'd probably never know the whole truth of what my father was trying to save when he'd given my mother the box of watercolors years earlier. But, as I stood back and read the words I'd painted, a peace settled over me as I realized the truth.

"Love Survives."

THANK YOU

This book has most definitely been a labor of love for me. I wrote the first draft of Drawing Free almost three years ago. It's since been through two complete overhauls and is now a very different book. There were many times when I wanted to give up on Drawing Free, but ultimately I believed in Becca and the story she had to tell. This wasn't an easy story to write, because it touches on so many elements that are close to me. Again, as always, Drawing Free is a work of fiction and all characters are created entirely from my imagination and not pulled from my real life.

I need to offer a huge thank you to my extremely talented writing group, The Easy Writers. Brad, Nancy, Trish, Leanne, Susan and Gigi, it's a privilege to be a member of such a great group of people and to spend every second Thursday with you. I am a stronger writer because of all of you and your scribbled notes on my early drafts.

A special thank you to Natalie Thwaites for her editing talents and for finding time during the busiest time of the year to read through Drawing Free and point out my punctuation errors and any Canadian spelling issues that snuck through.

To Charrissa Weaks. who read early drafts of Drawing Free and offered her wisdom, thank you!

An extra special thank you to my dear friend, Tammy Evans. She read so many versions of this story through the years and believed in Becca and her story as much as I did. And at time, more than I did. Thank you for your faith in Becca, and in me.

As always, a huge thank you to my beautiful children, Lincoln and Sydney and my wonderful husband, Rob, who put up with my writing weekends, endless hours holed up in my office writing, and even my last minute edits in the days leading up to Christmas! It's a joy and a privilege to be able to do what I love. Thank you for supporting me and cheerleading me through it all!

Nothing Stays In Vegas is Elena's debut novel, however she has numerous parenting articles to her credit and has been published in multiple Chicken Soup for the Soul anthologies, as well as the Seal Press anthology, How to Put a Car Seat on a Camel- and other misadventures travelling with children.

Residing in the Alberta Foothills with her husband and twins, Elena escapes to the mountains as often as possible and can often be found sitting by the lake plotting her next story.

To learn more about Elena Aitken and her upcoming books, please visit www.elenaaitken.com

Twitter - @elenaaitken
Facebook - www.facebook.com/elenaaitken.author

QUESTIONS FOR DISCUSSION
AND FURTHER THOUGHT

1) In the beginning of the story, Becca is overwhelmed by the daily tasks of her life and her children. Despite Connie encouraging her to do something for herself, she resists. Why do you think that is? Can you relate to the way Becca felt at the beginning of the story?

2) Becca seeks an endless stream of advice from books, yet resists the advice of her loved ones on more than one occasion. Why do you think it was easier for Becca to turn to books than her family? If you were her friend, how would you have tried to get through to her? Why are self-help books so popular ?

3) Becca's father is suffering from Alzheimer's and Becca struggles seeing the changes in him. How do you think her father's illness contributed to her leaving? Why do you think he kept the cabin in Rainbow Valley for all those years?

4) In the story, Becca and Jon's relationship is struggling, do you think it was reasonable for Jon to give Becca the negligee for a birthday gift? Would you have reacted the same way she did?

5) Right before Becca makes the decision to take a different exit off the freeway, she's experiencing a number of pressures that build to the breaking point. Have you ever thought about doing something like Becca? Why didn't you act on it? What would happen if you did? Or, have you ever asked yourself other 'what if' questions like, 'What if I married my first boyfriend?' or 'What if I didn't take that job?'

6) Becca's choice was a hard one, but one many mother's have thought about. Have you ever taken a 'mommy vacation'? Planned or unplanned? Why do you think it's important for mother's to get away every once in awhile?

7) The town of Rainbow Valley is filled with hippies and people who have 'run away' from something in their life. What is it about this town that makes it a desirable place to hide?

8) Why do you think Becca was able to open up to Jason? Do you think it was her physical attraction to him that led her to open up to him, or was it the fact that she was able to share her feelings with him that fueled her attraction?

9) Becca makes a very difficult moral decision regarding Jason and her marriage to Jon. Why do you think Becca's choice upsets some readers? Do you agree that the choice she made was right for her? Why or why not?

10) Sheena talks about auras, spirits and other mystical things on more than one occasion. Do you think there is any validity to what she says? What do you think is in the pouch that she wears around her neck?

11) Becca is drawn to Sheena long before she knows the truth about her. Do you think that on some level, Becca knew the truth about Sheena, or was Becca so desperate to find a connection with someone that she clung to Sheena?

12) When Becca rediscovers her passion of drawing and painting, she seems to experience an overall shift. Do you think that for Becca, art represented who she used to be, and her overall sense of self? Do you think a creative outlet is important for women?

13) When Dylan comes to Rainbow Valley to talk to Becca, she already has a sense that he's going to reveal something about her mother, but she's not sure what. When do you think she realized there was more to the story than she was being told?

14) Would you have reacted the way Becca did to hearing the truth? How do you think you would have reacted to such news? Do you think Becca would have returned home had Jordan not been involved in a car accident? Why or why not?

15) Becca's friend, Stephanie is angry with her for leaving, yet she still sat vigil at the hospital. Why do you think she did that? Do you have a friend like Stephanie?

16) Becca had repressed her true feelings for so long that the first tear that Becca cries is at Jordan's bedside. Do you think the tears started to flow because of the impact of seeing her daughter injured? Or was there more behind the tears?

17) When Becca leaves the hospital, she goes to see Connie. Why do you think Connie never told Becca the truth? Do you think she should have said something earlier? Would you be upset if Connie was your stepmother?

18) When Becca decides to tell Jon the truth about what happened between her and Jason, she tells him that she's sorry, but if it needed to happen for her to realize what was missing from her life, she's glad it did. Do you think she should have told Jon the truth? Do you think Becca's choices could be forgiven? Do you think Jon has anything to apologize for?

19) The theme of 'self' and losing yourself is a strong one in the novel. Could you relate at all to Becca? Have you ever lost your self in the pursuit of daily life and family? Why do you think it's important for women to retain their sense of self? Why?

20) Thematically, what struck you most about the novel? Did it lead you to think about any aspects of your own life?

Please enjoy an excerpt from Elena's
Contemporary Romance/Women's Fiction
novel-
Nothing Stays In Vegas

Chapter One

~April 2004~

The music was too loud. Maybe it was me. Was twenty-seven too old to sip an overpriced cocktail, wearing a too-short skirt and a too-tight top? Judging by what some of the other ladies were wearing, no.

I tugged at my skirt in a vain attempt to pull it closer to my knees. Preferably over them. Nicole was late, as usual; it would take at least twenty minutes to go back to the room and change. There was no time. One thing was for sure, I'd never again buy anything an eighteen-year-old sales girl declared, "Totally perfect for Vegas."

The fluorescent blue liquid swirled around my glass as I fiddled with my straw. A "Knock Out," the bartender had called it. It was going to knock me out. Every time I took a sip, the sweetness sent bites of pain through my teeth. Yet I couldn't seem to stop drinking it.

"Excuse me," a voice from behind said.

I swiveled in my seat to see a very blond, very clean cut, very preppy guy. Good looking if you liked the college boy look.

I didn't.

He was standing over me, not even trying to conceal the fact that he was staring at my cleavage, which there was way too much of.

"Yes?"

"Can I get you another?" College Boy gestured to my drink which I was surprised to see almost empty.

That would explain the dizzy feeling every time I

moved my head. Knock Out, indeed.

"I'm married," I said and turned back to face the bar. Where was Nicole?

"I'm Clark," College Boy said as he took the seat next to me, "and nobody in Vegas is married."

I twisted to look at him again. His smile dazzled. Clearly the result of thousands of dollars of orthodontic work. "Seriously," I tried again. "I'm not interested."

He leaned in and the smell of stale beer assaulted me. Over his shoulder I could see the table of his frat buddies, poking each other in the ribs and pointing in our direction.

Perfect. I was a bet.

"Listen, Kid." I couldn't have been much older then him, but maybe an insult would help. "I'm not interested in being part of your game tonight."

"Come on, Baby." His breath was hot and moist in my ear. I leaned back as far as I could without falling out of my seat but his arm snaked around me and yanked me toward him. "I just wanna have a little fun."

"Maybe I can suggest a playground nearby."

"Ouch," College Boy said and pulled back in mock injury. "That hurt."

"You think that hurt?"

"Come on," he leaned in again. "Don't be a bitch."

Really?

Changing my approach, I slid my hand up the side of his face, being sure to give his cheek a little caress as I went.

"Yeah," he murmured and closed his eyes. "That's what I'm talking about."

Without wasting anymore time I grabbed his soft, fleshy earlobe and twisted, hard.

"Ow!" His eyes snapped open and he jumped back but I still had a grip on his lobe. "Shit! Let go."

"Have I made my point?"

When he didn't answer immediately, I applied a little

more pressure.

"Shit! Yes, you've made your point."

I let him go and his hand flew to his ear. He shot me a look which made it clear that whatever he was feeling towards me, it was no longer romantic. I gave him an innocent smile and a little wave as he retreated to his buddies who were howling with laughter.

Yes, I was definitely too old for this.

I turned around intending to return to my drink but my eyes landed on a man standing at the other end of the bar. He was tall, but it was his black hair and matching dark eyes that caught my attention. From the grin on his face I could tell he'd witnessed what happened. I offered a little shrug but didn't look away.

He was handsome. No, more than handsome. He was gorgeous in a way that only guys who don't know how gorgeous they really are can pull off. And he was coming over.

"I'm not trying to interrupt you," he said. I looked him in the eyes. No, not black but perhaps the richest shade of brown I'd ever seen. Gold flecks caught the light making his eyes shine like onyx. I couldn't look away. "I saw what happened to the last guy," he continued.

"I didn't want to have to do that."

"No," he said with a grin. "It was great. I was going to offer my assistance, but it's clear you didn't need my help. I'm Leo." He extended his hand, which I took.

"I'm Lexi."

His skin was warm but a shiver went through me when he squeezed my hand before releasing it.

Leo turned and we both watched as College Boy threw money on the table and started toward us on his way to the door. When he got close enough he glared and said. "Good luck, man. She's married. And mean." He pushed past us and out of the lounge, his buddies tailing him.

Leo shook his head and turned back to me. "I only have a few minutes. Do you mind if I sit here?" He pointed to the stool at the bar next to me. "Or would you rather be alone?" He held up his hands in mock defense.

I laughed. "Go right ahead. I'm just waiting for someone."

"Since you're waiting anyway, can I get you a drink? I promise I won't try any bad pick up lines."

My defenses fell a little and I said, "Sure, since you promised not to try anything."

"Never," he said and smiled. His dark eyes lightened when he smiled which made them look even richer. I tried not to stare. "What are you having?"

I looked at the blue liquid at the bottom of my glass and shoved it away. "Anything but that."

Leo called the bartender over. "Mike, can I get a coke and a vodka tonic for the lady."

"Make that a vodka and soda," I interrupted.

Leo turned to me and gave me a sly smile. I shrugged. He turned back to the bartender and said, "Make that a vodka and soda. Thanks, Mike."

I watched while he made small talk with the bartender, who seemed to know him. There was something about his confidence that hypnotized me. But it might have been the effects of the Knock Out.

"So," he said turning back to me, sliding my drink over. "Is what that guy said true?"

"That I'm mean?" I took a long sip of my vodka, enjoying the sharp contrast of the soda from the tooth rotting sweetness of my first drink. I rolled the liquid around in my mouth before swallowing and added, "Absolutely."

"Well, I'll withhold judgment on that one," he said. "But what I really wanted to know is, are you married? Is that who you're waiting for?"

Was he flirting with me? "Actually, no. I'm meeting

my best friend. It's her birthday. Well, not tonight, but this weekend. She's always wanted to come to Vegas, so I caved."

I could've smacked myself. Instead I grabbed my drink to prevent anymore random ramblings. If he was flirting with me, he wouldn't be for long. But what was wrong with a little flirting? It might be fun if I had any idea at all how to do it.

"And the husband?"

"I'm here with Nicole," I said hoping that I could avoid that particular line of questioning. Thankfully, he didn't push it.

"So, what are you going to do to celebrate Nicole's birthday?" he asked.

I smiled, relieved to talk about something else. "Her actual birthday is tomorrow and I told her she could choose what she wanted to do. So, I guess we'll go out dancing somewhere." I winced at the thought of braving a Las Vegas night club. "But tonight we're keeping it pretty tame. We're going to see a Cirque show. I can't remember which one. They're all the same, aren't they?"

He laughed, smooth and natural. The image of warm caramel on an ice cream sundae popped into my head.

"No, they're not *all* the same," he said. "Similar, I'll give you. But each one has a different focus."

"You've seen them all?"

"I have. Some more than once."

"You must spend a lot of time in Vegas."

"You could say that," he said, taking long sip of coke. "I live here."

Before I could ask him about that, Nicole's voice, preceding her by seconds, cut in. "Well, hello," she said as she sashayed over with a little more enthusiasm than normal. She looked much taller than her 5'2" in spiky heels. I wasn't sure how she could breathe let alone walk in her emerald green dress that hugged her like a second skin. She looked good; she'd been working out twice a day for months and practically starving herself in preparation for this trip. I hated to admit that it paid off. I tried not to encourage that behavior in her, but she did look amazing.

"Who's your friend, Lex?" Nicole flipped her red hair over one shoulder and held out her hand in invitation.

Leo stood and took her hand. "I'm Leo. You must be Nicole."

"The one and only." Nicole took the stool he offered and slid in next to me.

"I was just keeping Lexi company until you arrived. But I should let the two of you get on with your evening." He spoke to Nicole, but his eyes didn't leave mine.

"You don't have to leave," I said.

"Unfortunately, I do. But maybe I'll run into you again," he said with a smile that made my stomach flip.

I struggled to keep my composure. "Maybe."

"Nicole," he said turning to her. "What are you drinking tonight?"

Her face flickered and the flash of a frown transformed into a smile so fast that if I hadn't known better, I'd doubt it had even been there. She ran a hand through her hair and said, "I'm kinda in the mood for something sweet. You know what I mean?" she purred. She couldn't help it. Whenever there was a man around, Nicole transformed. She would bat her eyelashes, throw on her sexiest smile and send out vibes of pure lust. She'd been that way ever since we were teenagers and she'd figured out that boys would do pretty much anything for her with a little flirting.

I felt a small burn of jealousy, which was ridiculous, when Leo returned her smile and ordered her a Knock Out.

"So, Lexi said you're going to a club tomorrow night for some dancing," Leo said.

"Well, when in Vegas..." she said and leaned forward

exposing a little more cleavage.

I rolled my eyes and looked out onto the casino floor where the lights from the slots flashed and waitresses traipsed back and forth on their stilettos carrying drinks to gamblers who were pumping money into machines at a surprising rate. Over at the blackjack tables, there was a crowd of people forming around a man in a Hawaiian print shirt. By the excitement surrounding him, he must have had a run of luck.

"Well, what do you think, Lexi?"

I shook my head and turned back to the conversation. "About what?"

"Leo has offered us VIP passes to Studio 54 for tomorrow. He tells me it's the place to be on a Saturday night."

"It's your birthday. If that's what you want to do, it sounds good to me." I did my best to sound excited. Night clubs were akin to torture. "Thanks, Leo."

"It's my pleasure." He held my gaze again.

I cleared my throat and forced myself to look away. I swiped a piece of hair behind my ear before asking, "So, how did you happen to have these tickets?"

"I have my connections." He grinned and because he looked so cute, I found myself grinning back. "Seriously," he added. "I work at the hotel. Speaking of which, I should get back." He pushed himself away from the bar.

"It was very nice meeting you, Leo," Nicole said.

"Likewise, ladies. Have a great night." He started to move to the door.

"Wait," I called and the second he turned around my face burned with embarrassment. That sounded ridiculous. "How will we get the passes?" I asked, trying to sound natural.

"Don't worry, Lexi," he said and I could tell he was trying not to laugh. My face got even hotter if that was possible. "I'll make sure you get them." And then he turned and disappeared onto the casino floor.

I watched him go, wishing with a great deal of absurdity, that he would turn around and come back.

"That's it. No more alcohol for me," I mumbled. I hadn't reacted to a man like that since, well, since ever.

Nicole didn't hear me. "He's yummy," she said licking her lips. "Now come on, we're going to be late for the show. And what are you wearing?"

I looked down and said, "What's wrong with this? The sales girl said this was totally Vegas appropriate."

"Seriously, Lexi? For such a hottie, you choose the strangest clothes." Nicole stood and pulled me from the stool. "Don't worry, we'll go shopping tomorrow and get you sexed up."

I turned to grab my purse and caught sight of my left hand. It still made my breath catch when I saw my naked finger where a ring had been for the last three years.

"Lex, come on. What are you looking at?"

I blinked hard. "Nothing," I said and grabbed my purse. "Let's go."